Bedding the Marquess

Spy Society, Book 3

Kelsey Swanson

ARE YOU SIGNED UP FOR DRAGONBLADE'S BLOG?

You'll get the latest news and information on exclusive giveaways, exclusive excerpts, coming releases, sales, free books, cover reveals and more.

Check out our complete list of authors, too!

No spam, no junk. That's a promise!

Sign Up Here

www.dragonbladepublishing.com

Dearest Reader;

Thank you for your support of a small press. At Dragonblade Publishing, we strive to bring you the highest quality Historical Romance from some of the best authors in the business. Without your support, there is no 'us', so we sincerely hope you adore these stories and find some new favorite authors along the way.

Happy Reading!

CEO, Dragonblade Publishing

Additional Dragonblade books by
Author Kelsey Swanson

Spy Society Series
Courting the Duchess (Book 1)
Seducing the Spy (Book 2)
Bedding the Marquess (Book 3)

Reformed Rakes Series
The Rake Needs a Bride (Book 1)

For Mom.

Prologue

London, 1823

GIDEON BRAY, MARQUESS of Swanleigh, signaled for another drink from a passing servant. It was hours into the annual Haverford ball, and the guests were becoming quite rowdy. Dance steps grew sloppier as more drinks were consumed. The atmosphere suited Gideon just fine because he could become lost in the crowd.

Yet another disappointing meeting with the newest Bow Street Runner he'd hired had left him in a bitter mood, so much so that several of acquaintances had commented upon his unusually dour demeanor. Of course, he'd brushed them off. He had no desire to discuss the root of his mood, nor did he wish to explain how he'd spent the last decade trying to locate a man who seemed to be a ghost—a specter who shared half of Gideon's blood. He'd finally tracked him to a Newgate cell more than a decade earlier, but then, the man had vanished. There was no record of a death or release. It was as if the man had evaporated through the stone walls.

He owed it to the man to find him.

Not only that, but after so many years of being alone, Gideon was driven by a primal, desperate need to have kin in his life. The isolation of being the last in one's line, of sharing blood with no living person, was achingly desolate. For so long, he'd harbored the hope of one day meeting the person who had been missing from his life that it felt like slicing off his own limb to cave into the growing despair following failure after failure.

His half brother was out there.

He knew it.

The servant arrived with Gideon's drink, which he accepted with a flourish and tossed back with aplomb. The burn of the whiskey ran like fire to his gut and consumed his veins until he felt his entire body alight with it. He ached for the numbness it promised.

"When Brinley said you were in a mood, I thought he was being his dramatic self; I see now his description was uncanny." The cultured voice of Gideon's longtime friend, Rafe Hart, Viscount Blackwood, came from over his shoulder. The man attached to said voice appeared shortly thereafter, looking impeccably polished, coiffured, and devilishly handsome. His aristocratic features bordered on pretty, and his fashion choices just on the harsher side of dandified. From the curl in his dark hair to the starch in his cravat, the cut of his coattails to the pattern of his waistcoat, everything he did and wore was either envied or emulated by many a nobleman. The constant adulation could make Blackwood unbearable—especially when women practically tripped one another to be the first to grab his attention—but he also possessed a quick wit and an unerring sense of loyalty that made him bearable.

"And what description was that?" Gideon asked, though he was not in the least bit interested.

"Like a recently castrated alley cat—all scowls and grimaces."

"I beg your pardon?" Gideon's head snapped toward his friend. He'd had low expectations, but that had sunk them all like a lead weight.

Blackwood lifted an unapologetic shoulder. "Take it up with Brinley. He provided the description; I am merely providing my agreement. Better yet, take it up with yourself. You are the one making the face that is scaring off half of London."

Gideon sighed. "I am not quite myself, am I?"

"We all have those days," Blackwood replied nonchalantly as he accepted a drink from a passing servant. A true friend, the viscount would not press him. He, like every other person in their little collection of London's notorious rakes, had demons they battled each day. The Marquess of Kempton, Lord Pearce Brinley, and Viscount Trenholm were not excluded from this. The more senior members of their group, the Duke of Foxton and the Earl of Prestwich, had once dealt with their own but appeared to be settling in quite nicely with women who both suited them and mended whatever cracks their souls had once possessed. Gideon had never said it aloud, but he thought their state quite enviable—to be cherished and understood and unconditionally loved like that.

This shared damage had drawn their group together and formed their camaraderie. Each had something he wished to outrun, and they were able to do so with the help of non-judgmental friends, diverting adventures, more than a little flirtation with beautiful women, a steady string of dalliances, and good food and drink. They did not need to bare their souls to one another to recognize when one of them needed a little lifting up…which was why Blackwood did not pester him. They merely stood together in that stuffy ballroom, sipping their drinks and surveying the crowd.

Gideon's eyes snagged on the shimmer of rose-gold hair, and he knew instantly he'd spotted their group's sole female member—Miss Caroline Wells. She looked radiant as the autumnal sunset in her yellow-gold gown, her smooth, glowing skin, and wide smile that could make a man's knees unsteady. She was not a conventional beauty, but Gideon had always found her beautiful—more so when he came to know her over the years.

She'd been dealt an unfair hand in life, but he'd always admired how she'd crafted an unconventional life from the ashes of a scandal without so much as a single kind word from her family. She was resilient, witty, adventurous, and slightly wild. She could also drive him to distraction if he weren't careful.

The two of them had never been more than the closest of friends. In fact, he'd made it his mission to take her beneath his wing when she'd been cast out of her family, and he'd shown her how sometimes friends could be an even more supportive family than the ones into which they'd been born. It had taken time, but Caro had found her stride.

At first, their group had been hesitant to admit a lady into their midst, fearing the dynamics would change. But Caro had proven them all wrong, just like Gideon knew she would. She rode just as hard and fast as they did. She was never one to shy away from a prank or lark. She was always game for an adventure and didn't become missish around drinking, smoking, or gambling on horses, dogs, or fights. Though—to the best of Gideon's knowledge—she chose never to take a lover or form a romantic attachment, she never judged them for theirs. (They wouldn't have been very good rakes if they didn't, now would they?)

Despite his incessant attraction to her, Gideon had steadfastly never crossed the line of friendship with Caro. She'd had enough poor luck with men in her life, and the last thing he wished to do was destroy the comfortable relationship they'd formed.

"You're staring at her a bit more forcefully than usual," Blackwood leaned in and murmured to Gideon.

Gideon snorted divisively. "What do you mean?" Though he knew bloody well what the man meant. Whenever Caro was around, Gideon was hard-pressed to pay attention to anything or anyone else. His gaze latched onto her, even across a crowded ballroom.

"Caro does look lovely tonight, doesn't she? That color suits her."

Gideon narrowed his eyes at his friend. "It does," he said cautiously. This was not the first instance where one of their friends had attempted to play Matchmaking Mama with the two of them. In fact, Gideon strongly suspected the men were placing bets behind their backs about when he and Caro might cross the line between close friends and paramours; they'd never admitted as much, but he knew them well enough by then to say with certainty that they were hiding something.

Whatever it was, their subtle and not-so-subtle nudges of him in Caro's direction over the years were beginning to erode his resolve when it came to her.

Caroline's clear green eyes found his, and Gideon's pulse thrummed with awareness. When the corners of her mouth lifted in a smile—a smile just for *him*—blood began to pool in his groin. He wanted to taste those lips. He ached to bury his face in the honeysuckle-scented flesh of her neck and chest. He needed her to wrap her arms around him and remind him that all was not lost, even though he might have to admit to himself that it was finally time to give up the search for the half brother he'd never known.

CAROLINE'S BODY FELT warm and tingly. Perhaps she'd imbibed one too many glasses of Lady Haverford's notorious punch that evening to calm her nerves. She supposed she should regret it more, but how could she, when the buoy to her courage was undeniable? She had, after all, made a life-altering decision just that day, and she knew, whatever the outcome, she required all the encouragement she could muster to see it through.

Gideon, her oldest, dearest friend, had received his usual invitation to the Haverford event. Curiously, an invitation had also arrived upon her table the following day. It had been years since Caroline had received one, and she knew in her heart that she had Gideon to thank for it. She didn't doubt that he'd wrangled an invitation out of Lady Haverford—he really could be unbearably charming when he wished to. Blackwood and the others had all received their invitations, so she was certain Gideon, weary of her exclusion, had called in a favor, though he denied he'd had a hand in it.

He'd stated on numerous occasions how deplorable Society's treatment could be toward women and how it was so much more forgiving toward men who committed the very same "sins." He reiterated quite frequently how she had never done anything worse than he and the rest of the lads had; in fact, Caroline would even dare to say she was less scandalous because she never carted along paramours or kept a mistress! Still, she was the one who was routinely looked down upon, the one at whom Society sneered.

All of this was to say that Gideon had, yet again, gone above and beyond in the name of their friendship and secured her a coveted invitation. He had a long history of doing such things for her, and, over time, it had endeared him to her in an irrevocable fashion. So much so that she very strongly suspected that she'd fallen quite helplessly in love with her friend somewhere along the way. Therefore, after much consideration, she'd made a decision—one which she refused to allow herself to back down from.

That night, she would invite Gideon to share her bed.

She'd sat with her thoughts on it for a long while, and still her hands trembled with nervous excitement as she set aside her final cup of punch and smoothed the skirts of her glittering goldenrod gown. She closed her eyes and breathed slowly through her nose, trying her best not to allow her nerves to overcome her.

Not for the first time, she considered that there was every possibility that Gideon would decline. Still, he was a man…and her many years of friendship with his gender had taught her that there were few occasions where a man would not take an opportunity presented to him. They could be quite the opportunists when it came to their baser needs, to be sure.

However, Caroline was also a woman with needs of her own.

No man had kissed her or so much as touched her since the dreadful night of her ruination when she was but seventeen and in her first Season. Even years later, the memories caused her skin to grow clammy and her abdomen to clench. She had spent far too long with those memories in the Fischer gardens as her only amorous experience. It was time to overwrite those memories with new ones, better ones, ones with a man whom she trusted, body and soul. Caroline's eyes sprang open, the light-green irises burning with the fires of determination.

She had resolved to have one experience with a man whom she adored before she was an old maid, and no one fit that description better for her than Gideon. Of course, it did not hurt that her heart had been his for years now, whether he was aware of it or not.

She'd already repeatedly promised herself that she would form no silly romantic notions about this evening being the start of a life and a future with him.

It was one night.

One.

And she fully intended to make that much clear to him as well.

If he declined…she would receive it with grace and save her tears for the privacy of her bedchamber in the wee hours of the morning after the ball.

If he accepted…

Oh, how she prayed he would accept.

As if summoned by her thoughts, the man in question suddenly turned, and his silver-gray eyes found hers across the overcrowded room. His gaze was as palpable as a caress; his familiar smile, as warm and as welcoming as a long-awaited embrace.

"Now or never, Caroline," she murmured to herself, not caring when a nearby lady raised a quizzical brow at her. As if navigating by the stars, she strode straight and true across the room toward Gideon.

And toward whatever the future held.

Chapter One

Four Months Later

GIDEON BOUNDED UP the stairs of Lady Night's high-end brothel, one of the thrumming heartbeats of Covent Garden. All his friends had prior engagements that evening, so he'd been left to his own devices. What better time to make his inaugural visit to this exclusive establishment? Its employees and atmosphere were touted as the best England had to offer, and, having seen some of Lady Night's women at Duke's gaming club on several occasions, Gideon could honestly say his interest had been piqued.

He handed off his hat and cloak to the waiting servant, casting his eyes over the opulent furnishings, ornate trimmings, and the large, black-dressed blokes standing surreptitiously in corners and watching the guests and employees interact. Everything about the space read *money*; it was a display of it, as well as a draw. The air was scented with a heady combination of fine tobacco and desire. Women strode about in various stages of undress as they served, chatted, flirted, displayed their wares, and began to seduce their patrons for the evening.

It had been too long since Gideon had enjoyed the charms of a woman, and he was determined that that evening would finally put an end to his dry spell. It mattered not that his body was only barely moved by the expanses of flesh and sultry voices he encountered as he moved from room to room, he would do whatever it took to feel like his carefree self again—the Gideon who wasn't so damned consumed with the memories of a single night months ago, that he'd been unwilling and unable to take another woman to his bed.

Soul filled with resolve, he discovered a long, open room that had been repurposed as a public house, complete with a long, lacquered bar top scrubbed to a golden gleam. Upon his arrival, it had been explained that many of the rooms were designed to give the guests varied experiences. Some liked the relaxed atmosphere of the pub room, others enjoyed performances put on by employees in specially decorated and outfitted spaces, and a few preferred to eschew all pretenses and head straight to the private rooms on the upper floors and the illicit delights on offer. With no particular plan in mind, Gideon was going to see where the evening led.

Propping a hip against the bar top, he signaled the serving girl for a drink. The room was crowded, but not overly so. A pleasant hum and buzz surrounded him, a mixture of excitement and unfettered joy. He recognized a few faces, but everyone did the gentlemanly thing and turned away without acknowledgment. What men did in their private time was their own business and, if rumors were to be believed, almost everything was on offer within these walls. These women were highly trained in all the illicit arts and, as long as a patron respected their boundaries and Lady Night's rules, he might find a pleasure unlike that to be found anywhere else.

He needed those rumors to be true.

If countless sessions at his pugilism club hadn't cleared his head, he hoped a good tupping would be precisely what he needed. Split knuckles, bruised ribs, and sore muscles were all well and fine, but they had done nothing to repair his sorry, preoccupied mental state.

Taking a cue from some of the other clientele, Gideon shimmied free from his brushed velvet coat and laid it across the bar top after checking it for cleanliness. Luckily, the establishment seemed to live up to its impeccable reputation. He rolled his neck and rotated his shoulders, enjoying the freedom of movement, when his drink was delivered.

"Anything else, sir?" the barmaid asked without a hint of flirtation or suggestion in her tone.

"Thank you, no."

The woman turned away with a nod and began seeing to another guest. Gideon watched with some fascination as she leaned toward the man to expose nearly her entire ample bosom above the gaping neckline of her unlaced muslin bodice. Her tone was markedly different as she inquired after that man's desires, and her fingers traced suggestive patterns on his knuckles.

Now, Gideon was just vain enough to recognize that most women found him attractive. It had never been a chore for him to locate female companionship, even less so if said companion was incentivized. It was not often that he was overlooked. The fact that he was in a brothel and had been treated with only polite professionalism thus far was more than a little bit perplexing. He resolved to brush it off and move on with his evening.

He took a healthy swig of his whiskey and enjoyed the fire it ignited within him as he turned to face the room. It was still early in the evening, so only a handful of patrons had arrived. From what he'd heard, the spaces would soon be overflowing with wealthy and titled men seeking excitement and companionship.

Gideon's optimism began to wane when an hour passed, and, other than many deferential nods, the most attention he'd garnered was from the barmaid who kept him well-plied with glass after glass of whiskey. Despite his efforts, all the women spoke to him with only polite deference before moving on their way. Did he smell off? He didn't believe so. He slyly checked his clothing for odd stains and found none. What in God's name was making him so repugnant that even prostitutes avoided him?

Fed up, Gideon gently touched the shoulder of the first woman who walked by him. She was a young woman—perhaps early in her second decade—with round, rosy cheeks and warm eyes. She wore her dark curls piled at the back of her head and a low-cut crimson gown designed to tease her curves to perfection. She was lovely and enticing in all the right ways…in all the ways his whiskey-blurred mind needed.

"Don't you look lovely this evening," he purred in his best seductive tone.

Her eyes widened almost comically, and she stammered, "W-Why thank you, sir."

"I have been looking for someone like you since I arrived." His fingers trailed down her arm and snaked around her trim waist. "I hope you are not already indisposed because I find myself in dire need of companionship." She squeaked in surprise when he tugged her against the length of his body.

"Sir!" she gasped, and the breathy sound sent the first spark of desire to his groin.

He dipped his head to whisper in her ear, his finger tracing the edge of her tight bodice just above where her areola would begin. "You are," he murmured, "a delicacy in which I cannot wait to indulge." Her floral scent filled his nostrils until it overcame all his other senses. Just as he leaned forward to press his lips to the fluttering pulse in her throat, he was suddenly yanked back.

Hard.

So hard, in fact, that the woman in crimson slipped from his hold and he staggered back a step. His eyes flew to the perpetrator and he was rather pleased to find she was a petite spitfire with sapphire eyes, white-gold hair, and the most angelic features he'd ever beheld.

"What are you doing?" the newcomer demanded of him, her voice loud and unsteady.

When he was once again steady on his feet, Gideon turned his most charming smile on her and followed it up with a wink. Was it his imagination, the drinks flowing through his veins, or was there a furrow of confusion in the little angel's brow?

"Don't worry, love; there's enough of me to go 'round."

In one elegant movement, he pulled her body flush with his, and her full breasts were crushed against the hard wall of his chest. His sluggish mind barely registered how she was wide-eyed and stiff with shock when he dipped his head and his mouth slanted over hers.

Only two heartbeats later, Gideon was jerked backward by his shirt collar far more firmly than another woman could ever have managed. The angel stumbled free from his arms. He was bent painfully back over the bar top, the back of his head cracking on the polished surface and making his vision flicker. The door to the attached card room still swung from where his assailant had burst forth in a black rage. Gideon winced and blinked up to find a fist cocked in the air to deliver what would likely be a knockout blow. He'd dealt enough—and been on the receiving end a time or two—to know one when he saw it. He grappled with the iron arm that held him bent back at an awkward angle, but he was unable to gain purchase.

The large hand with its scarred knuckles began to descend but stuttered and froze.

The man above him stared, unmoving, though his hold on Gideon's clothing remained firm.

Gideon stopped struggling when he finally looked up into the face of his attacker.

It was like staring into a reflecting pool; the images were near copies, but something was ever so slightly distorted the closer one looked.

The room grew silent as more people became aware of the situation.

The girl in crimson turned to the blonde; her face was deathly white when she stammered, "Mrs. Black—I never would've—I thought 'e was—I'm sorry. I didn't know how to react when Mr. Black behaved like that…now I see 'twasn't him, but his twin. I did not know he had a brother."

Gideon was not a man prone to fanciful imaginings, nor could he recall a time he'd ever drunk himself into such a state that he saw ghosts.

However, he was fairly certain his deceased father had followed him on his inaugural visit to this Covent Garden brothel and was standing over him, lips curled in a familiar snarl, eyes hard and cold, fist poised to strike. It was a sight he'd been subjected to numerous times in his youth but had thought never to see again when the man's body had been interred in the family plot some five years earlier.

The ghost's features suddenly softened into confusion, and Gideon seized his opportunity to wrench himself free. It wound up taking far less effort than he'd judged, so he stumbled forward and barely caught himself before he tumbled face-first into the floor.

Judging from the gaping expressions around him, he wasn't the only one taken aback by the situation—two men, near mirror images, standing wide-eyed as they stared one another down.

Gideon straightened his shirtsleeves and ran his hand through his dark hair just as his father's ghost performed the same gesture. The two of them froze mid-motion.

The angelic little prostitute he'd kissed moved forward and spoke to the other man in soft tones, her blue eyes dancing between them. The next thing he knew, Gideon was ushered into a back room at Lady Night's. He and the other man stared one another down across the space like dogs in a fighting ring, wondering which of them would be the first to make a move.

The woman—brave little thing that she was—spoke first. "Who are you?" she asked Gideon. Her voice was clear, but its slight tremor gave away her unease.

Gideon offered her his most charming smile as well as a bow. "Gideon Bray, Fourth Marquess of Swanleigh. And you are?"

"Mrs. Emily Black," the other man growled dangerously. *"My wife."*

"Oh. Oh!" Gideon's drink-addled brain caught up, and he turned to Mrs. Black. "My apologies for mistaking you for a prostitute." There was another low rumble from her husband's direction. "You must understand, you are lovely and, in the context of this establishment—" His word died when he caught sight of the other man's glare and clenched fist. Gideon cleared his throat, deciding it was prudent to quit before he proceeded down that avenue. "And you are?" he asked the man.

"Oliver Black," was the flat reply.

Neither exchanged hands or pleasantries.

Mrs. Black took it upon herself to break the silence again. "There must be some explanation for this…situation." She looked between them once more. "There is more than a passing resemblance here. Even I had difficulty telling you apart at first, and I am Oliver's wife."

Gideon experienced the simultaneous effervescent and sinking realization that the day he thought might never come had finally arrived. The drinks he'd enjoyed that evening had delayed the weight of it, but now it sat on his chest with the crushing heft of a building. He'd told himself time and time again that the possibility was slim…that the odds of finding this man and recognizing him were almost nonexistent—especially after his years of searching. Alone in the world, he'd been driven by the inexplicable desire and naïve hope that he would find kinship with the bastard his father had sired, and years of searching had turned up fruitless. But there he was, facing the man whom he'd only seen once from afar when they'd both been children.

Though his heartbeat was deafening, he forced himself to meet Oliver Black's eyes—eyes so uncannily like their father's—a pair he'd once believed would never stare him down again.

"The reason we share such similar appearances is because…you are my brother."

There was a heartbeat of silence before Oliver snorted disbelievingly. "Impossible."

"I assure you, it is possible as it is the truth."

"You're much too deep in your cups," Oliver insisted.

Gideon scoffed. "Did your mother ever work for my family? Is the name 'Bray' or the title Marquess of Swanleigh at all familiar?" He watched as Oliver raked his memory.

"She was employed by a marquess, yes, but that could be

easily explained as a coincidence. There is more than one marquess in London, each with many maids in their employment. The odds are simply astronomical."

"Is it only a coincidence? There is a reason your mother was a maid in the household of a marquess, and you and I share such physical likenesses," he drawled.

The words were formed only one second before Oliver charged him more quickly than Gideon's eyes could follow. To a man who was no stranger to the fighting ring, it was shocking to be caught so unawares once, let alone twice in the evening. How the hell did the man move like that? The wind was knocked from Gideon's chest as he was thrown up against the wall.

"Are you calling my mother a whore?" Oliver roared in his face.

"Never." Gideon shook his head as best he could, grappling with the hands at his throat. "I simply know the kind of monster our father was."

Oliver released him as abruptly as if he'd been scalded and scrubbed at his scalp as if trying to scour his very mind.

Gideon sucked in a gulp of air and straightened. "You were born in the spring of 1794, correct?" Oliver's eyes met his, and Gideon didn't need to hear an answer; the silver irises said it all. Gideon nodded and pressed a hand to his own chest. "July of 1794." He saw the moment the truth set in in the other man's mind as his storm-cloud eyes darkened: He was Gideon's elder brother. And, had he been born on the right side of the sheets, he'd be the current Marquess of Swanleigh instead of living and working in Covent Garden.

Oliver's eyes were wide, and his breathing grew ragged and uneven. Gideon had known for years the atrocities committed by his father; he'd had time to come to terms with them. This conversation must have been nothing short of earth-shattering to a man who'd made it three decades without ever questioning his sense of self.

Gideon scrubbed his face, suddenly feeling far too sober to

confront these demons despite the drinks he'd imbibed. He pulled a card from his pocket and handed it to Emily. "Feel free to call when you've both had time to process this information. I am happy to discuss this at your convenience."

She examined the embossed card before looking back up at him with doe-like sapphire eyes. "You are taking this remarkably well."

He offered her a sad smile in return. "I knew I'd have to face Father's sins sooner or later. 'The sins of the father are visited upon the son' and all that," he said, waving dismissively. He tilted his head in another bow to her. "Again, I do apologize for what happened earlier. And, do not fret, I'll not be frequenting this establishment again. Nothing against the business or its fine employees, I merely think it prudent to keep pleasure separate from family in this situation." He turned on his heel to return to the bar room, retrieve the rest of his clothing, and return home to his dark, quiet house and the ghosts awaiting him.

So much for that evening being the cure to his addled mind.

EMILY BLACK TURNED back to her husband. He stood, palms braced flat on a table, eyes wide and haunted as his mind sped. To watch a man usually as composed and unflappable as he experience an existential crisis was nothing short of unnerving. So often, he'd been her shelter and her anchor, but he was now the one adrift.

She didn't know what to think about it—the confrontation, the story, the possibility that Oliver was not who he'd always believed he was: the son of a maid and a dockworker. Emily knew Oliver's parents had wed eight months before his birth, but, even if it was frowned upon, this was not unheard of. Oliver's arrival, approximately four weeks earlier than expected, would not have created a great stir and might not have raised a moment of question. Whether Mrs. Black had known she was expecting another man's child at the time she'd wed Mr. Black was something she'd taken to her grave.

Of course, there had been no love lost between the deceased Mr. Black and his son, but that didn't mean it made the possibility that Oliver had, in fact, been sired by a marquess any less shocking. Emily wondered if the man had known—or at least suspected—Oliver was not his. If so, perhaps that might explain the enmity he'd aimed toward a defenseless boy. It did not make it right, but it made a sick sort of sense. His wife had died, so any animosity was now solely directed at the child he was left to care for.

There was no denying the uncanny resemblance between Oliver and the current Marquess of Swanleigh, and he'd somehow correctly predicted the general date of Oliver's birth. Oliver's mother had at one time been a maid in the household of a marquess, but she knew Oliver had been too young—or perhaps, not even born yet—to recall the circumstances of her departure from that position. No one who might be able to confirm it was alive any longer. There was little tangible proof above these things; however, the encounter had clearly left her unshakable, worldly husband rocked to his very core.

Oliver started a little when she touched his sleeve, but he allowed her to hold him as he took stock of everything he'd ever believed about himself. Emily buried her face in his chest, sinking into him as he lowered his head and pressed his lips to her collarbone.

Emily knew one thing for sure: She'd do everything she could to protect her husband because he'd never before had anyone to do that for him.

Chapter Two

THE NEXT MORNING, Gideon woke with a splitting headache and an unholy level of nausea. Following his leave of the brothel, he'd gone home and dragged a chair to face the portrait of his father, which, regrettably, still hung above the hearth in the library. Several times, he'd nearly given in to the impulse to burn the damned thing, but he'd stopped just shy of tearing it off the wall. He kept telling himself that he'd move it to another wing or another estate entirely, but that would have deprived him of the many joys of cursing the man to his face, subjecting him to rude gestures, and, perhaps most importantly, serving as a reminder of why Gideon continued to search for the sibling he knew existed somewhere in the world.

That evening, he'd nestled in for a long night of all three of those activities, spending hour after hour glaring and drinking, toasting the man who still seemed to be sending him jabs from the grave. He'd been gone half a decade, and Gideon was still caught treading in the wake of his father's tumult, his rash behavior, and his selfish, poor decisions. The man had likely left behind at least several bastards, but Gideon had only snippets of information about a single one of them. Before that night, everything had led to a dead end…until his brother found him…

Gideon was barely awake, swathed only in a coverlet, when his butler, Perry, arrived to advise him of a guest.

"What person of my acquaintance would call at this ungodly hour?" Gideon groused, his voice hoarse from sleep and drink.

"A Miss Emily," his butler replied with a disdainful sniff, clearly put out by the stubbornness of their visitor.

"Emily? Just Emily?"

"Indeed."

Gideon heaved a weighty sigh and had the butler show her into the parlor, where he would join her presently. There was only one Emily he knew. He hadn't known her long, but she seemed just feisty enough to intrude upon a marquess's home well before proper visiting hours.

Absently, he wondered why she'd come to see him alone—especially after how close her husband had come to pummeling him the prior evening—but she must have deemed it important enough for her to arrive so soon after their unorthodox meeting.

It took far longer than it would have had he not finished the second bottle of brandy, but he survived washing up and dressing after choking down one of Cook's headache remedies. A deep-brown coat and buff breeches provided a nice contrast to his emerald green waistcoat and polished black Hessians. He bemoaned the purple shadows beneath his normally sharp eyes, but there was nothing to be done about them now; hopefully, his refined attire would make up for his lackluster expression.

He found Mrs. Emily Black examining a landscape hanging on the far wall of the blue parlor. Not for the first time, he was struck by the prettiness of her face, though her true charm lay in the smooth, sensuous elegance with which she moved, and how she held herself. She couldn't have been older than three-and-twenty, but there was an uncommon worldliness about her. No wonder his brother had snatched her up.

His brother.

Now that was a notion that would take some getting used to—especially after spending three decades as an only child—the sole son and heir to the marquessate. Gideon's head throbbed painfully, and he winced. How much had changed in the span of a single night? Exhaling a measured breath, he greeted his visitor.

"Mrs. Black. A pleasure to see you again so soon." He strode over and took her hand, bowing over it as he smiled warmly.

"Lord Swanleigh," she greeted him in return with a deferential curtsey. She'd donned a modest, gray-striped gown and matching spencer that morning, along with a plain bonnet, gloves, and an unadorned reticule. Despite its simplicity, every piece she wore was of uncommon quality and impressive tailoring. Whoever she was, she was a woman with some money and connections despite her presence in a brothel the night before, and it made him wonder about her husband all the more.

She plucked her hand back and laced her fingers together before her as she stood stiffly. Her luscious mouth was drawn into a taut line; her large eyes darted across his features; she appeared as if she were addressing a rather unpleasant intrusion upon her marital bliss. Gideon supposed he couldn't blame her.

Before he could inquire as to the reason for her call, she blurted out, "You must forgive me for staring, but the similarities between you and my husband are unnerving—even more so in the light of day. I'd almost convinced myself that it had been a trick of the evening, but I see now that was not the case."

Gideon's winning smile dimmed slightly. "Our appearances run quite strongly in the male line of our family. The hair, eyes, and build are traditionally passed from father to son."

She eyed him for several long seconds before speaking again. "I am here to protect my husband."

Gideon chuffed. "The man seemed rather well-equipped to handle himself."

She ignored the comment, continuing on as if he hadn't spoken at all. "You see, he has not had the easiest of lives, and I feel it is my duty to do what I can to learn more about the circumstances of the…situation, as you put it, before we become too embroiled."

"While I appreciate your looking out for him, I believe it would be prudent for your husband to be present for this conversation."

"And I would prefer to speak to you alone first," Mrs. Black replied steadfastly. "I am determined to protect my husband in any way I can—especially if it turns out to be a ruse."

"And what, madam, would I seek to gain from such a ruse?" he asked, cocking a haughty brow. Wasn't it usually the lower class attempting to gain something from the wealthy in this sort of situation? She remained unmoved. "Very well," Gideon sighed resignedly. "What would you like to know?"

"How did you know of Oliver's existence?"

"A fair enough inquiry and as good a place to begin as any." Gideon gestured to the nearby chairs and offered her a seat. "This will take some time. Might I offer you any refreshments in the meantime?"

She considered his offer for a few more seconds before sitting. "Thank you, no," she answered with a shake of her head. She did not intend to stay long, it seemed.

It was probably for the best; even if he hadn't been suffering from the aftereffects of overindulgence, Gideon didn't think his stomach could handle anything. He took up a seat in the other chair and went on to explain how thoroughly his parents had hated one another.

"It was not a love match in any sense. Their families forced the marriage from the cradle despite their obvious incompatibility. My mother loathed my father for his drinking, spending, volatile temper, and, of course, his blatant dalliances. She found them humiliating, and I cannot blame her for that." He watched Mrs. Black nod in agreement, her keen eyes watching his every gesture as he continued speaking. "My father, in turn, hated my mother for her disgust of his behavior, her censorship, and how she attempted to bring him to heel by any means necessary. This included causing public scenes, berating him, hurling vases at his head, even removing the soles from all his right boots so he would not leave for a holiday with another woman." Gideon shook his head—that last one had been creative, if childish.

"The only reason I was conceived was my father's fleeting sense of duty following a near-death experience. After being thrown from his horse and remaining unconscious for the better part of a day, he dedicated himself to wooing and apologizing for his wicked ways enough for my mother to allow him back into her bed. Little did she know, he'd already molested the new upstairs maid."

Gideon watched the dread bloom in Mrs. Black's luminous eyes—she was quick enough to predict where his tale was headed.

Gideon waved a negligent hand. "Some years later, a former maid arrived with a little boy in tow, claiming he was Swanleigh's son. He had a shock of black hair, silver eyes, and a sturdy build despite his malnourishment and tender years. She said she could barely afford the extra mouth to feed since she'd been forced to find employment elsewhere, and all she asked was for a bit of money so the boy might eat." Bile rose to the back of Gideon's throat, but he choked it back. His voice was rough, and he averted his eyes in shame when he continued. "My father had her turned out without even bothering to see her or the boy." Mrs. Black remained silent, but he could see how tightly her hands were clasped together.

"It is important to note how, in the course of my parents' marital war, the servants had divided themselves into factions of their own—the marquess's side and his wife's. A maid on my mother's side of the divide caught wind of what had happened with the former maid and the young boy and told her. From then on, the bitterness exploded with new rancor. Infidelities had been committed before, but not to my mother's knowledge had there ever been a child born of them. That was a blow she simply could not stomach."

"But you couldn't have been more than a small child when Oli—when the boy was brought 'round. How did you know of it?" she asked in a small voice.

"Because my mother made sure to tell me at every opportunity what a lecher my father was, how disloyal a scoundrel he'd become." As harsh as his words were, his tone was flat with acceptance. He'd long ago resigned himself to the tragedy of his youth wasted in a household devoid of kind words. "She didn't doubt that he'd raped the young maid and then crawled into her own bed shortly thereafter to get her with child—with me. Apologies for speaking so bluntly." Mrs. Black inclined her head and urged him to continue. "For my father's part, hardly a day passed that he didn't remind me that all women were like my mother: controlling, ungrateful harpies. He did his best to discredit everything she said." Gideon didn't say it outright, but he could not recall a time when he wasn't used as a pawn between his parents in their war, each spilling as much venom into his young ears as possible. Even now, decades later, he still experienced the echoes of their arguments and heard the tinkle of shattering crystal.

"On her deathbed," he said, forcing himself to continue, "my mother was feverish and insensible, ranting again about the bastard child my father had sired, but letting slip that she'd once located his family in London, that he was only a few months older than I..." Gideon had to clear his throat. "I never found out why she'd tracked him down, nor what she'd intended to do with the information, because she lapsed into delirium. Despite trying to follow the little information I had, I was unable to discover where my half brother was, following a stint in Newgate, but it had confirmed to me that there was a possibility—no matter how slim—that I would one day encounter him. I'd just about given up hope, but last night was that moment."

Though she'd listened intently, he could still see disbelief playing around the edges of her expressive features. There was one more thing that might just make her believe in the truth of all this, as he did. Gideon stood and held his hand out to his brother's wife. "Come."

He led her out of the room and down the hall.

"Has my brother had a truly terrible life?" he asked, snapping the tense silence between them. Her tight lips were answer enough, and it made every inch of him ache. "I'd been afraid of that."

From the time he'd first heard of Oliver's existence, Gideon had wondered what life was like for his mysterious half sibling. If he enjoyed riding as much as Gideon did; if he preferred dogs to cats; if he struggled with Latin; if he excelled in math, too. If he'd had enough food or any education to speak of. As he'd grown older, however, Gideon had realized more and more that it was far more likely that the bastard who shared his blood had had none of the privileges Gideon did, and likely even fewer comforts. The tragic reality was that bastards bore a stain upon their very existence, and the world did not take kindly to anyone who did not fit a prescribed mold. The child of a working-class family in London could struggle, the bastard child of a disgraced maid whose employment had been terminated...that child would suffer. Often, he'd gone between wishing the brother he'd never met had died young without experiencing the cruelty of the world, and hoping that he'd been strong enough to grow into a man whom Gideon could one day meet.

Gideon was so lost in his thoughts that he hadn't expected Mrs. Black to delve into her husband's upbringing, but, when she did, he wasn't certain it wasn't intended to twist the knife in his gut just a little bit. "His mother died of the drink—probably not that long after Oliver had been brought to your doorstep in an attempt to seek aid from the old marquess." Gideon's fragile stomach lurched. He couldn't blame the woman for seeking solace at the bottom of a bottle—not if her rape had brought about a child she could not support and cost her a stable position. Life had dealt her a cruel hand and, had he been a religious man, Gideon might have crossed himself and said a prayer for the unfortunate woman, hoping that she'd found peace in death she'd been denied in life. "The man Oliver had always believed to be his father exhibited no love or gentleness toward him... Now it makes more sense, in a horrid sort of way. He may have married Oliver's mother and at one time believed Oliver was his son, but somewhere along the way, the truth must have been revealed, or perhaps the child's appearance offered doubt as to his sire."

"I suppose he didn't take too kindly to raising the child—the by-blow—of another man, begotten on his wife."

Mrs. Black made a thoughtful sound.

It was likely no consolation after a life such as he'd had that Oliver was actually the son of a peer, so Gideon refrained from pointing that out. Instead, he showed Mrs. Black into the library. The scent of parchment and leather would have been comforting, were the room not haunted.

"The timing makes sense, and there are similarities in your appearances, but I am still unsure as to why you are so certain my husband is this missing child." Mrs. Black was looking up at him, and he could see her clutching her skepticism like a weapon. Most women would have jumped at the chance to have their husband welcomed by a wealthy, titled relative, but Gideon recognized Emily Black was, at her heart, unique. She wished only to protect her husband, even if it cost them connections and anything else they might gain from being kin to a marquess. Gideon found that more than a little admirable.

His lips twisted into a sardonic smile, and he gestured up at the larger-than-life painting mounted above the hearth. "Meet my father, Harold Bray, Third Marquess of Swanleigh, philanderer, vile bastard, and man absent of morals."

He should have felt satisfaction over her reaction, the evidence of her belief, the blatant astonishment splashed across her face, but he experienced only intense sadness.

She clapped her hands over her mouth.

As similar as Gideon and Oliver had appeared to be, the painting of the young man looked as if Oliver, himself, had sat for the portrait.

"And that, dear sister, is why I am so very confident."

EMILY LEFT SWANLEIGH House a short time later, silent and contemplative. Before she'd stepped from the Mayfair townhouse and into the burgeoning bustle of London life, the marquess had extended an invitation for both her and her husband to call at any time—especially if Oliver had any questions. "We are, after all, family," he'd said. And now, that was a nearly impossible statement for her to refute; she'd all but stared down the evidence hanging in the Swanleigh library.

It had been overwhelming to listen to everything the marquess had to say about his history and what he knew of the tragic circumstances of Oliver's early years, but it had been downright shocking to come as near to face-to-face as one might with a dead man. One thing was certain: she hoped there was a hell so that man might burn for how he'd damned Oliver to his lot in life…and also how he'd treated his only legitimate child. Emily never thought she'd pity a lord—a man born to money, power, and unfathomable privilege—but it was difficult when he was humanized in such a way. She could almost imagine him as a child, torn between bickering parents and privy to all manner of things to which a child should never have been exposed. The old marquess had clearly been a man who damaged indiscriminately.

As she walked along the street, Emily felt more than saw a tall, dark man fall in step beside her. She wasn't at all surprised when Oliver spoke up.

"I see your curiosity won out." His voice was low and perfectly modulated.

"How did you know where I went?" she responded without looking up. She could, however, feel the droll look he aimed at her.

"Compared to my past profession, tracking my wife when she sneaks out of bed is child's play."

She should have known better than to try to pull one over on a former spy for the Crown. Though he'd been retired for some time now, he'd not lost any of his finely honed skills or his fighter's physique. Following her had likely been one of the simplest things he'd done in years, but she'd had to try to meet with Swanleigh on her own to gauge his intentions. It was absurd to believe her husband needed protecting, but she couldn't help herself. He'd spent so long putting the greater good before his own well-being, and it was well past time someone looked out for him.

She sighed in resignation. "Are you very cross with me?"

As a reply, Oliver gently pulled her arm through his and they walked together in perfect sync, him slowing his long-legged pace to match hers.

"What did the marquess have to say?" he asked her after they strolled for a few minutes in the watery late-morning light.

Screwing up her courage, Emily vowed to tell him everything. She wanted Oliver to have all of the information at his disposal so he might sift through it and decide how to move forward with it in his life. Carefully, she proceeded to share what she had learned. She described the old marquess and his wife, what Swanleigh had learned both as a child and while his mother rambled on her deathbed.

Then, she described the painting.

"It was as if the artist had painted you, my love." Oliver's arm tensed beneath her fingers; she wrapped her other hand around it as well. She longed to fully take him into her arms as she'd held him the previous night, but that would need to wait until later. "My gut is telling me Swanleigh is being truthful. I think…" She paused to nibble her lower lip. "I think you should meet and speak with him on your own."

Oliver's only reply was a terse, "We shall see."

RATHER THAN FEEL relieved after Mrs. Black took her leave, Gideon experienced only white-hot anger.

Anger that his father had begotten a son upon a poor woman and cast her aside without so much as a single thought to her well-being or that of her child.

How the man had robbed Gideon of knowing his half sibling and damned that child to a life in the gutters.

Then again, even if he had been acknowledged, Oliver might not have fared much better in Gideon's household—trading one hell for another. The old marquess had not been one to spare a rod or a rapier-sharp word, and certainly no solace would have been found with the marchioness.

As he sat heavily in one of the chairs in the library and cradled his leaden, aching head in his hands, Gideon wondered if it was still too early to begin drinking again.

Chapter Three

CAROLINE STARED DOWN the snarling bronze griffin knocker of the Swanleigh townhouse for a long while before she even considered raising her hand to announce her arrival. Despite being one of her dearest friends—"her partner in crime," the tabloids had once cried—she hadn't seen Gideon in a month. It wasn't for his lack of trying, however. He'd certainly extended invitations to her; tried to convince her to accompany him to their usual gaming haunts, wild fetes, to spend an evening carousing in Covent Garden with their group of mutual friends and fellow hell-raisers. Caroline, however, had declined them all.

She'd decided she couldn't face him until she knew precisely the right words to say…and now the time had come. After three months—perhaps a bit too long due to an abundance of caution—she was finally ready to reveal to Gideon the consequence of their impulsivity.

Well, she supposed *consequence* was an unkind label to apply to the little being growing inside of her.

Caroline's heart had hardly slowed its pace since the physician confirmed to the best of his abilities that she was expecting. Fear and excitement, dread and anticipation had all warred for supremacy inside of her. Her position was a precarious one—if not downright dangerous—in their Society. She had no husband, no supportive family, and, if there were any shreds of her reputation remaining, they were about to be ignited and burned to ash.

She supposed her apprehension over the upcoming conversation was only natural, but her heart told her Gideon's reaction would be kinder than most men in his position.

Still…

She was a woman accustomed to being let down, so she had not foregone formulating alternative plans. Didn't women in her situation usually leave London to give birth in secret? At least, those were the whispers she'd caught. That was likely her best option should Gideon wish to step aside. While she abhorred Cornwall, it was the farthest, safest option for her to see the pregnancy through, enter confinement, and give birth.

She had not yet sorted out what would be done once she needed to care for the child on her own, but that was a storm she would weather. She had no choice. She refused to consider abandoning the baby to the care of strangers, no matter what Society dictated.

In her secret heart of hearts, Caroline hoped it would not come to that, and Gideon would be pleased by the news and wish to offer support. After all, these circumstances were as much her fault as his—if not more so, because she had been the one to proposition him.

She had thought it over a great deal and decided that she would not demand that he marry her…though she would not lie and say the idea of marriage to him had not crossed her mind.

She adored him.

She was enamored of him.

A place in her heart would always be reserved for her dearest friend.

But she would love him from afar if that was his wish.

"You can do this," Caroline murmured shakily to herself. She'd already screwed up her courage, completed the process of donning her favorite marigold-colored morning dress and peony-pink spencer, allowed her maid to spend the better part of an hour shaping her rose-gold hair into an artful style of ringlets and pins, and taken a hired hack from her small townhouse to

Mayfair. She wouldn't allow all of that to go to waste now. She raised her hand and knocked before closing her eyes and retreating into her memories for support while she waited for the butler to answer.

It felt so long since she'd been a starry-eyed girl in braids who begged Nanny for more stories of knights and daring battles. She'd mourned the loss of that innocence many times over at that point, but only in recent years had she come to acknowledge to herself that the true demise of her childhood had come about in preparation for her debut into Society, and the fallout shortly thereafter. Gideon had been the only one who saw her for who she really was and appreciated her as more than just a salacious tabloid headline.

Back when he'd been only the Earl of Eastwich, Gideon had been the only ray of sunlight in her bleak new existence after her ruination. Everyone knew his father, the Marquess of Swanleigh, to be quite dark and domineering, so Caroline had initially been shocked that Gideon had been allowed to interact with her. She had learned very early on, however, that father and son were not particularly close, and Gideon was not one who deferred to his father's preferences.

She and Gideon had met on several occasions before her scandal, and his easy smile was always quite charming. At first, she'd been afraid he'd only come to harass her or offer a vulgar proposition, given her new status as a "fallen woman," but he offered only the sincerest friendship. He worked quite diligently to earn her trust, bringing her new books to read when she felt too low to venture outdoors, making her laugh when she would rather cry. Though she'd lately realized she was a horrendous judge of character, she could sense no ulterior motives in him. Through it all, he afforded her time and space when even she was unaware it was something her healing soul required—not only after the assault upon her person by a man who was supposed to be her sweetheart, but the banishment and condemnation from her family. He always had the uncanny ability to bring sunshine and joy wherever he went and morph himself into whatever it was a person needed most. In him, she'd found a true friend who could see past the scandal to what lay within her.

Throughout the past decade of their friendship, she and Gideon had become quite the infamous duo in London, both of them used as a cautionary tale for mamas who sought to rein in willful daughters—"Take care with your reputation lest your options dry up and the only men who will want to keep your company are rakes and reprobates." Naturally, it had bothered her at first, but, as she matured, Caroline had realized that the "rakes and reprobates"—her friends—were truer and more dedicated than any man she'd met at Almack's. And Gideon was at the top of her list of good men at whom the *ton* looked down their noses simply because he lived life a bit more loudly than was acceptable.

Naturally, she and Gideon had been connected by numerous gossip rags, each one salivating at the possibility of an illicit relationship playing out between a future marquess and the disgraced eldest daughter of a viscount. She didn't miss the titillated whispers, everyone expecting them to be longtime lovers, but they would have been wrong…at least up until a few months ago, following a night of drinks, dancing, and poor choices.

She'd have been lying if she claimed she'd never found Gideon handsome—most women did with his midnight hair, thundercloud eyes, and tall, trim build—but, to her, he'd always been just a friend, and one of the very select few who had remained with her after her youthful rebellion and a miserable judgment of character. He'd stayed by her side even after her family had chosen reputation over blood and turned their backs on her with no support other than a small income as a bribe to keep her distance. His steadfast presence in her life had long provided her with solace enough when she was otherwise tragically alone. Even if he'd never directly witnessed the vitriol with which her parents treated her since what had been dubbed *The Incident*, he'd done nothing but remain by her side and do everything in his power to show his support, cheering her when she might have otherwise wallowed in despair, making her laugh when tears felt like her only option.

Now, as she waited for the Swanleigh butler to open the door, Caroline hoped she wouldn't lose Gideon, too, after she revealed her pregnancy to him. She didn't know how she would weather that.

"Good afternoon, Perry," she greeted the butler with what she hoped was a convincing smile.

"Miss Wells." The man of middling years inclined his head with proper deference and immediately showed her inside. It was a standing order at the Swanleigh household that Caroline was to be granted immediate entrance; she and the marquess did not stand on ceremony. Still, there was something in the butler's dark eyes that gave Caroline pause—as if the man was second-guessing allowing her in despite his master's instructions.

"What is it, Perry?" Caroline asked bluntly, removing her gloves and hat before handing them over.

"My lord has had…a difficult morning." His reply was accompanied by a shift in his gaze, clearly discomfited by revealing even that much to her.

"A long night, then?" she guessed.

"As well as a long day. I am certain he could do with some cheering."

Interesting.

Not prone to fits of the blue devils, Gideon was usually the one who did the cheering. What could have happened to create such a change in his demeanor?

Caroline pondered that and prepared herself for what she might see as she was led down the hall and into the library. There, she found Gideon already present and sprawled out in an armchair upholstered in a garish green-and-brown pattern.

Just as Perry had warned her, her friend had no easy smile for her, no joke or comment about a mutual acquaintance. Gideon, instead, saluted her with a cut crystal glass in his hand and said, "I hope you are here to brighten my day, sweet Caro, because I've certainly experienced a hellish past twenty-four hours."

This suddenly felt like a bad idea with even worse timing, but it had taken Caroline more than a week to build up the nerve to call at the Swanleigh townhouse. She affected a brave demeanor and approached him.

"Who has crossed you now?" she asked lightly as she claimed the other chair and spread the embroidered skirts of her morning dress around her legs. Despite what her parents might say, she did have some dignity and manners.

"My father, the bastard he is." He sipped from his glass. "Was."

Caroline frowned. "But…he's been dead for years now." And she couldn't recall the last time Gideon had mentioned the man. Even though he glared at it, she refused to allow her eyes to stray to the nearby portrait of the old marquess. It had always unnerved her how Gideon and that man could appear so similar and yet have such very different souls. She had never asked why the portrait hadn't been moved in all this time—there certainly had been no affection between father and son—but that was Gideon's business and she was sure he had his reasons.

"Precisely the problem…" Gideon went silent for long, heavy minutes. She allowed him the grace, patiently waiting for him to be ready to discuss whatever had set him on this path. She'd begun the day with the intention of unburdening herself, but she realized it would not be fair to do so until Gideon did. "I have a brother," he finally said, the words dropping between them like a shattered glass.

Caroline reared back, her mind struggling to comprehend the words he'd just said. It took her several minutes before she was able to ask, "Are we happy about this?"

"I haven't decided yet," Gideon replied flatly and then paused thoughtfully. "Yes and no, I suppose." He leaned forward and set his drink on the nearby table with a sharp click. "On one hand, there is something reassuring about knowing I am not the last with my blood—the world suddenly feels a great deal less lonely—but I'm wracked with guilt."

"Why? You had nothing to do with it." Her heart ached to see her friend thusly. His bloodshot eyes with their purple shadows, the furrows his fingers had carved through his once immaculately styled hair, the rumpling of his usually impeccable clothing…it was not who he was. Of course, he could be serious when the need arose, but she'd always been drawn to his determinedly light spirit in spite of all he'd weathered, his easy smile and genuine laughter, his penchant for mischief.

"Because I grew up *here*," he gestured to the grand room around them, "and he…did not."

"You did not have the rosiest of childhoods either," she reminded him gently. She twisted her fingers together to prevent herself from reaching for him when she wanted nothing more than to hold him close.

"Hardly a comparison; I had the benefits of plenty of food and shelter." He stared into the golden light refracting from what remained of his drink on the table as if it were stained glass in a church. "You know what really makes me ill, Caro?" he asked, seemingly not expecting an answer when he continued without waiting for her. "He is my *elder* brother. All of this would have been his if he hadn't been born on the wrong side of the sheets. Instead, he bears the mark of a *bastard*, and I live as a marquess."

Caroline cringed at the way he spat the word *bastard*, but she said nothing. Gideon was a man whose very nature would have made it difficult for him to stomach such inequality. The what-ifs would buzz through his brain like a swarm of insects.

If the other boy had been legitimate, then he wouldn't have suffered a life of deprivation. All the privileges Gideon enjoyed would have also belonged to his brother.

She did not know the full story yet, but Caroline got the sense that the other boy had suffered because of the circumstances of his birth. It struck unnervingly close to the reason she'd dropped by Gideon's home that day and it made her momentarily lightheaded.

In one swift move, Gideon snatched up his glass and tossed back the rest of his drink before launching to his feet.

"I'd always known my father was vile, but it is another thing to finally be faced with the consequences of his actions," Gideon ranted as he strode over to the sideboard and poured himself another few fingers of whiskey. "Even worse, both he and my mother *knew* of my half brother's existence and yet neither lifted a finger to see to it that he was cared for."

"What has brought this on?" Caroline asked gently, examining the tenseness of his shoulders beneath his tailored brown coat.

Gideon turned to her with a wry smile on his lips. "A case of mistaken identity. I accidentally propositioned his wife, to which he did not take very kindly.

"Oh, Gideon."

"Believe me when I say none of us left that encounter unshaken." He returned to the chair beside her and dropped down, barely making it onto the seat rather than tumbling to the floor.

"And you are so certain this man is your illegitimate kin?" she asked.

He tilted his chin to the cursed portrait as part of his response. "The man looks like he could have bloody well sat for that painting."

"I see…" she trailed off.

"More than two decades I've known of his existence, but I never thought to find him in this city. What are the odds?" He emitted a cruel, disbelieving laugh as he slouched back in his chair.

"I would imagine very slim, indeed."

Gideon heaved a sigh and rolled his glass between his palms before giving his head a little shake. "My apologies, Caro. I have so rudely monopolized the conversation when you were the one to call upon me. I am horrible company, as you can see, but to what do I owe the pleasure of this surprise visit? I feel as if it has been an age since we last saw one another."

As a hint of his usual mischievous glimmer twinkled at her over his glass, Caroline experienced a sudden flashback of Gideon over her, his hard body atop and inside of her, wringing from her the most exquisite pleasure with his mouth and hands, and cock…

"Christ, Caro. You are incredible. You've no idea how long I've dreamt of this."

Caroline clenched her trembling hands as her body flushed hot and cold from the erotic memories. She could still taste him on her tongue.

She couldn't do what she'd gone there to do—not when, only the evening before, he'd already suffered the strange and disconcerting situation of meeting his half brother for the first time.

She could not tell him yet.

Not today.

"Nothing of any import," she replied lightly as she stood and shook the wrinkles from her skirts. "Is there anything you need? Shall I request Cook make you something to eat as I make my way out?" Gideon caught her hand when she would have walked by him on her way to the door. She steadfastly avoided his gaze and, instead, stared at the pattern on the rug beneath their feet. His thumb brushed over the bumps of her knuckles, the heat of his fingers was searingly warm against her skin. He pressed a quick kiss to the back of her hand, and her eyes fluttered closed. It wasn't anything he hadn't done a thousand times before, but it was the first time he'd done so since their shared night. What a fool she'd been to believe they could explore carnal desires and return to the way things were—well, what a fool *she* had been to think she could move on after knowing him that way.

"You can tell me anything," he murmured.

Finally, Caro met his eyes. She knew she could tell him anything…she also knew he could read her so well that he'd press until she finally admitted to what was bothering her. Even deep into his cups, he exhibited such care and understanding of her that it made the backs of her eyes burn with emotion.

His fingers gently squeezed hers once more, unleashing the words with a frisson of both fear and excitement, until they leapt from her lips as if from a cliff. "I am with child."

Chapter Four

G IDEON COULD ONLY stare up into Caro's shimmering green eyes as his drunken brain struggled to comprehend her words. *With child?* Surely she was jesting—it wouldn't have been the first time one of them attempted to make sport of the other. But, no. She was deathly silent and more serious than he'd ever seen her before.

Pregnant.

Caro is pregnant.

His body went cold and numb as the deep thud of his heart became deafening in his ears. Blindly, he reached out to set his glass on the table, nearly missing.

As most unmarried men would in his position, it was on the tip of his tongue to ask for confirmation that the child was his...but he stopped shy of speaking the words. Even in his inebriated state, he recognized what a grave insult it would have been to his friend. He knew Caro better than most; contrary to the vulgar rumors, she never took lovers.

It would be just his luck that the only time she did, she'd put her faith in the one man with the world's most rotten luck.

He sat back in his chair and speared both hands into his hair. His gut had warned him that sleeping with Caro after their many years of close friendship was going to be a miserable mistake— regardless of how beautiful he'd always thought she was and how much his drink-addled mind screamed to possess her—but he'd assumed it was regarding their relationship...not *this*. Any fool could explain how introducing physicality would likely ruin a friendship or complicate feelings. An utter idiot would, in favor of giving in to both their desires, conveniently ignore another very real possibility: A child might come of the union.

It wasn't that the thought hadn't crossed his mind—it was more a force of habit now than an act that required planning—but here was evidence that nothing was foolproof. He'd heard stories of just such accidents happening before; he'd simply (naively) thought it was unlikely to happen to him. When it came to his single night with Caro, he'd been too overtaken by drink and lightheartedness, too overcome by his long-simmering attraction to her for any sense to win out. He'd made a mistake; the onus was on him. Caro had requested one evening with him, and he'd agreed. No one had forced him; she hadn't truly coerced him. As soon as she'd whispered in his ear that she desired a lover and trusted him to teach her what passion could be like, he had quite literally leaped at the chance, springing to his feet and ushering her from the Haverford ball with astounding speed.

And now he would face the consequences.

The world began to spin, and Gideon was forced to rest his elbows on his knees and hang his head as he rubbed the back of his neck.

"I plan on retiring to the country before I begin to show—perhaps in the next couple of months," Caro rushed to say. He could hear the tremble in her voice and he didn't care for it one bit. God, this must have been terrifying for her, and he wanted nothing more than for her to know she was not alone. "I have relatives in Cornwall—"

"What? Your horrid elder cousin, Edith?" Gideon looked up at her and narrowed his eyes, knowing Caro would be miserable if she followed through with that plan. Not a day would go by that that pompous, pious vicar's wife wouldn't remind Caro what a sinful burden she and her unborn child were. It was out of the question. He could not allow her to travel to Cornwall, but he also recognized how limited her options were.

None of her other family would provide her assistance—especially not if they discovered *he* was the sire of her child. He'd never interacted with them directly, preferring to keep his distance from the people who had disowned his dearest friend after she'd been nothing more than a girl who placed her trust and her heart in the hands of the wrong man. He'd also never witnessed Caro interact with them, but Viscount Fischer and his wife had been very vocal to everyone who would listen that they disowned their "rebellious" daughter, denounced her scandalous behavior and companions. They felt Gideon was a poor influence…and hadn't he just proven them correct?

The taut lines of Caro's face made his heart squeeze uncomfortably. He didn't know how long she'd sat with this knowledge, but he knew he couldn't allow her to bear the burden alone any longer. A sudden thought smacked him upside his head.

"Have you been to see a physician?" He hoped she hadn't also been feeling ill. Didn't that happen to women when they were with child? He seemed to recall someone mentioning that it was a common experience. Caro nodded in response to his inquiry. "And you are feeling well? All is well?" She nodded again.

"The doctor said it was still too soon for the morning illness to begin, but it will likely appear in the next several weeks."

There was his answer. He felt absurdly proud that he'd gotten that much correct; unfortunately, that was the sum of his knowledge of pregnancy after the point of conception. "I am pleased that all is well so far," he added earnestly. He'd caused this, so it was reassuring that Caro hadn't suffered any ill effects without him unawares.

There was another heavy pause. "I do not expect anything of you. It was not my intention to force you to the altar," she reassured him. "I will find a way to withdraw somewhere safe so I might wait out the pregnancy and give birth in secret."

Gideon shook his head more forcefully than he should have, given the amount of whiskey he'd drunk. "Did you not hear anything I just said? About my father? How could you believe I'd not take responsibility for you and this child? *Our* child?"

"That is not what I was saying at all!" Caro responded hastily. "I merely wished to absolve you of any feelings of obligation."

"I will not become my father," he said with all the finality of a judge's ruling. "I refuse."

"What are you saying?" The tears had disappeared from her eyes, thankfully, without ever actually falling. She had beautiful eyes with tilted corners and fringes of thick chestnut lashes. A smattering of freckles was painted across her cheeks and nose, constellations he'd long ago memorized.

A memory floated back to him—something his consciousness had swept aside, but his soul had never forgotten...had cherished, in fact.

Caroline had been with him when he'd received word of his father's death following a brief illness of an undisclosed nature. The man's life of excess was likely what had finally done him in.

Gideon had allowed the news to roll off him like rain on oiled canvas, maintained his cool façade despite his confusing emotions, and insisted they all continue their planned evening of gambling at Duke's. He'd gone to great lengths to secure a pass for Caroline to accompany the rest of their group, and he would not allow his father to ruin one more thing for him.

It was clear that his reaction—or lack thereof—unnerved his companions, Caroline included, but they'd eventually capitulated and moved on with the evening. He never made a secret of his dislike of his sire. They may have possessed a striking physical resemblance, but that was where the similarities ended. There were few pleasant things to say about the man, and fewer people who would voice them. He had been a powerful, unpopular man who'd often overindulged in spirits, women, and other vices. He displayed uncouth outbursts and a haughtiness that was most unbecoming. And he had been none of the things a father should have been.

He hadn't been a kind man, a decent man, a patient man, a warm man, nor a protective man. Both he and Gideon's mother had cultivated a hostile garden in which Gideon had been forced to grow…and it was a wonder he'd survived at all, let alone turned into a relatively decent human being.

Gideon wasn't cold; he was numb from the news.

He'd long believed he'd feel relief at his father's passing. He did not long for the title and wealth he would inherit, but for the freedom. He would finally be released from beneath his father's hulking shadow to break away from the legacy his father had built and forge his own way.

What Gideon hadn't expected was the way it felt as if his heart was splintering in his chest, the shards scraping his ribs and organs with every breath.

At the conclusion of the evening, Gideon had insisted upon seeing Caroline back to her home, as he usually did. He knew she was strong and independent, but he could not sleep well unless he knew she was safe…not to mention, he hadn't quite been ready to be alone. As he drove the two of them through the streets in his gig, Caroline finally mustered up enough courage to ask him about his father. His response had choked him so unexpectedly that he lost his breath. He actually forgot how to breathe. The reaction was so sudden, so unanticipated, that he'd nearly lost control of the reins. He could sense her growing uncomfortable beside him, unsure whether he had taken offense to her query, and he'd finally been able to force words from his chest.

"I am not ready to speak of him." His voice hardly sounded like his own, thick and raspy with blasted emotion. "But I will come to you if and when I am."

Caroline had nodded in acceptance and did not continue to press him. Her quiet presence eroded his composure more than any further questioning would have. By the time they reached her building, his chest had felt as if it was going to split in two.

He couldn't stop himself from taking her hand to stall her. He knew from her eyes that she read the pain in his; she heard all the words he could not form and understood all the emotions he could not name. He'd had a horrible father, but he'd also lost the slim shard of a chance of ever forming the relationship for which he'd longed his entire life.

He'd wrapped Caroline in his arms and crushed her to him. To her credit, Caroline did not flinch at his strength nor protest the contact; instead, she held him back just as tightly to let him know she, too, would not disappear from his life. She propped him up when he was too weak to stand. She did not shame him for faltering. She grounded him when he felt as if he was falling through an endless pit. He had no idea how long they'd remained like that, but it mattered to neither of them who witnessed the display. He'd needed her, and, without having to utter a single word, she let him know that she would be there for him.

And he would be there for her—not only because he owed it to her, but because he wanted to be.

He'd probably do a horrendous job of it. He had nothing in his past that led him to believe he might even make a passable husband or father—he didn't know what a man like that would even look like—but, for Caroline, he would bloody well try. She deserved better than a man who had no idea if he could be what she needed, but he vowed to do his best to, at the very least, improve upon the examples he'd had. Granted, that mark had been set extremely low, but at least it gave him somewhere to aim.

The way Caroline looked at him, disbelieving in her hopefulness, made Gideon proud to utter his next words. "I intend to procure a special license so we can marry as soon as possible. You need not do this alone."

"Surely, you are not serious," Caroline gasped. "I cannot be your marchioness! This is something you must think on, it does not do either of us any good to make rash decisions, since those are clearly not something in which you and I excel." He enjoyed the flush spreading on her cheeks and throat. "Besides, you've been drinking and should sober up some before we proceed any further."

"Fine," he bit out. "But I will not change my mind."

Chapter Five

TRUE TO HIS word, Gideon arrived at Caroline's townhouse only two days later, special license in hand. Her housekeeper showed him in and then left them to their private conversation. She knew it was only a matter of time before the entire staff knew about the pregnancy, if they didn't already. It had actually been Caroline's lady's maid who'd alerted her to the fact that she'd missed her monthly courses. Their time for managing the consequences of their actions was growing slim.

"I called in a favor owed to my father," Gideon explained as he held up the signed, sealed document that would allow them to forego the reading of the banns and marry as quickly as possible. "It is nice to know the man was good for something." He dropped onto the sofa beside her with all the grace and negligence of an overindulged hound, making her bounce a bit and scramble so her sewing wasn't lost in the cushions. Most would be surprised to realize how prolific an embroiderer she was, but she'd always enjoyed the task. It felt as if she were painting with thread instead of a brush. The repetitive motions and mindless counting served as a pleasant counterpoint to the joyful chaos of the rest of her life.

Hastily packing her work away in its basket, Caroline supposed she shouldn't have been surprised that Gideon had followed through. The world might think him an unreliable scoundrel, but she and their closest friends knew the truth: There were few people more trustworthy than him.

Her reaction had more to do with the fact that she'd long ago given up any hopes of a proposal, let alone one that would make her a marchioness.

Never mind marriage to Gideon, her closest friend.

Her mind simply could not fathom the speed with which her life had careened onto a new path.

"Really, Gideon, you needn't do this." She tried to sound convincing, but she feared her tone gave away how she'd lain awake the previous few nights mulling over her very limited options. Either she disregarded Gideon's insistence that they marry and she disappeared into the country, thereby absolving him of what he saw as his responsibility, or she allowed him to press forward with this marriage of necessity and trust that he knew precisely what he was doing.

She'd also have been lying if she claimed the thought of marriage to him didn't unleash a bevy of flutters in her stomach. No matter how tempting the prospect, she would never forgive herself if, down the line, he felt as if he'd been trapped. That was not why she'd mustered the courage to invite him to her bed with no strings attached, and that was certainly not how she intended to move forward now that her choices had caught up with them.

Gideon was an honest, loyal, terribly generous person. All of these were admirable traits in a man, and they were desirable in a mate. Still, he was also first and foremost her friend. The last thing she'd ever intended to do was ruin his life on a whim. Granted, he'd been a willing participant in said whim, but neither of them had intended this outcome. Caroline knew she could do far, far worse than Gideon, but that didn't change the fact that the outcome felt hollow—that she'd somehow cheated her way into a prestigious place in Society by extending the illicit invitation.

At least, that was how she knew her family and many others like them would see things.

The truth of it was far less nefarious than entrapping a good man into marriage…she'd only wanted to, just once, experience intercourse with a man whom she cared for and trusted. Her experience was tragically limited, and she'd only wished for something to help blot out the memory of it—to replace it with something better.

"Of course I do," Gideon replied lightly, snapping Caroline out of her scattered, rambling musings. Despite the joviality of his voice, there was no mistaking the adamancy in the message. He would not budge.

"This is entirely my fault," Caroline sighed, deflating somewhat. She fought to maintain her composure, but it was a vicious battle. She'd never been an overly emotional person before, but this child in her womb was making her rather weepy—what an inconvenient side effect.

"I am certainly not blameless." She could hear the kind smile in Gideon's voice as his hand covered hers in her lap and his thumb stroked her knuckles in that familiar way. "My curiosity finally got the better of me," he jested gently. Caroline tried to smile in return, but it was nearly impossible.

"I am…" She trailed off with a shaky sigh. "I am worried that, one day, you will resent me…and the baby."

"Caro…" he chided, gently lifting her chin until she finally met his eyes. His dark brows were knit together in concern. The hard angle of his jaw was tense. The sincerity in his storm-gray eyes, however, was what finally caused a single tear to spill onto her cheek. "It won't be such a bad arrangement. We've always gotten on well. We share history and common interests." He went on to detail all the ways they suited, but, to Caroline, she couldn't help believing it all sounded as if she, the baby, and the marriage were a consolation prize into which he'd talked himself into accepting.

Taking a slow breath through her nose, she reminded herself that her emotions were high and she bit her tongue. Gideon was doing his best to be reassuring in their unorthodox situation.

"Besides," he continued, "I'd have to marry and produce an heir sooner rather than later. As I see it, you've saved me a hell of a lot of trouble and given me a head start." The last finally made her crack a smile. He took both her hands now and squeezed them warmly. "I suppose we shall have to tame down a little bit as parents, no? Fewer visits to Duke's and Vauxhall? And the child's first words probably should not be 'win,' 'place,' or 'show,' so less time at the races is in order."

Caroline's smile finally bloomed in full. "The only change I will request from you is to put an end to your drunken jousting career."

Gideon threw his dark head back and laughed heartily, the sound booming through her chest. "I thought you found that hilarious," he chuckled.

"That was when I had no right to dictate your behavior. Now, as your supposed fiancée, however, I may have to put my foot down against anything that might result in you snapping your neck."

"For you, I just may make a concession." He inclined his head gallantly. "Speaking of fiancée…" Gideon trailed off, reaching into his coat and pulling a dark-blue velvet pouch from an inner pocket. Unfastening it, he dropped into his palm a glittering gold ring set with a sizable pigeon blood ruby and a quartet of diamond baguettes. Caroline immediately began shaking her head.

"I couldn't—"

"It wasn't my mother's," he hastily reassured her, "nor was it ever part of the Swanleigh estate. I didn't want you to have anything tainted by their bad blood." She eyed the beautiful piece longingly, knowing it must have cost a small fortune. She all but melted when he said, "I purchased it with you in mind, Caro." A soft smile tugged at the corner of his mouth. "I won't force you to wear it—I wouldn't presume that I can force you to do anything because I *know* you—but I hope you will at least accept it and keep it."

She was utterly helpless in the face of this information. Biting her lip, she plucked the stunning ring from his hand. It was deliciously warm from the heat of his body as she slid it on her middle finger—the only one it would fit.

"We can have it resized," he reassured her as he took her hand and examined it. Was it her imagination, or did he linger a bit longer than he should have? She was so lost in examining the contrast of his long, square fingers as they cradled her much smaller ones that she nearly jumped when he spoke again. "Now, would you like to accompany me to speak with your family, or shall I go alone?"

Caroline blanched immediately. "Why would you do that?"

"Because we should still obtain your father's consent to wed…unless you wish to run away together?"

If only he knew how appealing that sounded—especially now.

"I am six and twenty; I reached my majority five years ago." She spoke rapidly, her insides clenching at the thought of being in the same room as her parents for the first time in years.

"I understand your reticence, but I have thought it over and feel it would be beneficial for us to begin this marriage with their support."

"They won't offer it." Caroline couldn't recall a time when they'd ever supported her in anything; there was no reason to believe they would start now.

"We cannot know that unless we ask." He was achingly optimistic. How had he managed to hold onto that after all this time—after all he had experienced? "I will go regardless of whether you accompany me or not, though I would prefer we present a united front." He squeezed her hand again, grounding her in the moment and reminding her she was not alone.

Caroline had not faced her family or spoken to them directly in nearly seven years. Following the scandal of her debut Season, when she'd been caught in an extremely compromising situation with a young man, they'd immediately cut ties with her. Her last conversation with her parents had consisted of them handing her paperwork outlining a small pension as bribery to stay away from them and Caroline's younger sister, Grace. To keep the stain of her shame well away from all of them. Gideon knew of *The Incident* that had precipitated the falling out with her parents, but did not know the full extent of her family's censure, their bitter venom at the disappointment she was to them.

She could only imagine how her father would react to Gideon's showing up on their doorstep, forcing an introduction, and then explaining that he'd impregnated their scandal-ridden daughter and planned on marrying her in a rushed ceremony with a special license. That would quite possibly be an even bigger disaster than her first debacle.

Unfortunately, she realized that, if there were no dissuading Gideon, then she would be forced to accompany him. It was the only way she might try to mitigate a disaster. "I will join you," she finally said in a tone brimming with resignation. Dread threatened to boil over within her breast, but she knew she had to take solace in the fact that she would not be alone. If anyone was going to protect her from her family, it was Gideon.

His grin was nearly blinding in its beauty. "Brilliant. We shall go later this afternoon, then."

It continued to cause Caroline no small amount of pain that the thought of interacting with the two people who were supposed to care for her and support her the most in this world were the ones whose vicious verbal barbs had filled her life with discomfort and anxiety. It had always been that way with them.

Mama and Papa had sat her down shortly before her seventeenth birthday and informed her in no uncertain terms that her debut marked her recognition as an official representative of the Wells family and the Fischer viscountcy; as such, she was expected to maintain the utmost decorum and comport herself in a manner befitting a lady. Rather than bolster her, their firm warnings had only increased her nerves exponentially, making her feel as if she'd swallowed an entire hive of angry bees.

Caroline would have gladly sold every beautiful dress they'd ordered for her first Season if only Mama had held her hand; if only Papa had smiled and reassured her that all would be well. Unfortunately, that was not the household she'd been born into.

In place of affection, she was peppered with warnings and lessons. Instead of praise, she was told only how she might have improved. She lived in constant fear of making a mistake.

Nearly every night leading up to her debut, she awoke in a cold sweat from nightmares where she'd done something wrong; her mother wailed over the embarrassment, and her father's scowl could freeze a kettle of boiling water. Those nights, she would crawl into Grace's bed and take comfort beside her sweet younger sister's warm body as they held one another close. Grace always smelled of sunshine and sweets, and she was the best comfort Caroline had in that home. Unfortunately, she had not spoken to her sister in years. Her parents made formidable gatekeepers. They hadn't deemed her appropriate company for their *unsullied* daughter and had refused her any access to Grace since the day of Caroline's disgrace.

"Have you heard from your brother again?" she asked, abruptly changing the subject when her eyes began to sting.

Gideon shook his head. "Though I cannot blame him. It was a remarkable discovery. I am certain he requires time to process it." He stared off, unseeing, at the nearby window. The sofa was positioned just right so she might watch the passersby as she read or sewed. Several silent seconds passed like this until Gideon shook off his unease, the glint in his eyes returning. "Why don't we see your parents now, hm?" Caroline's stomach plummeted when she realized her plan to switch topics had backfired spectacularly. Rather than preoccupying him with another conversation, it had only turned his mind toward family and made him want to settle matters with her parents at that very moment.

Caroline attempted to splutter a refusal, but he heard none of it as he pulled her to her feet and went about having her spencer and other traveling accessories brought down. The Swanleigh carriage was already waiting in front of the townhouse, so, in less than a quarter of an hour, Caroline was—much to her horror— swept out the door and set on her way to visit her childhood home.

Chapter Six

U PON ARRIVAL AT Viscount Fischer's townhouse, Gideon and Caroline were shown into a small parlor by a very put-out butler who either suffered from allergies or found it impossible not to sniff with disdain each time he looked their way.

"You'd think we were asking the man to go above and beyond his duties by admitting us to the house," Gideon said out of the corner of his mouth as the servant fled from the room as quickly as he could. The comment had its intended effect—Caroline was forced to bite her lip to stifle a giggle. She had been stiff and tense since they'd departed her home. He knew full well that she and her family did not get on well, but his intent was not to torture her, but to give their union more legitimacy and acceptance in the eyes of the *ton*. The quickest and simplest way to go about that was to have her parents on their side, publicly supporting the match. There would be enough whispers and rumors without it, and, as uncomfortable as it might be, he hoped it would be worth it. Whatever Viscount Fischer might think of him, there was no denying that it would be an advantage for him to have a marquess as a son-in-law. He was hopeful that this would entice the man enough to bite his tongue and finally give his daughter the recognition she deserved.

Gideon had sat by for far too long while they ignored Caroline, pretended she did not exist, and did nothing to naysay the negative things written about her in tabloids. One thing was certain: Gideon would do everything he could to put a stop to their cruelty as soon as Caroline had his name.

He narrowly fought the urge to hold Caro's hands as she fidgeted while they waited.

And waited.

And waited.

At first, he'd thrown out little comments and snippets of conversation to cheer Caroline and pass the time, but, as the long minutes passed, the more anxious and annoyed Gideon became. He also noticed Caroline began to curl in on herself, growing smaller and smaller. That, somehow, made him angrier than the blatant rudeness of their treatment by Fischer. Caroline was not a meek little mouse; she could be sunshine personified. This was part of what had initially drawn him to her. Her joy was infectious, her adventurous spirit was intoxicating. The woman sitting in the chair beside him in that parlor was most assuredly *not* the Caro he knew, and it disturbed him. What was it about this house that had changed her so? What had her family done to her?

Finally, the door to the parlor opened to admit Viscount and Viscountess Fischer, and Gideon was reminded how little Caro resembled her parents. The red hue to her golden hair had been inherited from her father, her green eyes from her mother, but that was where the similarities ended. Fischer was stout and jowly; his wife was short with ruddy cheeks and watery eyes. Perhaps she'd once been a pretty young woman, but the fishlike downturn of her thin mouth counteracted any attractiveness. *Unpleasant* was the word that came to Gideon's mind. These people were the very definition of the word, and, with their unwelcoming looks, wrinkled noses, and deplorable manners, they affirmed his assessment. When they spoke, they underscored it.

"Swanleigh," grunted Fischer, his icy eyes darting to his daughter, but not saying a word to her in greeting. Gideon's fist clenched. He had to remind himself that laying the viscount out flat would be counterproductive, so he took a bracing breath, rose to his feet, and greeted Caroline's parents with his most amiable smile. He tapped into his bountiful well of charm, only to have it disregarded.

"To what do we owe this visit?" asked the viscount. Caroline's mother had not even turned to greet her yet. With every passing second, Gideon's ire was rising.

Gideon turned and held his hand out to Caro. She took it, her fingers like ice as he helped her to stand. "We have not previously been formally introduced, but I have some things to discuss with you, and Miss Wells was kind enough to accompany me."

Her father's eyes flicked to Caroline. "If there was any reticence in her joining you here, that is because she knows full well she is unwelcome within these walls."

Gideon's brows snapped down. "I beg your pardon?" Caro flinched at his side and it was everything he could do not to pull her against his side. He hadn't expected a warm reception filled with embraces and fond words, but this?

This was hostile.

"And you, Swanleigh," the viscount continued, his cheeks quivering like an obese hound's, "why have you come here? It is no secret that you are connected with Caroline, but that is hardly a reason to call here, dragging sin and gossip in your wake." Viscountess Fischer was nodding along with her husband's words, as if she were a puppet in a child's play, righteous indignation fairly oozing from her pores.

"That is hardly the way to treat guests in your home," Gideon ground out, barely keeping himself in check. Throwing a punch would feel so bloody good.

"I will speak to people in my home in any manner in which I see fit." He leveled a stubby finger at Caro. "Especially when they have been told in no uncertain terms that they are never to darken our doorstep again."

"Lord Fischer—"

"You grew tired of staining our name from afar, so you had to come here and flaunt yourself before us?" Fischer finally addressed Caro, but it was far from what Gideon had expected. The vitriol was astounding. "You were to stay away, and now the whole of Mayfair will be discussing your visit by the end of the day. How dare you bring this upon us?"

"See here," snapped Gideon, stepping between Caro and her father. He couldn't stand by one more second as she shrank into herself while her father spewed his vile words. "Take care with the way you are speaking."

"This is no matter of yours," Fischer snarled, spittle flying from his loose lips, "even if she is acting as your current whore."

Gideon snapped. He drew himself up to his full height and adopted a cruel, frigid tone eerily reminiscent of his deceased father's. "It damn well is my concern because Caroline is my betrothed. And I will *not* allow you to speak to the future Marchioness of Swanleigh in such a manner."

Fischer's hand fell and the room went deathly silent. Lady Fischer turned gray, her fish mouth gaping, making her look like a beached trout. The viscount began to stammer and spluttered, "This cannot be true." His eyes darted between Gideon and Caro several times before landing on his daughter. "Surely, you cannot have made yet another horrendous mistake? Chosen to throw what remains of your life away? It is bad enough that your antics are bandied about in the gossip columns, speculating about what sort of sordid relationship you share with this reprobate, but now you must feed this bit to them? Marriage will not scrub away your sins."

"How can you do this to us?" wailed her mother. "Grace is only just making her debut and you will destroy everything we have worked for." She plopped dramatically onto the sofa, fanning her face as if she were near to fainting.

In response, Caro was more silent, more cowed than Gideon had ever seen her. The protective monster inside of him roared in fury.

Gideon closed the gap between where he stood and Viscount Fischer in three long strides until he towered over the older man.

"Part of being a 'reprobate' means I've become quite adept with both sword and pistols. I suggest you bite your tongue before I am forced to show you just how accomplished I am." Fischer began to stammer, but Gideon did not offer him another chance to speak. "I came here out of respect for Miss Wells—to offer you, as her parents, an opportunity to bestow your blessings upon our union, but I can see what a mistake that was. You are not worth the courtesy. You are not worthy of another second of Miss Wells's time. She has not needed you in seven years, and I will personally ensure she will never have need of you again." He leaned in close. "And if you ever cause her a single ounce of pain again—if I hear one more vile word tumble from your disgusting lips—then you will answer to *me*."

Gideon wasted no time in bundling Caro up and back into his carriage.

"What utterly horrid people," Gideon fumed. "I don't bloody blame you for staying away from them for as long as you did."

"As you now know, it wasn't entirely my choice." Her voice was so small that he almost missed it in his rant. He heard her, though, and his tirade came to a screeching halt. He crossed the carriage and sat beside her on the forward-facing seat. Caro was impossibly pale, the cinnamon sprinkles of her freckles standing in stark contrast on the sickly apples of her cheeks. She was shaken by the confrontation with her parents; there was no other way to describe how it had left her. He couldn't blame her. If that was how they treated her in front of someone else, it sickened him to think how they behaved behind closed doors. Even if Caro had been cast out as a girl of less than twenty years of age, it might have been a minor blessing compared to being subjected to that venom on a daily basis.

He wrapped an arm around her slim shoulders and pulled her close to his side. She immediately melted into him like a candle left too near a flame. He savored it.

"I apologize for coercing you into joining me. I should have listened to you."

"You were trying to do the right thing."

"That doesn't make it any better."

Caro tilted her head back and looked up at him. The color was beginning to return to her cheeks. Finally. "Having you stand up for me—making my father look as if he was about to piss a puddle in the middle of the parlor floor—made it more worth it."

Gideon gave a gentle chuckle. "How could such vile people create so incredible a person?"

Her answering smile was soft and fleeting. "At their heart, they are trying to protect my younger sister, Grace. They've failed with me and want to give her the best chance at a good match."

"They have more than one daughter."

Caro pulled her lips between her teeth and averted her eyes. She could not argue with the truth. Just because her parents wanted to protect Grace from the stain of Caro's reputation and influence, that did not give them leave to treat their elder daughter in such a deplorable fashion. She gave a little sigh.

"Is there anything I can do? Anything you need?" he asked gently.

She shook her head. "I would like to return home."

"Very well," he agreed and set their course with the driver.

Chapter Seven

T HE FOLLOWING TWENTY-FOUR hours gave Gideon time to sit with the knowledge that he was well and truly the only person Caro had in the world. The meeting with her family had been both disturbing and eye-opening. He would be a husband in hours and a father in months; not only that, but he would be their sole system of support. He was emotionally damaged enough for that to be unnerving. What kind of example did he have to be a husband and a father? A terrible one, that's what. How could he hope to fulfill the roles with any sort of grace and dignity if he had no experiences from which to pull? It did not make him second-guess his decision to wed Caroline—that was never in question— it made him question the possibility of his success.

Would their longstanding friendship be enough of a foundation?

He did not know the first thing about babies or children.

Could he be trusted to make the right decisions, to say the right things when his family required it of him?

Gideon had been alone for so long—had eschewed Society's dictates with relish and savored their shock—he was unsure he could act any other way. He'd been so concerned with unfettered pleasures after a childhood so devoid of joy and security that he did not know if it was in him to be anything other than the unworthy man he'd been.

Regardless, he had to try.

After he'd deposited Caro at her townhouse and lingered long enough to ensure she was indeed all right after the confrontation, these thoughts struck him with a gravity he hadn't been expecting.

It felt more real than when he'd procured the special license for their marriage.

It washed over him anew when he and Caro stood before the bishop and a very small gathering at Swanleigh House, which consisted only of their closest friends. Lords Kempton, Blackwell, Brinley, and Trenholm rounded out their sextet of hell-raisers. There was a decided lack of females present at the event, but Caro had assured him that all was well, saying she was the only woman patient enough to tolerate their lot.

Though he was supremely grateful for their friends' support on that day, Gideon still felt the lack of family rather keenly—both his and Caro's. Of course, his parents were deceased, and the day before had extinguished any flicker of hope that Caro's parents might one day support their union, but he now knew there was someone else who shared his blood... It had crossed his mind to invite Oliver and his wife to the hasty ceremony, but he'd stopped just shy of it. It felt somehow too desperate...and awkward, given the fact that Oliver still had not contacted him. He didn't want to exert any pressure upon the man, so he let it be and told himself he and Caro would be content having just their friends with them to celebrate.

Finally, his mind made a full stop when Caroline entered the room wearing a morning gown of the clearest blue in nature. The color complemented her pale skin and her rose-gold hair, which had been plaited and pinned to the back of her head in a simple, elegant style. The scooped neckline afforded a glimpse of just the right amount of cleavage to be fashionable and respectable. He had an instant flash of memory of kissing her just there, the delectable valley between those perfect globes...

He had to force his eyes upward and into her face, but that did nothing to calm his racing pulse. She smiled at him and the world faded away around them. It was no different than any other smile she'd shared with him over the years, and yet, it was entirely new. This was the smile of Caro, his soon-to-be wife. The mother of his unborn child. A woman he'd cared for, for years, and now, it was as if she'd been cast in golden light.

The bishop's words passed in a haze. Gideon could hardly remember repeating the necessary phrases, slipping the slightly-too-large ring on Caro's finger, and reminding himself that he would have it resized for her as soon as possible. And then the time came when the bishop instructed Gideon to kiss his new wife.

He actually froze.

Not because he did not wish to kiss Caroline, but because he was nearly overcome by how much he did. His abdomen flexed with the desire to taste her again, just like when they'd crossed the line of platonic friendship months before.

When he finally bent his head, he pressed his lips to hers in a chaste caress…but it was still as if he were tasting liquid fire. He found her as sweet as his hazy memory recalled. What he wouldn't give to slip his tongue between her lips and lick into her mouth…

Gideon lingered longer than was perhaps proper for two friends marrying to legitimize an accidental pregnancy, but he could not bring himself to care. The second she softened against him, however, he had to force himself to pull back lest he lose control before their audience.

Following the ceremony, there was a simple wedding break-fast during which Blackwell clapped Gideon on the shoulder, his dark eyes dancing with mirth as he said, "I'll be honest…we've all been placing bets on when the two of you would end up together."

"Of course you were," Gideon replied with a roll of his eyes.

"Thick as thieves, as they say," added Lord Kempton.

"And I won," crowed Brinley.

Gideon and Caro shared a knowing look. The kiss at their ceremony had been the first time they'd touched in any way other than friendship since their shared night. They'd decided to keep the truth of their rushed marriage a secret, but they both knew the rumors would spread quickly enough. They were already suspected of having an illicit affair. Why else would a marquess need to marry a woman in haste? They agreed not to give any satisfaction to the tabloids, however, and remain as tight-lipped as possible when it came to the pregnancy.

Gideon and Caroline were seen off with ribald jabs and friendly winks—none of their friends being aware that the sum of their sexual history was a single night. They accepted them all in stride and with good humor, both avoiding contemplating too much what would be expected of them that evening.

As GIDEON FINISHED seeing their guests out, Caroline followed Gideon's housekeeper—*their* housekeeper—to the upstairs bedchamber that would be hers. The marchioness's quarters consisted of a beautiful corner suite with a flood of glorious natural light. There hadn't been time to completely redecorate the room in preparation for her arrival, but the windows had been opened and the room, aired; every surface had been thoroughly dusted; the linens were new; her belongings sent over from her townhouse had been carefully unpacked and put in their proper places. Vases of fresh flowers were set beside the bed, on the escritoire, and on the tables in the adjoining private sitting room—pink roses, her favorites. She didn't doubt that Gideon had had a hand in that touch, and it made her skin tingle from head to toe.

Her maid, whom she'd brought with her to Swanleigh house, helped her undress and prepare for bed. Each passing minute caused Caroline's anxieties to swell. She was nervous—more nervous than the night she and Gideon had first shared a bed; probably because she'd spent her entire wedding day painfully sober and achingly aware of what was supposed to lie ahead once she had a husband. Consummation of the union was not only expected but a necessary part of the marriage contract.

She'd lain awake the entire evening prior, kept awake by fevered memories of Gideon holding her and touching her, kissing her, like he had that first and only night. A night that now felt like a lifetime ago.

Regrettably, they hadn't expressly discussed what would happen after their nuptials—would they truly live as man and wife, or would her pregnancy suffice as consummation enough? Would they share a bed, or would they live only as friends from then on? And what if the babe she carried was female—would he wish to try for a male heir? Would that coupling be purely transactional, or might it be as transcendent as the night they'd already had?

At once, Caroline dreaded the answers to those questions, even while desperately wishing to know them. She did not doubt Gideon cared for her, but she knew nothing of what might happen—what might change—between them now that they were wed. She knew what she desired and how she felt about him. She cared deeply for him. He held her heart, whether he knew it or not. She longed for little else above being once more held safely in his arms. She only wished she knew what he was thinking.

Sitting before the low-burning hearth, Caroline pressed her palms to her flat abdomen and wondered how much longer she would have to wait until she felt the little life growing inside of her. The physician had told her it could be a few months yet, but she hoped it would be sooner. For a woman who'd spent nearly a decade believing that she would never make a respectable match or bear children, this was a novel situation…and she ached to have evidence of it. The physician she'd seen had confirmed the pregnancy with as much certainty as the limitations of medicine could, but it didn't feel real. None of it did. Even the wedding had felt like a fantasy as she strode across the room, through the small gathering of their friends, and toward a darkly handsome Gideon dressed all in black and white, as immaculate as always.

And now, in the eyes of the law, he was all hers.

She'd never harbored serious fantasies of marrying the man

who'd been her closest friend for years. Of course, she'd been attracted to him from the start—had felt enough for him to want him to be the man she invited to her bed—but this... This was beyond even her wildest imaginings.

Caroline jumped as the door to the chamber clicked open and Gideon slipped inside. Having changed from his formal clothes into a loose shirt and breeches beneath a loosely tied robe in burgundy silk, he looked relaxed and breathtakingly handsome. She tried not to feel self-conscious about her own state of dishabille, but she struggled when he managed to look like *that* without trying.

Sinfully handsome.

Erotically charming.

Every fantasy she'd ever held rolled into one.

And now...he was *her husband*.

"How are you? Not too fatigued by today?" he asked, his tone gentle and solicitous.

"Not at all," she murmured in reply, wanting to add that she wouldn't object if he decided to toss her over his shoulder and have his way with her. She cast her eyes back at the fire and hoped he would not see the flush on her cheeks at the memories of how he'd done just that and brought her to shuddering releases again and again.

"I hope the rooms are to your liking," Gideon said, joining her by the hearth and dropping into the other armchair. It was a marvel that his large frame did not cause it to collapse entirely. "The staff did their best on such short notice. We can change anything you do not care for."

"Oh no! It is lovely, thank you." It was not lost on her how Gideon did not take any of the credit for the care taken with her rooms—not even for the flowers or the comfortable chairs positioned perfectly between the hearth and the windows. "I enjoy the view of the gardens quite a bit. There is nothing about the room that cannot wait to be changed or updated should I decide in the future."

Gideon nodded, seeming pleased by her answer.

They sat in silence for several minutes after that, both lost in their thoughts and unsure of how to approach the new status of their relationship.

Finally, Gideon blurted out, "We do not need to consummate the wedding night if you do not wish to. I know it is expected, but since when have we done anything the proper way?"

"Oh…" Caroline's stomach did a swooping loop. Was she relieved? Disappointed? Hurt?

"Or, if you wish to…"

"Do you? Wish to…consummate it?"

"No—I mean, yes," he laughed and raked a hand through his dark hair, making it curl boyishly. "I have never been at a loss for words in my life. Since when did we become so awkward around one another?"

They both laughed at that, helping evaporate the tension between them. He leaned forward and covered her hand on the arm of the chair with his own. Did he feel the same tingle there that she did?

"Please know, Caro, that there is no pressure for anything. This situation will take a great deal of adjustment for both of us." She nodded in agreement. "For now, we can resume as friends while we learn one another's private habits. I dare say we have a better foundation than most married couples with our years of friendship, but that doesn't mean there is still not a great deal to learn."

"I could be a horrible snorer," Caroline said mischievously, then laughed heartily at Gideon's stricken expression.

"You aren't, are you?" She shook her head. "Thank God," he breathed a dramatic sigh of relief.

"Though I suppose that is the benefit of separate bedchambers."

"Who says we will always inhabit separate rooms?" he asked cheekily. There was a brief moment where Caroline thought that might have been an invitation, but the flirtatious glimmer in his gray eyes told her that he was no more serious than any other time he'd jokingly propositioned any number of other women who struck his passing fancy. He'd been dubbed a rake for a reason, after all. She needed to bring herself under control before her pregnancy-addled brain made more of this situation than it really was.

Yes, Gideon was her husband.

Yes, he was the father of her unborn child.

Yes, she'd always found him intensely attractive both in physical appearance and manner.

But he was her friend.

Despite the fact that they'd shared a bed once and then married due to the consequences of their choice, even though she would be the woman to bear any legitimate children he had, he'd likely never viewed her as anything above a close friend. She'd convinced herself that she could be like most males and set emotion aside from physical pleasure, but this was proving her sorely mistaken.

Their marriage was all about making an inconvenient situation more convenient, of allowing Gideon to fulfill his sense of right and duty, and of assuaging his guilt over what his father had done to this mysterious half brother of his.

Caroline forced herself to return Gideon's quip with a good-natured eye roll and, with effort, settled back into her role as his good friend... even though the last time they'd been in each other's presence in such a state of undress, they'd wound up panting and sweating in bed. Suddenly, a thought occurred to her. "How do you expect we shall pass the time?" she asked steadily. It was humbling and slightly mortifying to realize that everyone—even the staff—believed them to be busy copulating.

Gideon cocked a brow and it sent her pulse racing. After a beat, he said, "Shall we play some cards? I believe there is a deck of cards somewhere in my bedchamber." He spoke so casually, as if his look hadn't sent awareness curling through her veins like fire.

GIDEON DID NOT return to his bedchamber until the wee hours of the morning. Caroline had been a good sport for several hours, but he'd recognized the undeniable signs of fatigue upon her face as the clock ticked over past midnight. Despite her denials and determined efforts, her stamina wasn't what it once had been.

As he all but deposited her into her bed, he wondered if this was common in pregnant women. He'd done what he could the past several days since learning Caroline was expecting to learn of what a woman went through when she was enceinte, what she might need, what changes might occur. Of course, he'd learned precious little; few men he knew were fathers (intentionally or otherwise), and a man could only make so many subtle inquiries of his staff before people grew suspicious. It had been uncomfortable and deuced awkward, but he knew it was something he needed to do to better understand what Caro was experiencing— even more, he *wanted* to do it for her. It was the least he could do after impregnating her; it was something he owed to her. To be honest, it allowed him to feel even closer to her than he already did. He'd believed he understood her like no one else, but this line of inquiry afforded him a very personal insight into her life as she lived it. He was starved for every bit of knowledge he could obtain. She'd become as much a part of his life as his right arm; without her, he would be lost. It was a privilege to have the opportunity to care for her, and it was thrilling to realize that he no longer had to mask his gestures beneath the guise of simple friendship. He was her husband and could do whatever he damned well pleased.

Now, if only he knew how she felt about him in return.

Gideon had lingered in Caro's bedchamber just long enough to see her crawl beneath the coverlet, looking small and virginal—and unaccountably enticing—in her white lace nightdress, before forcing his legs to move lest he give in to his impulse to follow her there. More times than he could count, he'd pondered what it would be like to hold her as she dreamed, to be lulled to sleep by the gentle sound of her breathing.

He knew enough that this was not simple male desire for a

woman; this was nothing he had felt before. Rather than slaking his desire for her, sharing her bed had only torn open whatever sensible defenses he'd prepared to safeguard their friendship.

From the day they'd met, he—and likely every other man who knew her—had been of the opinion that Caro was remarkably enticing. Her sultry laugh, playful sense of humor, willingness to explore, sense of adventure, and, of course, her attractive figure were all intensely pleasing. This, however, was different.

And it hadn't begun the moment they repeated their vows.

This went back to the night they'd shared in each other's arms. He needed to possess her in a quintessential way. He'd already planted his seed, but he wanted more.

Oh, yes, he wanted her.

In a way, he always had.

It had been apparent from the first that their personalities meshed with the simplicity and ease of two people who were meant to be in one another's lives. They'd become so comfortable as friends, so much so that it became painful to consider asking if she might want more for fear that it would send what they had up in flames. Caro had become an integral part of his life, and he liked to think she felt the same after all this time.

Gideon supposed this was the reason why, when she'd propositioned him that night, he'd thrown all caution to the wind and relinquished control to his baser instincts. He'd desired her for so long, had given up all but the slimmest of hopes that she desired him, and then, faced with everything he'd secretly longed for and never hoped to act upon, he'd dove in without forethought or sense. To be fair, she seemed to lose a bit of control, herself.

His back bore the marks of her passion for days following their assignation…and he'd *loved* it.

Gideon climbed into his cold bed, now aching and frustrated by the memory of that glorious night and the fact that the object of those desires was just on the other side of a wall, and well within his right to claim.

Instead, he lay awake a long, long while, wishing he wasn't so alone.

Chapter Eight

THE FOLLOWING MORNING, the Swanleigh household packed up to retreat to the country house in Kent for the duration of Caroline and Gideon's honeymoon period. Caroline had attempted to insist upon the unnecessary effort and expense, but Gideon remained steadfast in his belief that they take some time away from the stir that would strike London as soon as news of their wedding took flight.

While he was preoccupied with a last-minute meeting with his solicitor, Caroline was busy directing the loading of the last of the luggage when a young woman arrived on the doorstep. She was angelic and ethereal with white-blond hair and doe-like glittering eyes, full lips, and pleasant curves. In all, she was beautiful.

Caroline paused in the doorway of the home as the young woman sidestepped a footman and reached the top step.

"May I help you?" Caroline asked, hoping her pleasant smile masked her confusion and wariness.

"I believe so. I am Mrs. Emily Black," the young woman introduced herself in a confident, steady tone. Her accent was clean, but there was something far more worldly about her carriage than a well-bred lady of her age should have possessed. If Caroline had to guess, the woman was in her early twenties—likely a few years younger than her.

Caroline inclined her head politely, still no less confused. The woman read this immediately and quickly pulled a card from her reticule, adding, "My husband and I very recently became acquainted with Lord Swanleigh. I realize now this is likely inconvenient timing with your packing up house, but I wanted to personally deliver my congratulations on your recent nuptials. I read the news in this morning's paper. You are the new Lady Swanleigh, are you not?"

Caroline examined the card only to discover that it was Gideon's own, engraved with its familiar flourish. This woman could only have possessed it if he'd given it to her.

"I am, indeed, Lady Swanleigh," Caroline answered, her mind turning over the possibility of this woman's identity. Hadn't she mentioned a husband? A recent acquaintance with Gideon?

Her heart skipped.

When she'd come to Swanleigh House to tell Gideon of her pregnancy, he'd been in such a dour mood…because he'd finally located his half brother after years of searching. Could this woman be the wife Gideon had mentioned?

"Your husband isn't…that is, is he Lord Swanleigh's…" She huffed, aggravated that she couldn't spit out the words. "Are our husbands relations?"

A wave of relief washed over the other woman's delicate features. "It seems that way. I was beginning to fear that you knew nothing of our existence and I just unleashed the secret."

"Yes, I know!" Caroline said, then added in a lower tone so servants passing by wouldn't overhear, "Please, do come in." She didn't give Mrs. Black an opportunity to demure before she took her hand and ushered her inside and through to the parlor, where they might speak more privately.

"It was not my intention to interrupt your packing," the other woman said, seeming self-conscious for the first time. "I heard of your wedding and wished only to leave a congratulatory letter." She held out said letter, which Caroline accepted with aplomb.

"You are not an intrusion or an interruption at all. Please do not ever feel that you are! And you must call me Caroline—is it alright if I call you Emily? We are family, are we not?" Emily nodded, her smile broadening. "I fear our wedding was a small affair; I feel terribly that an invitation was not extended to you and your husband."

"Do not dwell on it. This…relationship is so new, and it likely would have introduced more questions than our husbands are yet ready to answer. It is a very delicate time."

That was the first time Caroline heard Gideon addressed as such, and her stomach did a little flipping motion. In the eyes of Society, that was who he was to her.

"I can understand that."

"They look so alike that it would have been impossible to pretend otherwise," Emily added with a chuckle.

"Are they truly that similar in appearance?" Caroline asked.

"Truly," she replied before detailing the very unconventional circumstances of their first encounter. Caroline found the entire thing utterly hilarious, and she took Emily's laughter as permission to show her amusement. "It was far from amusing at the time, but I can see the humor in it now."

"And this occurred at a brothel?" Caroline asked as she wiped away a tear.

Emily nodded and caught her lower lips between her teeth. "My mother spent years of hard work building her business, and I am proud that it is known as one of the finest houses for women and men to work, but I understand the stigma that comes from a connection with such an enterprise. I have always handled the bookkeeping and deliveries, and I still do now and then. My husband helps out when needed. We have no plans to cut ties with Lady Night's, but we do understand that such a connection might be detrimental to your reputations. It is not something we have yet discussed with the marquess—" Her words died when Caroline grabbed her hands.

"Believe me when I say I am certain that Gideon having family is far more important to both of us than anyone's background or reputation." She leaned in conspiratorially and added, "Besides, he and I are quite notorious ourselves. I am sure it would surprise very few if we were connected to Lady Night's. There are far less polished establishments—at least you come from the very best!" This seemed to comfort Emily somewhat, and she squeezed Caroline's hands in return. "Now, might I have your address so I may call upon you when we return to town? We are just leaving for our honeymoon trip."

"I would like that a great deal."

Caroline took her directions, a tidy little area not all that far from where Caroline's own townhouse had been, and they exited into the hallway, nearly colliding with a distracted Gideon.

"There you are, Caro," he greeted her with a smile so warm that she felt her muscles begin to melt. His eyes flicked to their guest. "And Mrs. Black! What an unexpected pleasure." He handed the papers he held to his solicitor, muttered a few words about being in touch, and the man took his leave with a polite nod to the ladies.

"Emily stopped by to pass along their congratulations on our wedding," Caroline explained. Her husband's immediate warmth and pleasure at seeing Emily were not lost on Caroline. As she suspected, he was desperate for a relationship there; she only hoped Emily and her husband felt the same. The last thing she wanted was for Gideon to place his hope in people who might let him down—he had experienced it enough in his life. If this small interaction with Emily was any indication, however, Caroline chose to take it as a positive sign...even if her husband hadn't accompanied her.

"How kind of you," Gideon said with a grin. "And your husband? How is he?" Caroline recognized something cautious and hopeful in his tone, though his pleasant expression did not waver.

There was a flicker in Emily's blue eyes before she replied. "I hope you understand that his absence is no reflection on his opinion of you, Lord Swanleigh. He is coming to terms with a great deal of new information, and, by nature, he is not a very open man."

Gideon nodded in understanding, though Caroline did not

miss the momentary sadness in his eyes, the color of a dreary day. It made her heart ache.

Together, Caroline and Gideon saw Emily to the doorway and bade her farewell. They watched in silence as she descended the steps and turned down the street.

The butler handed over their hats and gloves. "The carriage is prepared, my lord."

"Very good," Gideon replied, all traces of his earlier melancholy evaporated as he turned to Caroline with a blindingly handsome smile and held out his arm to her. "Shall we?"

CASTLE BRAY, THE ancient country seat of Gideon's ancestors, was a remarkably well-kept structure whose foundations dated back nearly two centuries. Constructed of gray and brown stone, it was sturdy and made up in width what it lacked in height. The main wings were three stories tall, ending in red slate roofs and neat clusters of spiraled chimneys similar to those Caroline had seen in drawings of Hampton Court Palace. The grand entrance was the oldest part of the building, Gideon explained. It was crafted in the old fortress style, square with arrow slit windows and square turrets built into every corner. It reached nearly two stories higher than the rest of the building. With its enormous arched gateway and working portcullis, it wasn't difficult to imagine the Bray men guarding England's shores from this very place. In fact, it was precisely why the Swanleigh marquessate had been granted to his family; they and their land had played quite a role in English history.

And she was now one of them.

Caroline found it all more than charming. She was in utter awe of her new surroundings, the fairytale-esque nature of her new life. Despite its age, the most well-used rooms of the castle were beautifully appointed and more modern than she would have expected.

"Not every one of our homes is this well-kept, mind you," Gideon cautioned her during the tour. "For all their faults, this property happened to be my grandfather and father's favorite. I have merely kept up the tradition. There is something enchanting about it, isn't there?"

"I think it's just remarkable." This was a place she could see herself relaxing. It was peaceful and secluded, but not too far from the excitement of London or the thrill of the coast. She might even picture herself entering confinement here.

To be sure, it was leaps and bounds better than anything she might have been able to coordinate on her own, and she knew she had Gideon to thank for that. She didn't doubt that she would have figured something out, had he decided to allow her to retreat to the country and give birth on her own, but it most certainly would not have been anything like this! She was instantly, wholly in love with Bray Castle and, judging from Gideon's knowing smile, he was quite pleased about it.

While the grounds were stunning and there were seemingly endless corners and corridors for her to explore, she guessed Gideon would be bored to tears in a few months. Before her pregnancy, she probably would have felt the same, but so much had changed. She did not know when it began, but she was suddenly viewing everything differently. While she might miss the long, hard rides on the mare Gideon kept for her use, she was becoming just as excited about the thoughts of quiet picnics where she and her child could doze in the dappled sunlight. Spending her evenings laughing so loudly with her friends that they drew disapproving looks was being replaced by imagining what her child's laughter would sound like.

She wondered how and if Gideon would change, too—not that she really wished for him to change; she was simply curious about how he would adapt to fatherhood. However, there was plenty of time for that yet. She'd once heard it said that a woman became a mother when she learned of her pregnancy, but a man became a father when he finally held his babe.

The image of Gideon cradling an infant in his strong arms was enough to make Caroline's knees weak. She knew how gentle and tender he could be, and also how much power his body possessed. He knew precisely when to employ both.

She was lost in just that thought when Gideon entered the library and discovered her gathering wool. "I've always found that particular bit of wainscoting extremely interesting as well," he remarked, mirth bubbling in his tone.

Caro jumped a little at the sound of his voice. "Gideon! Do not sneak up on me like that," she admonished, but her ire died away as soon as he pulled her into his side and dropped a chaste peck to the top of her head.

"My apologies. I only came to tell you that all our belongings have been unpacked. Would you care for a broader tour of the grounds now, or would you prefer to rest?"

She gave this a moment's consideration before answering. "As much as I would love to explore, I think I should have a bit of a lie-down. I've been so fatigued lately."

Concern instantly narrowed Gideon's eyes. "Are you feeling unwell? Shall I send for a physician?"

"No, I am fine," she said quickly and placed a hand on his arm so he would not bolt from the room. "I am told it is common in early pregnancy. I struggle to make it through a single day without a nap." She screwed up her face, annoyed with how she'd become a doddering old lady. "It's terribly inconvenient."

"Luckily for you, we have nowhere to go and no one to see, so you might avail yourself of a lie-down whenever your heart desires." He leaned in close until his warm breath tickled her ear. "And I promise I shall never judge you for it." Then, he scooped her into his arms, ignoring her squeal of surprise, and began carrying her from the cavernous library.

"Where are you taking me?" she demanded, a little breathless from surprise and the feel of him holding her. More so the latter.

"To bed, of course."

Caroline met his eyes. He couldn't mean—

No.

He gave her his cheeky wink, that damned flirtatious gesture he'd used on her and so many others countless times over the years. He was merely jesting—using suggestive language to get a rise out of her as he always had. He no more meant to consummate their marriage than she could sprout wings and fly from the top of the parapet. Caroline did her best not to allow her disappointment to show on her face.

"I will see you to your chamber, ensure everything is to your liking, and then stretch my legs. I shouldn't be more than an hour or two. I expect you will be wanting to eat then?"

She forced a grateful smile and reminded herself that he was only looking out for her. "Perfect." It was everything she could do not to press her face to the curve where his jaw met his throat above his cravat and breathe deeply his scent of leather and tobacco, dark and rich and intoxicating in the best way.

"Do you remember that horse race with Kempton and Brinley?" Caroline murmured, already teetering on the edge of pleasantly drowsy and nearly asleep within the safe cradle of Gideon's arms and his familiar scent.

She felt his chuckle against her side and heard his smile in his voice. "You felt poorly after we were caught in the rainstorm."

"And you still insisted upon being admitted to my home. My poor maid did not know how to turn away an earl, and I could not blame her. You can be quite intimidating when you try." That earned another chuckle.

"When I *try*?" he scoffed lightly, but Caroline was already drifting back into her memories.

She'd been hardly decent at Gideon's arrival, wearing nothing more than her nightshift, a wrapper, and an enormous pile of blankets; however, he'd seemed neither to care nor notice.

"You brought with you a parcel of your cook's best shortbread and two new books from Thorpe's. I tried to make you leave, but you'd already ordered tea and bone broth for me."

Gideon had taken command of her tiny household and refused to hear any of her protests. He'd dragged a chair from another part of the flat and into her bedchamber and settled in for an afternoon of chatting and reading. The man had even stoked the fire himself!

Even years ago, there had already been rumors about a relationship between the two of them. Caroline had believed that, if the world only saw how kind and caring a man he was, how he treated her like his most cherished friend rather than a lover, then they would not say such things. She'd tried convincing herself that there were not a thousand reasons for her to develop feelings for him.

The facts that he always seemed to know when she was not feeling herself, that he remembered when she mentioned she was looking forward to reading a new publication, and how she adored his cook's shortbread because the batches from her kitchen always wound up too sweet were not reasons enough alone to assume they shared an explicit relationship...though they were wonderfully endearing benefits. This cozy blanket of comforting memories finally lulled Caroline into a deep and restful sleep, so deep that she did not stir when Gideon carefully placed her on the bed, covered her, and, after a moment of indecision, lay down beside her, his planned ride long forgotten.

CAROLINE AND GIDEON spent the first week of their honeymoon trip walking and talking, reading with the windows open on rainy days, and staying up late into the evenings playing any one of the countless card games they'd learned over the years. The two of them fell into a comfortable routine, both entirely unaware that, as they retired separately each night, both were frustrated by the ongoing lack of intimacy. Neither was willing to take the first step and risk the amiability of these early days of marriage.

For Gideon's part, there was little he desired more than to share Caroline's bed again; however, she'd taken such pains to let him know that they would be together only one night. With her history, the last thing he wished was for her to feel pressured to follow through with anything she did not want. Unless she came to him expressing interest in exploring their chemistry in bed once again, he would remain respectful and silent.

"If I'd wanted to be a monk," Gideon grumbled to himself in the wee hours one morning as he palmed his aching cock, "I'd have joined the order or wed a woman I could not stand."

Caro certainly was not that woman.

In fact, he enjoyed her company far too much.

He was used to seeing her several times each week, but this constant dose of her sharing his home was having a curious impact upon his senses. He became attuned to her in new ways, began to learn her private quirks and habits. She preferred breaking her fast with fruit and tea, but she was not picky about the variety, so long as it was fresh. Following that meal, she enjoyed walking outside if the weather permitted, but laps around the residence worked in a pinch. She detested fish in all its forms, and this was only exacerbated by her expectant state; however, this did not diminish her enjoyment of the salty sea air that often whistled through the castle's windows. He'd learned over the years how she enjoyed a hearty laugh, did not shy away from elaborate pranks, and could hold her drink and gamble with even the most seasoned of lords, but this was different. Now he witnessed Caro in her quiet moments, and he could not seem to get his fill of watching and learning.

He memorized the curve of her cheek as she tilted her head when she read, the quiet sounds she made when she accidentally fell asleep on the settee in the library, and the new and wonderful smile she displayed when they were in private.

This was, of course, not to say that there were no moments of uncertainty or awkwardness between them, but they worked through them to find a rhythm to their days.

At the start of their second week at Bray Castle, Gideon collected Caroline at the door to her bedchamber as usual. She greeted him with her usual smile, but it wobbled almost immediately. All color drained from her complexion and she scrambled away, practically diving for her porcelain washbasin before she tossed up her meager accounts. Gideon hurdled his shock to follow her. He hadn't known such sounds could come from such a fragile body. He rubbed soothing circles along her back as she heaved and groaned. He felt helpless and lost as he asked, "Is there anything I can do? Anyone I can send for? Does this call for the physician? Are you in pain?" His questions grew progressively more alarmed as her illness continued, and his mind ran in circles.

Caro shook her head as she attempted to regain her composure, breathing in slowly through her nose and out through her mouth. "It is…normal." She spoke in carefully modulated words as if speaking too loudly or rapidly might set her off again. "Expected."

"Expected," he snorted, feeling the worst sort of bastard that this was something she was simply *expected* to endure as a part of pregnancy. It bothered him to no end that this was the case while he suffered not one bit—his sympathetic nausea notwithstanding. "Is there anything to be done?"

She closed her eyes and exhaled a shaky breath. "Ginger. The doctor suggested sucking on candied ginger or sipping ginger tea might help with—"

"I will find you some ginger," Gideon said with all the gravity of a Holy Crusader. She slackened against him, drained, and he easily scooped her up and settled her on her bed.

"Don't," Caro groaned in mortification when he went to take the washbasin.

"Please," he scoffed, offering her his lopsided smile to disarm her sensibilities. "I've dealt with far worse on an average evening. D'you remember that night with the brandy and the acrobatic dogs?"

"And Blackwood thought he could walk on his hands, too?" Caro chuckled and groaned, holding her abdomen. "Please do not make me laugh; I don't think I can bear it."

"Very well. I will return shortly." Gideon slipped from the room, taking care of the washbasin and summoning the proper staff to have a fresh one brought to Caro in case she required it, and every other set of hands was sent to locate as much ginger as existed in their corner of Kent.

It wasn't long before Gideon returned to Caro's chamber bearing a tray of ginger tea, candied ginger, ginger biscuits, dried ginger leather, even a fresh, raw hunk of ginger—anything he could think of to help her. Some maids had returned bearing other home remedies for nausea; Gideon accepted them all and began a list. He was determined to tick them off one by one until Caro improved.

She was sleeping when he ducked back into her bedchamber, her breathing even and comfortable though she looked pale. He hoped she would not miss her fruit and her walk that day, and that his offering would be recompense enough. Quietly, he set the tray on the table beside the bed and was pleased to note that a fresh basin was already waiting, as was a damp cloth to replace the one already resting across her forehead. After carefully testing its dampness, Gideon decided to change the cloth on her forehead, gently swapping it for the fresh one. She purred and turned into his touch. The sound was as if she'd run her finger down his spine, a delicious chill traveling in its wake.

He could not resist dipping his head and brushing his lips against her cheek, running the pad of his thumb along her lower lip. Before he did something stupid, he forced himself to straighten and exit the room.

CAROLINE'S EYES FLUTTERED open at the sound of the door latch clicking shut. Her fingertips grazed the fresh, cool cloth on her forehead, and the scent of ginger drew her eyes toward the tray laid nearby. Beneath the powerful spicy aroma was the familiar fragrance of the man whom she longed for with every ounce of her soul.

His nonjudgmental care of her that day had shown her a new side of him. She'd always suspected he was putting on a bit of a show whenever they were out with their group of friends— exaggerating his behavior a bit for laughs and shock—but this more relaxed Gideon, this quietly caring and thoughtful man, was even more endearing and attractive to her. As wonderful as he'd always been, "Gideon in the country" was something else entirely. It was easy to be with him…and it was even easier to fall more deeply for him.

The last thing she'd expected that morning was for him to comfort her while she was ill and then immediately jump into action to tidy up and do what he could to make her feel better.

She pressed her hand to the cheek he had touched, telling herself that they could either ache separately or make the most of this marriage.

Chapter Nine

T HE EVENING FOG hung heavy and low that evening, making the air thick with moisture and filling Oliver's lungs with the dankness of the streets. He knew from experience that the scent of mildew and refuse would cling to his clothing long after he'd returned home.

He walked with purpose and confidence—the biggest deterrent to pickpockets and thieves—but he was not foolish enough to traverse Covent Garden unarmed. A man with a past like his was never caught so unprepared, nor did he possess such hubris to believe himself unapproachable by those living desperate lives in London's slums. Not for the first time, he was grateful Emily had remained home that evening. Of course, they would have hired a hackney rather than travel by foot, and Oliver never would have left her side, but he was still more at ease with her safely ensconced within the walls of their home rather than deep in the heart of Covent Garden on a night such as this.

Earlier that day, Emily and Oliver had shared a late luncheon and then went about their usual preparations for an evening at Lady Night's. It was immediately apparent to Oliver that his wife was not up for the long hours necessary to fulfill her obligations. He witnessed her yawn no less than three times as he helped her unlace her dress in preparation for donning another to wear to her mother's brothel. The quality was slightly less than her usual wardrobe and the color was much more muted—anything to avoid drawing attention to herself should she need to leave behind the books and see to other business within the building. It had taken Oliver a long time to come to terms with his wife flitting through the brothel and managing the employees, but she'd proven time and time again to him that her mind craved the stimulation and her skills with Lady Night's employees were unsurpassed. She was unfailingly kind and nonjudgmental. It was part of why he loved her so.

It did not take his keen observation skills to recognize the drowsiness in her doe-like eyes, the fatigue furrowing her brow, the slight slump to her shoulders.

"Why don't you remain at home this evening?" Oliver had presented it as a gentle suggestion, though he took his time fiddling with the laces of her gown to delay her dressing.

"Because my mother has been feeling poorly. She could use the extra set of hands and eyes once I finish with the books," Emily insisted, barely managing to swallow another yawn.

"And that is why I will go. The books will keep for another time, and I will lend myself wherever it is needed." Oliver could see in her impossibly blue eyes how tempted she was by that, so, in an effort to clinch her decision, he added, "I will return and crawl into bed with you where we will sleep however late we desire tomorrow morning."

Emily had narrowed her eyes at him. "Will you be nude?"

Oliver chuckled and shook his head at her incorrigibility. "Would you have me sleep with you any other way?"

"Never." She slung her arms around his neck, stood on the tips of her toes, and pressed her lips to his. "Very well, I shall remain home this evening. I do not know why I am so exhaust-ed—"

Oliver had dropped the garment he held and scooped Emily into his arms. Her little trill of surprised laughter unfurled a tendril of warmth low in his belly, like it always did. He carried her to bed in three quick strides.

"Because you work too hard," he'd said flatly. "You know you needn't do that."

"I enjoy it, and I enjoy spending the time near to you," Emily replied with a sigh as he tucked her beneath the coverlet.

"I have my savings and a small pension," he groused as he fussed over the bedding until he was satisfied that she was comfortable enough. "It should keep us sufficiently comfortable."

"You, of all people, should understand my desire for activity and mental stimulation."

He emitted a toneless huff of laughter. "I may, but this is a slower pace from my previous life. You, Angel, have never slowed down." She turned into the pillow, and he brushed a lock of her white-gold hair from her cheek. "Perhaps we should go on holiday," he suggested. "Spend some time in the countryside; enjoy the clean air."

"If you aren't careful, you may fall in love with it and never return to London." Emily's voice was already thick with sleep.

"The worst parts of London are thick in my blood, love; there is no leaving it behind for me. For you, though, I would go anywhere." His heart swelled at her dreamy smile. He pressed a lingering kiss to her forehead, knowing she was already asleep before he finished dressing himself.

Oliver mulled over that exchange as he continued his winding path through Covent Garden toward home. Dawn would break soon enough and burn away the fog swirling about Oliver's legs, but there was still enough time for all manner of dangers to lurk in the night's long shadows.

Parts of London never slept. Even in the latest hours of the night and smallest hours of the morning, the noises of life provided an undercurrent of sound to Oliver's footsteps. Were his senses not so attuned to his surroundings, he might have missed the pair of feet following in his wake. Their owner was skilled, timing his steps to Oliver's with near perfection, but Oliver was not most men. From the echo of their sound, his pursuer was less than one block behind him. Heartbeat slowing, senses sharpening, mind running, Oliver maintained the cadence of his steps and continued his circuitous route home. Never had he been more pleased that he'd ignored Emily's annoyance that they always took a different and indirect route back to their townhouse. She'd believed him to be overcautious but had capitulated when she realized his habit had been born both from years of secret service to the Crown and his unimpeachable desire to see her safe. Though he'd retired, following the mission that had brought him and Emily together, and had buried his most recent alias of shipping heir, Marcus Holden, some reflexes were never forgotten.

He took two carefully timed turns down side streets and alleys, effectively leading his pursuer away from his home and toward the Thames. The continuation of the subtle sounds of someone behind him solidified his understanding of the situation. This was no mere coincidence. His eyes scanned his surroundings, gained his bearings, and remembered how, just ahead, there would be a false alleyway on his left—an alcove of what had once been a Medieval passthrough between buildings, but had since been closed off. The footsteps had advanced and whoever was there was now less than half a block behind him.

Muscles tense, Oliver turned left at the very last second and ducked into that alcove. As he spun to face whoever followed him, he ripped his knives from their sheaths within the waist of his breeches and waited...but there were no more footsteps. He listened carefully over the rush of his pounding pulse, but there was nothing.

Oliver sprang from the alcove and found only a deserted street cast in murky shadows. The watery light of dawn was beginning to lighten the cloudy, soot-streaked sky, but it would take a while before any of it filtered down to that darkened part of London. His eyes scanned the foggy street scattered with leavings and trash, but there was no indication that he wasn't alone. No sound. No movement. No hint of who had been following him almost since he left Lady Night's doorstep.

Palming his blades and slipping the handles up into the cuffs of his coat sleeves, Oliver decided to spend as much time as it took wandering the mazelike streets of London until he could be certain he was no longer being followed. The last thing he wished to do was lead anyone to Emily.

Maybe leaving London for a spell was not a bad idea at all.

Chapter Ten

THE WEEKS PASSED like the lazy clouds over Bray Castle. Caroline's stomach began to round and she spent each evening examining the new shape of her body before the looking glass. She'd always possessed a pleasing figure and had been just vain enough to wonder what pregnancy would do to it, but she was discovering she quite liked the new fullness of her tender breasts and the gentle curve of her abdomen. There were still several months until the baby would arrive, so she anticipated a great deal of change to come, but she was content with her current progress. She'd even felt the baby move.

The first incident occurred during supper one evening. Gideon had been describing the book he'd been reading that day—something about political satire disguised as a description of pastoral life—and then she'd felt it. At first, she thought she might have been imagining the whisper of a flutter, but then, when it happened a second time, she suspected something about the meal disagreed with her. When Gideon laughed as he told his story, there was no mistaking the reaction inside her body.

Caroline had dropped her fork and clamped her hands over her abdomen, eyes wide with shock and joy. Gideon had immediately tossed down his utensils and knelt at her side. "What is it?" he'd asked with impressive calmness given the panic in his tight expression. "The baby? Are you in pain?"

"No," she reassured him. "I—I felt it."

"You...felt it?"

She'd nodded vigorously and, without hesitating, she took his hand and placed it right where she'd experienced the flutters. It was the first time Gideon had held her stomach and felt the small curve of her body as it swelled to accommodate the life within. His large palm nearly spanned the entire width as he cupped her protectively.

Another tiny flutter.

"There!" She practically bounced in her chair from excitement. Gideon frowned down at the place where his hand rested against her.

"I feel nothing." The disappointment in his tone squeezed her heart uncomfortably.

She covered his hand with hers. "It is still early days; I am certain the movements will grow stronger and you will feel him soon."

Gideon looked up at her from where he knelt on the floor. The molten silver of his eyes was breathtaking; even through her layers of clothing, the heat of his hand on her was intoxicating. Her skin ached to feel his once more. Her mouth watered with the desire to taste him once again, to feel his silken tongue dueling with hers. They were so very close to one another. She had only to lean forward and they would be kissing.

Immediately, she grew wet between her thighs, the persistent hum of need slowly drowning out all her rational thoughts. She'd had desires before, but nothing like what she'd been experiencing since the very beginning of her pregnancy. Most nights and mornings, she awoke damp and needy, mewling in desire, wishing it were Gideon who pressed his fingers through her dripping folds and found that sensitive bud that set her every muscle on fire.

Her every sense flared with his nearness; the slight hitch in his breath as she involuntarily leaned forward made her press her thighs together. She didn't know how much longer she could stand this tension—the simmering desire—between them.

And, when he pressed his lightly stubbled cheek to hers, she nearly combusted.

"D'you think…" he asked slightly unsteadily before trying again. "D'you think we might one day revisit what transpired between us after the Haverford ball?" Caroline couldn't prevent her little shudder of pleasure when the tip of his nose grazed the sensitive lobe of her ear. Her cheeks warmed with a combination of need and nerves.

"Perhaps…" she said on a tight exhalation, the power of her own desire making it difficult for her to breathe, let alone speak.

"Good." Gideon rocked back on his heels and stood. "Please excuse me."

He turned quickly and beat a hasty retreat from the room, but there was no masking the thick, prominent ridge of his arousal as it strained against the falls of his breeches.

"Oh my…" Caroline shivered and began to fan her face. She didn't know how much longer she could stand this.

The baby fluttered once more within her womb.

GIDEON WOKE AT dawn the next morning, dressed quickly and silently, ignored the painful hardness and heat in his groin, and stormed out of the castle to the mews. As instructed, his chestnut gelding had been prepared and danced on anxious feet as Gideon approached. His large, dark eyes wide, nostrils flared, muscles trembling in anticipation, it appeared they could both use a long, hard ride to start their day.

Offering a quick nod in acknowledgment to the groom, Gideon swung up into the saddle in one fluid movement.

They were off like a cannon.

Gideon gave himself over to the beast's thundering hooves, the heaving of his broad back beneath him as they flew across fields, down dusty paths, and skirted the village. The air grew saltier as they neared the coast. The wind stung his face and whipped the air from his lungs, but it felt glorious. It had been too long since he'd ridden like this—so hard and far that the rest of the world fell away. Everything around them was reduced to blurs of color and physical sensations. He allowed his mount to choose their direction and speed, giving him his head as they both worked off their pent-up energy, enjoying the strain upon their muscles. It wasn't precisely the release he ached for, but it would have to do.

For now.

Caroline had given him hope at supper the evening before, and he'd bottled it and clung to it like a superstitious man would a talisman. Everything about Caroline drove him nearly insensible with need. Her smile suffused him with warmth; her laughter buoyed his soul; the way she cared for him brought comfort to his soul, the likes of which he'd never known before she came into his life. She was his, according to the letter of the law, but he was brimming with the desire to possess every part of her. He wanted her to ache for him as he did her. He wanted to know she, too, counted the minutes until they were once again in the same room. He wanted her body to burn for him with the same flame he experienced every time he looked at her or heard the melody of her voice.

And the hope she'd given him brought him one step closer to that.

The golden light of morning was in full force by the time they slowed to overlook the white chalk cliffs and the crashing waves far below. Gideon dismounted and rubbed the white splotches on the horse's velvety nose.

"Good boy," he praised, both of them catching their breath. Holding the reins in one hand, they walked along the cliff. Gideon tilted his head toward the wheeling seabirds, their screeching calls ripped away on the wind. He raked his damp hair back from his face, but it was an exercise in futility with the sea breeze. It plastered his linen shirt to his sweat-slicked chest, chilling his overheated skin and causing gooseflesh to rise over every inch of his body. The heat deep within him refused to be quelled, however.

It haunted him when he tried to sleep.

It plagued him when he attempted to distract himself with other tasks.

Each time he thought it was beginning to cool, Caro would walk into the room and it would roar to life once more.

It was Caroline.

She was the catalyst of all that was slowly driving him mad with need.

She filled his eyes, his lungs, his blood. Even when he left the grounds on his punishing rides, he could not fully escape her. His damned gelding was named *Posy* because of her.

"Don't the white markings on his nose look like flower petals? He looks as if he were sniffing a posy and some of them became stuck."

He could still hear Caro's words and her joyful laughter as he collected the animal from Tattersalls five years prior. Even though the yearling had had a much more regal, official title, the name had stuck. Gideon could only call him Posy. It was engraved on his tack and above his stall. He came to that name when called. There was simply no escaping Caro for either of them.

"Bloody hell..." Gideon groaned as they ambled along. Though his embarrassingly persistent erection had flagged, the ride had done little to clear his head.

Her words at supper ran through his head again and again. She'd left the possibility open to their being more between them, and it was at once his greatest relief and fear. He ached to possess her again; something primal had been unleashed within him when she'd felt his child—their child—move in her womb. It suddenly felt more real. And he wanted to claim her all over again because of it. She wore his ring, she had his name, she carried his babe, and now he wanted her in his bed. For good.

He was beginning to admit to himself that he was *allowed* to want Caro, *allowed* to desire a family, the likes of which he'd never known. With the volatility of his upbringing and the poor examples his parents had provided, Gideon had always felt somewhat inadequate and untutored when it came to relationships beyond the carnal. How could he ever hope to be sufficient when he had no training? No one after whom he might model his behavior? These first few weeks of marriage had taught him one thing: He could make up for a great many shortcomings if he just continued to adore and care for Caroline as he always had.

They were married now, besides. Didn't that mean they could pursue their physical desires to their hearts' content without fear of it destroying their friendship?

He had never known a marriage forced from mutual trust and affection, but he'd heard they existed—like unicorns and dragons in fairytales. Was it possible that this was what he could have with Caro? Could he have been so lucky that he could continue to have her in his life *and* share in their mutual physical desires?

As much as he longed for it, as torturous as it was to sleep one room away from her and not possess her, as much as his body screamed at him to reenact their night of passion, he forced himself to wait. He was still adamant that they move on her time.

Caro had said they might "perhaps" revisit what they'd shared; she had not expressly invited him to her bed that instant. The last thing he wished was for her to feel obligated to perform simply because she was his wife.

Then again…

The darkening of her eyes, the catch in her breath, the slight heaving of her bosom over her deep-green gown… Gideon was a man who knew when a woman desired him, and *that* had been desire.

He groaned as a fresh wave of longing pounded through his veins like a tidal wave of liquid sunlight and shot straight to his groin. Not a day went by that he didn't contemplate the sounds Caro had made as he guided her to completion again and again. How wet she'd been. How she'd tasted.

"Dammit!" Gideon snapped, so loudly and so suddenly that Posy danced to the side and threw his head. "Steady, boy," he said soothingly and gave him a firm pat on his thick neck. "I'm just torturing myself over here. Don't mind me." Both males heaved aggrieved sighs and resumed their walk.

His patience was running thin, as was his sanity, but he had a lifetime with Caro. He could wait until she came to him again. Only then would he be certain that she came to him out of desire and not obligation or duty. His every nerve longed for her. He loved her. And the little boy inside of him ached for that feeling to be returned without coercion or ulterior motives. He yearned for it with all the desperation of a man too long neglected.

"What say you, Posy, hm?" Gideon asked the animal's soulful eye. "Will I survive this, or will Caro finally do me in?" The horse tossed his enormous head. "That is about what I suspected as well." Posy's nose met his shoulder in an affectionate nudge. "I know how you feel about her—don't think I've missed all the apples she's snuck away from the breakfast table—you are a biased party. I don't know why I bother asking you anything." The gelding whickered, entirely unaware of the warring emotions inside of Gideon's chest. Like the frothy waves at the base of the chalk cliffs, his stomach churned with the need to be everything Caro wanted, and to have her give all of herself in return.

He remounted and turned Posy inland.

Toward home.

Toward Caro.

Toward his new life.

With a sharp whistle and a kick, they were off.

Upon his return to Bray Castle, Gideon did not have a chance to bathe and change his clothing before encountering the woman who so completely consumed his every thought. As he walked past Caro's private sitting room, he noticed the door was open wide and she, garbed in a mint-green morning dress embroidered in little white flowers, was draped across the burgundy chaise. She, with her ivory flesh, pastel gown, and hair the color of rosy sunshine, was like a breath of fresh air in the room populated with heavy and slightly outdated furniture.

She held her chin propped in her hands, not even attempting to feign interest in the book that lay open in her lap and rested against the soft swell of her abdomen. His fingers twitched with the memory of how that curve had felt beneath his palm, how intimate and domestic the moment had been when she, in her unbridled joy, had taken his hand in hers and pressed it there to feel their child.

Her expression was soft and her eyes, dreamy. Her freckled cheeks displayed a healthy blush so faint that it might have been missed if he did not know her so well. Whatever was on her mind, she certainly found it much more entertaining than the words on the pages before her.

"Thinking of me, are you?" Gideon crossed his arms and leaned his shoulder against the doorframe.

Caro jumped and the book fell to the floor. "Christ, you startled me!" she screeched and pressed a hand to the graceful column of her throat.

"The name's Gideon, but I thank you for the comparison," he joked with a wink.

"Infuriating is a better name for you," she grumbled and rolled her eyes. He breezed into the room and retrieved her book before she could lean over to do so.

"So…were you?"

"Was I what?" Her tone was still slightly snippy from the shock, but he knew she'd not hold it against him long.

"Thinking of me."

"Of course not." Her words said one thing, but her deepening blush said another.

"I think you're lying," he purred, taking her hand in his and pressing a kiss to the fluttering pulse on the inside of her wrist. He handed Caroline her book and sat back on his heels so they were relatively eye-to-eye.

"Very well, I was."

"That is nothing to be ashamed about."

"I am not ashamed."

"Pleased to hear that."

"I was merely…thinking of your birthday." It, too, seemed like a lie, but Gideon decided he'd teased her about that enough for one morning.

"What birthday?"

"Again, you are utterly vexing."

"I thought I was infuriating." He chuckled when she gently bopped the crown of his head with her book.

"*Your* birthday. Your *thirtieth* birthday, so it is a rather important one." She huffed a dramatic sigh when he feigned ignorance and cocked a confused brow at her. "I know you dislike being reminded how old you are. It is an utterly nonsensical complex for a man such as you to have—especially because you are fitter than many men a decade younger."

"D'you think so?" He was shamelessly fishing for compliments, but he cared not one bit when her gaze raked him from his wind-tousled hair to the sheerness of his damp shirt. He particularly enjoyed how her eyes lingered on the visible muscles of his bare forearms, where he'd rolled up his sleeves when rubbing down Posy after their excursion.

"You are shameless," Caro charged, tearing her eyes away from his body even as her flush deepened.

"Perhaps." He was enamored by the widening of her eyes— the way they glowed when compared to the paler hue of her morning dress. "Now, are you hungry? Have you broken your fast yet? I apologize for how long my ride took this morning, I—"

"Gideon, stop!" Caro couldn't completely mask her bubble of laughter. It was adorable, and it made him want to kiss her and never stop. "Yes, I have eaten. You do not need to apologize for missing *one* meal on this honeymoon trip. And would you enjoy a party or not? I believe it would be fun to plan a celebration for you."

Unable to bear it any longer, Gideon leaned forward and pressed a kiss to her petal-soft cheek. "Don't you make a wonderfully doting wife?" he commented lightly. "I do not require a party, but I appreciate the thought. I am entirely content with a quiet evening with you. We will return to London and, before we know it, the chaos of our *utterly scandalous* marriage will inundate our lives. We'd best enjoy the peace while it lasts."

He rose and pressed a kiss to the top of Caro's head, hoping she did not notice how he lingered a few seconds too long because she smelled so damned good, before excusing himself to bathe…and likely frig himself into oblivion because he was so bloody hard that it was excruciating.

Chapter Eleven

IT DIDN'T TAKE Caroline long to decide that she would go through with planning a surprise party to celebrate Gideon's birthday. What had begun as a ruse to disguise the fact that she'd been daydreaming—again—about her only night with her husband quickly transformed into a full-fledged notion. It was only fair, given how he'd helped her to celebrate her first birthday outside of her family's home.

Gideon had been summoned by his father to their Northumberland estate. Having ignored the last several summonses, he'd told her that he could not continue to do so or risk his funds being cut off as punishment. He'd apologized profusely to her, knowing this trip meant he would miss her birthday, but Caroline had assured him that she understood and would be fine on her own—especially because Blackwood, Kempton, Brinley, and Trenholm had not been subtle about some secret celebratory plans. Little did she know, Gideon had had a hand in coordinating all of it.

He may not have been in London, but he'd left express instructions that the men were to follow to the letter on pain of death. A morning of riding in the park before the usual slow-moving carriages and *ton* gawkers had been followed by a picnic luncheon and a boat ride on the Serpentine. They'd made quite a sight, Caroline accompanied by four of London's most notorious rakehells as they toted along an enormous wicker basket and rowed the tiny boat! She was certainly the simultaneous envy and butt of all Society's gossip that day, though she could not have cared less.

Especially when she'd finally returned home to discover Gideon had planted one final surprise for her.

A box had been delivered in her absence, and it waited for her on the entry table. The small note confirmed he'd been its sender and inside lay the most beautiful pair of sewing scissors she'd ever beheld. Made from polished gold and silver with artful craftsmanship so stunning, they appeared more like a piece of jewelry than a sewing implement. They dangled from a delicate gold chain that glittered in the light. To many, it might have seemed an odd gift, but for her, it had been perfect. Though contrary to what most believed her personality to be, Gideon knew of her true enjoyment of embroidery in her contemplative times...and her penchant for always misplacing her scissors.

She still possessed those scissors, cherished them, and thought of Gideon each time she used them. Because of this, she had an enormous task ahead of her in planning a surprise party worthy of such a man.

Plans and ideas to return the favor of that lovely birthday flitted through her brain like excited birds. All the possibilities thrilled her. Decorations, menus, and entertainment, each thing was more exciting than the last.

She enlisted the help of the staff the very next day, swearing them all to secrecy. Everyone seemed to enjoy the idea of opening up the castle for an evening of excitement. The great hall would be transformed into an elegant ballroom; adjacent parlors would be transformed into dens for Gideon's favorite games of cards and chance; and local musicians would be hired to lend their talents for dancing and entertainment. The west lawn would be cleared and staked for a special event. The china would be unpacked, the silver would be polished, and every corner would be dusted and swept. She also spent a great deal of time in the kitchens with the Bray Castle cook. Together, they designed a menu filled with Gideon's favorite foods—from roast venison all the way to his beloved cake with the ripest, sweetest summer strawberries to be found. A large order of his favorite whiskey was placed; red and white wines to match the dinner courses would be pulled from the castle stores. They were also in agreement that not a single mushroom would be allowed in the kitchens since Gideon could not abide them.

Caroline spoke with the housekeeper about obtaining flowers from the village and surrounding areas, determined to keep as much business as local as possible. Additional staff would be brought in a few days before the event to learn the layout of the sizable grounds, as well as their duties. The stables needed to be readied, as did additional bedchambers if guests were expected to travel from abroad. Some of the *ton* retreated from the city this time of year, but she knew most of their acquaintances preferred the bustle of town to any quiet country house, so they would not be difficult to track down.

Even after Gideon retired to his bedchamber for the evening, Caroline stayed up late compiling a list of guests. Nearly fifty names filled the page when she was done. It was a small party for a venue as large as Bray Castle, but these were the people whom she knew Gideon would have invited had he been aware of her plans. To him, pomp and circumstance meant little; he far preferred honest companionship and good laughter over pretenses. This birthday celebration would be precisely that.

It was unconventional for a newly married couple to host a party while still on their honeymoon trip, but since when had she and Gideon done anything properly? Beyond celebrating her husband, this would serve as their introduction as a married pair to Society—a demonstration of their unity and affection. She also harbored a secret hope that it would help dispel any nasty rumors that had blossomed in the wake of their departure from London.

Invitations were sent off to their close circle of friends, Gideon's nearest associates, kin, and neighboring families whom Gideon had spoken of fondly on their walks. Though she had yet to meet him, she also addressed one to Gideon's half brother,

Oliver, and his wife. Emily had been lovely during their only meeting and Caroline liked to think the man a woman like that had married would be as charming. As soon as the invitation was sent off for delivery, Caroline reminded herself not to allow her hopes to reach too high—that she would understand if they did not accept. At least the gesture had been made. Part of her truly believed it was the right thing to do. She'd seen the disappointment on Gideon's face the day they left London; a part of him wished to know Oliver, and, if this helped to facilitate the blossoming of a relationship between them, then so be it.

It had been a long time since her lessons in comportment and household management, but Caroline was impressed with what she managed to accomplish for her first attempt. She beamed with pride as her eyes ran over her neat lists of items, tasks, and names.

"You've done well, Caroline," she said to herself, unashamed by her pride. She hadn't set out to prove anything other than to give Gideon a party the likes of which he'd never had before, but she'd realized that this was something her mother would have told her she'd never accomplish unassisted. Even a gathering of this size was a massive undertaking for a lady who'd not coordinated such an event before, let alone a lady who still suffered with daily bouts of nausea and fatigue so rampant that she could not survive the day without a little nap in the sunshine like an overindulged feline.

And she'd done it.

"Did you say something?"

Caroline whirled around and just managed to shove her list beneath a stack of scattered pieces of parchment. "You really must stop this sneaking around," she snapped at Gideon.

The maddening man chuckled, and the intoxicating sound shot straight to her core. "I have been here for several minutes. I assure you, the 'sneaking' was entirely unintentional. What are you concentrating on? You were scribbling away so furiously, I was afraid you might wear a hole straight through to the desk."

"Nothing." Caroline stood and shook out her skirts. "Nothing important. Just some correspondence. It can wait."

"Wait for what?"

Why did he have to be so handsome when he was confused? He made her want to melt into a puddle at his feet. Ever since they'd arrived at Bray Castle, every glance he sent her made her heart stutter, each wink made her clench her thighs together, and every flirtatious phrase made her flush. She'd cared for him for many years, been attracted to him for nearly as long, been able to admit to herself that she desired him physically for the better part of a year, but lately everything about him drove her mad with need. It was terribly inconvenient to be so preoccupied when one had things to accomplish.

"A walk," she said matter-of-factly and slipped her arm through his to guide him from the room. "I've spent far too long indoors today and I am jealous of your riding. Sitting still for so long is beginning to bother my back."

"Your back?" His steps halted and she was pulled to a stop. "Should I—"

She clapped her hand over his mouth. "Do not say the word *physician*. I am fine, I merely wish to stretch my legs." His sensuous lips curled into a smile against her palm and she yanked her hand back before the heat could spread up her limb to her heart.

How could she have forgotten about how caring he was? *That* made her tingle from head to toe regardless of whether their skin touched or not.

GIDEON LANDED FACE-FIRST into his pillow and groaned long and loud, doing his best to release every bit of his pent-up frustrations as he did so…but it was a lesson in futility.

Following their walk around the grounds, he and Caro had enjoyed a light supper before continuing their regular ritual of retiring to her bedchamber for games. That night, they'd played several rounds of cribbage. Gideon had not won a single game. It hadn't been for lack of trying, of course; Caro was famously good at the game of cards and pegs.

"Lucky ducky," he'd grumbled and leaned back his chair.

"This is also a game of skill," Caro had replied haughtily. Her delicate fingers shuffled the cards with an elegant combination of speed and dexterity. "You are not playing at your usual level. You are making it too easy." She feigned an exaggerated pout, and it was all he could do not to pounce on her and take her plump lower lip between his teeth. She wasn't making things easier.

If anything, she increased his suffering daily because she had no idea what she was doing. Blackwood had once described Caro as "an innocent flirt," and Gideon had agreed it was an apt description. It came to her naturally, yet she knew not quite the strength of what she wielded. If she put even the smallest bit of effort, she could have any man she desired as clay in her hands—hell, he was already as malleable as possible as far as she was concerned. She could ask him to dance a reel on his hands while wearing nothing but a loincloth of nettles, and he'd give the request some serious consideration.

Wait for Caro to come to you was repeating in his mind almost constantly at that point.

His entire past was riddled with rash decisions and poor examples of proper, healthy relationships. Caro had her own wounds, besides, and the last thing he wished to do was reopen them or make them worse. He didn't wish to impose his hopes and desires upon her.

It was no secret that his childhood had been far from loving. While being sent away to school had been a relief, it had also served to underscore just how much he'd lacked. Watching the other boys receive letters and packages from adoring parents and family made him long for a companionship he hadn't even known existed. Eventually, he'd discovered a closeness with a few classmates—Kempton and Brinley, followed closely by Blackwood and Trenholm, who were a couple of years behind them—and this helped to fill in some of what was missing; however, their friendship did not heal all of his wounds.

Gideon had been used as a pawn by his parents for many years, and in doing so, they'd taught him to allow someone into your life meant relinquishing a certain amount of power in the dynamic. To a lad who'd only ever known vitriol and despair, this was terrifying. The love of his friends helped provide a counter-balance to the disquiet at home, but would anyone be able to heal him if things between him and his wife turned sour?

This left him anxious and wary, desperately desiring closeness and intimacy with her, but afraid of what it might do to their dynamic. Their friendship. These were all fears that had kept him from pursuing her in the first place. Without the buffer of space and separate households, she was quickly filling in every gap in his life, every crack in his soul. Even without sex, she was becoming so much more to him.

How could she not, when she brought him so much joy each day? When she looked like she did that evening, with her liquid sunset hair plaited and tied with an ivory ribbon, the sway of her full breasts beneath her nightrail and the shadows of her dark nipples teasing him with her every movement?

A man could lose himself—could lose control—but he was not that man, and he respected Caro far too much to take the decision of their intimacy out of her hands.

She wanted you once, he reminded himself; *she will again.*

Well, she would...if she forgave him after their marriage experienced its first argument that evening.

Caro had dropped her carved peg during the *show* portion of their cribbage gameplay. Of course, he'd laid aside his cards to help her search for the piece. It was lost in the pile of the rug, but it was located after several minutes of looking. Caro rose back to her seat and stared blankly at the cards and board, completely frozen.

"Caro?" he'd finally asked in a soft tone.

"I—I can't remember where we were." She still did not blink, as if focusing all her energy on the game between them might somehow help her remember. Then, a tear spilled from beneath her long, sable lashes, leaving a trail of dampness on the curve of her cheek.

"Caro…" he said in as placating a tone as he could manage. "It's all right. We can start the hand over again. I cannot recall either—"

"That is not the point!" she cried and stabbed her peg into a random hole. "I never lose my place in a game of cribbage." Her tears were falling in earnest now, carving trails through her constellations of freckles and dotting the virginal lace trim of her nightshift.

"Perhaps you are simply fatigued," he'd suggested, not quite sure how to proceed, but trying his best to be helpful. "Women in your condition can sometimes become overwrought quite easily—especially if they are overtired."

One snap of the green fire in her glistening eyes told Gideon that had been precisely the wrong thing to say.

"My condition?" She sat up straighter and narrowed her gaze at him. He had the sudden impression of being a hare in a hunter's sight. "With whom have you been discussing *my condition?*"

Gideon winced, gradually realizing the gravity of his mistake. If his wife could have killed him with her eyes, then he'd have been dead twice over already. "Mrs. Kant, the housekeeper, has been managing this estate since my father was a lad. I've known her my entire life. She also happens to have six sisters and three sisters-by-marriage, each of which birthed no less than three children of their own. She's quite well-versed in all things to do with children and pregnancy since she is proud of the fact that she was present for every single birth." He reached for her hand. "After your illness began and I scrambled to locate ginger for you, I only wished to understand what you are going through. I never told her you were expecting—"

"You didn't need to." Caroline snatched her hand back. "She is an intelligent woman. I am sure she has heard by now from the staff that I've not experienced my courses since we arrived. Having you make such inquiries likely only confirmed any suspicions she might have formed. We agreed to keep the pregnancy a secret for now; little did I know, you were making inquiries of the staff. News such as this spreads, Gideon."

"Is that such a bad thing to confide in someone? You and I have so little family…so few to rely upon and ask these questions. Wouldn't it be a comfort to have someone on our side?" Caroline's tears had begun to flow in earnest, causing fresh fissures to open in his heart. This was rapidly growing out of hand. He was doing his best to remain a calm counterpart to her inexplicable emotional state, but he was unsure how much longer he'd be able to manage it. "Darling Caro," he murmured.

"The very last thing I need right now is a reminder of just how alone I am."

"But you are not alone. You have me." And Gideon was struck by the truth of it, as well as its reverse. She had him, but he also had her. For better or worse.

He wanted nothing more than to pull her into his arms and hold her, kiss away her tears, but she leaned away from his touch. "Don't," she said, quiet yet firm. Her unsteady breath and the wetness of her cheeks made him feel as lost as when he'd been a child trapped in a house where nothing was in his control. "Please leave. I wish to retire."

"Do not send me away."

"I wish to be alone, Gideon! I—I am not feeling myself."

"And that is why I wish to—"

"Go," she snapped with a sob. Gideon was helpless to do anything other than obey her wishes, not wanting to upset her further.

And this was how he'd wound up lying face-down alone in his cold bed, growling his frustrations into the pillow.

The situation baffled him, her reaction concerned him; he'd wanted so damned badly to help her, but he hadn't known how. Nothing in his life experience had prepared him to nurture and care for another human being, let alone a wife expecting his child. He was a flailing fish dropped onto the shore and flopping in the wrong direction. Gasping. Lost. Having one goal in mind—to cherish Caro—but unsure how to accomplish it. When he thought they might be making headway in their marriage, something like this happened to set him back on his heels and remind him that he truly did not know what he was doing when it came to relationships.

The lads he'd met at school had gradually taught him how to manage friendships, but a romantic attachment…one as powerful as what he felt for his wife…that was something else entirely, and Gideon felt woefully unprepared for it.

Too frustrated and despondent to move, Gideon drifted off to sleep like that, still wearing his linen shirt and breeches, sprawled out across the coverlet.

He did not know how long he stayed like that, but he did not wake until a small hand grabbed his shoulder and shook him.

"GIDEON?" ANOTHER SHAKE. "Gideon," Caroline said more firmly. The man apparently slept like the dead.

She'd spent the better part of the last two hours alternately weeping, berating herself for weeping, then weeping because she was berating herself for weeping. It was a vicious—and embarrassing—cycle and, if she had one thing to be glad about, it was that no one had borne witness to it. She'd honestly been upset about the slip in her mental faculties, which had then fed into the feeling of betrayal over Gideon inadvertently revealing her pregnancy to the staff. As soon as he'd obeyed her and quit the room, however, her regret had been nearly instantaneous. Gradually, rationality had returned to her; what had seemed so upsetting and serious before melted away into something far less dire.

So, she'd forgotten where they were at in their game? They could have taken his suggestion and replayed the hand; it really would not have been that serious a situation and they were only playing for fun.

So the housekeeper knew of her pregnancy? The staff were often the first to know when the lady of the house was expecting. They'd already spent a month on this honeymoon trip. If they were afforded the benefit of the doubt, then it was plausible that she'd only just found out about it as well. Besides, she could scarcely believe Gideon had taken the initiative to investigate and procure remedies for her pregnancy-related ailments. *Gideon.* The man who had no maternal figure and limited experience with enceinte women had proven to have impeccable instincts. She should not have snapped at him when he'd only been trying to do what he could to understand what she experienced and find a way to help her.

And he had been right. She was tired—she was always so bloody tired. She'd been putting so much of her energy into planning the party for Gideon and keeping it all a secret. She hadn't realized how much it had worn her down until that blasted peg had fallen from her fingers. Gideon had been so kind and understanding, and she'd snapped at him.

The guilt only made her weep harder.

It took her far longer than it should have to free herself from the quagmire of emotions, but she'd eventually managed. She also knew that she'd never be able to sleep until she spoke to Gideon and apologized for her behavior—would he understand that it had felt perfectly rational and justified in the moment? She hoped so. They'd never quarreled before and it made her skin feel as if a thousand ants were crawling beneath it. All was not right with the world if she and Gideon were not on good terms.

Though splashing cool water on her face did little to counteract the redness and puffiness, she did it anyway. Not remotely satisfied with her appearance, she bit back more tears of frustration and made her way to Gideon's bedchamber.

She hadn't expected to find him so sound asleep, let alone still as dressed as when he'd left her. She was uncertain if she was disappointed at finding him in his loose linen shirt and breeches rather than gloriously naked.

"Gideon," Caroline repeated herself even more loudly, trying to stave off the wave of images her excited imagination was attempting to conjure.

Finally, he groaned and rolled to his shoulder. He blinked up at her sleepily, his midnight hair tousled and flattened on one side where it had been pressed to the pillow. His angular jaw was already freckled with stubble. She wanted to test its roughness against her cheek…her impossibly sensitive nipples. He stared at her with one eye until his mind finally awoke enough to register that it was she at his bedside.

She didn't know if she'd expected him to be cross with her for her earlier treatment of him or annoyed that she'd disturbed his sleep; what she hadn't expected was his immediate alarm. Gideon snapped up and instantly reached for her. His eyes, once dark and hazy with sleep, were alert and dancing silver with concern. Still kneeling on the enormous mattress, he grabbed her hands and held them tightly, as if afraid she were an apparition.

"Caro! Are you alright? Are you ill? The baby—"

"I am fine," she reassured him, squeezing his hands back with equal force to help ground him. For a man who was not usually so excitable, he'd been remarkably skittish when it came to her health.

Yet another reason she loved him.

And love him, she did.

Even if he might be too damaged by his parents to say the words aloud to her or recognize them in his actions and behaviors, she knew he felt the same.

A new wave of emotion began to clog her throat like a lodestone, and she struggled to speak around it. She should have known he'd read her distress in her eyes…

Immediately, he enfolded her into his arms in an embrace that was, at once, tender and bracing. His warm lips pressed to her hairline where he murmured reassurances and tender phrases. He called her his darling Caro, praised her strength, and told her to lean into him as much as she needed to. And she did just that. Caroline wrapped her arms around his lean waist, feeling the firmness of his body, the heat that rolled off of it like a blazing hearth. Never had she felt safer, more supported, more cherished than when she was in Gideon's arms.

It took some doing, but she regained her composure and leaned back enough to look up into his face. He was devastatingly handsome cast in shadows, her vivid memory filling in the gaps left behind by the night.

"I am better now," she said, her voice so small when confronted by at least fifteen stone of man.

Of tender *man*, she reminded herself as he offered her his gentle, lopsided smile of encouragement.

"I came to apologize." His dark brows rose at that, but he remained silent and allowed her to continue. "I may have displayed a slight overreaction earlier. You were infinitely patient with me and I am sorry if I seemed ungrateful of your support. You must have thought me such a ninny for crying like I did. I—I do not know what came over me, but I could not help it. I am sorry." His long, square-tipped fingers barely grazed the underside of her jaw, unleashing a shiver of pleasure from the nape of her neck down to her bare toes.

"While I appreciate the apology, it was not necessary. Nothing was broken—inanimate or otherwise—so I shall consider no harm done."

Caroline had to bite back her smile as she dug her fingers into his sides and made him bark in laughter. "Can you take one thing seriously—just one? I am busy apologizing for my irrational behavior."

"And I accepted your apology, though it was unnecessary. I may be a man, I may be woefully unprepared and undereducated, but I am trying. What I saw was nothing above what I was told I might expect. If you display a bit of irrationality from time to time, then so be it. I would prefer there be no tears, but I understand it cannot always be helped."

"Are you asking me not to cry?" she snorted incredulously.

"No. I only say that because it wounds me to see you in such a state."

Caroline's heart stuttered, reminding her how very, very close they were. Tired of fighting her impulses, she slid her hands up the hard wall of his chest and wound them around his neck, pulling Gideon's lips down to meet hers.

PINWHEELS OF SENSATION and light burst behind Gideon's eyes the second Caroline's mouth grazed his. The well of concern he'd felt at waking to find her standing over him with her eyes red rimmed and puffy evaporated along with the world around them until there was only her lips on his. His body reacted with instantaneous ferocity, hardening with such swiftness that it made his knees weak. She pulled them closer, pressing her unbound breasts against his chest until her pebbled nipples teased him through the thin fabric of their remaining clothing, and the firm curve of her belly grazed the hard ridge of his cock. He ached to grasp her delectable bottom and yank her more closely together so he could grind against her until there were no doubts as to the voracity of his desire.

His restraint wore thinner and thinner with every pass of her tongue on his, every stroke of her nails in the short hair at the nape of his neck. He trembled with it. He ached from it. Something primal roared to life within him, demanding that he pull her to the bed and claim her. She was *his*. She carried *his* child. She would never belong to another. Never.

Gideon held himself in check, but just barely. Even when she arched into him and whimpered at the friction of her breasts on the hard wall of his chest, even when she nipped at his lower lip, even when she gasped and shivered as his fingers traced the outline of her perfect curves.

She breathed his name like a plea.

"Hmm?" was his reply, too absorbed in every point of contact between them to break away and form a coherent question.

"Might we…please…make…love again…?" she asked, each pause punctuated by another kiss. God's wounds, what her words did to him. Her request was like angels' song to his forsaken ears. For months, he'd been without a woman's touch. No one had quite lived up to her since their night; no one had driven him mad with naked desire. Oh, he'd tried to hold up his bargain that they would share one night and one night only, but he'd desired her for so bloody long that he'd been unable to stomach the fact that the only way he'd have her again was in his dreams. It was what had driven him to Lady Night's the evening he'd met Oliver and Emily.

Following two generous glasses of whiskey, he'd made his way to the exclusive Covent Garden location in an attempt to slake is ceaseless lust for the woman he could not have. His attempts had been half-hearted and, of course, failed. But he did not regret it. He did not miss the novelty of new women in his bed. He'd discovered the intimacy to be had with one person who knew him the best in the world, and there was no earthly way to top that. No matter how hard he tried, no matter how much he fought it.

He broke their kiss and gazed down at her delicate features, her cinnamon constellations of freckles, her passion-glazed emerald eyes, her kiss-plumped lips. His chest heaved with his every breath, struggling to pull in enough air when faced with her honest beauty.

"I have thought of little else..." Gideon replied, his voice rough as gravel. "I'd once fooled myself into believing what I felt was a purely physical attraction to a beautiful woman, but the years only transformed my attraction into a desire. You drew me like a flame, Caro, and I told myself I was content to have you in my life and remain at arm's length, so our friendship was not affected. But when you asked for a night in my bed..." He groaned, his abdomen clenching at the memories that were unleashed. "That fanned my desire rather than slaking it." Her lips parted on a trembling sigh and he had to rip his eyes away from her mouth before he began devouring her all over again. "It was terrifying to finally fulfill my fantasies—all the things I'd imagined doing with you...*to* you—but the worst part came days later when I finally admitted to myself that I would never stop wanting more of you. That is unnerving for a man who never learned how to open himself up to a real relationship because you and I both know I've only had the worst sort of example to follow."

"Oh, Gideon," Caro sighed and nestled into his throat, pressing her lips to the hammering pulse she discovered there. "I've wanted this too…for so long."

That was all he needed to hear. With a feral noise bursting forth from his chest, Gideon hauled Caro into his arms and dragged her onto the bed. Enough sense remained that he did so with enough care that he did not injure the babe in her womb, but he vowed as soon as she was able, he would remind her just what he was capable of. He'd pin her down and spread her wide until she was at his mercy. He'd make her sob with pleasure again and again until she begged him to allow her relief. He'd haul her astride him and let her use him for her own enjoyment, as her toy.

Each one of his imaginings was more erotic than the last; he could feel the head of his cock growing slick with beads of moisture as his body pulsated with desire.

Despite the force of his need, Gideon was determined to display the patience and restraint he should have during their first coupling. Even in the moment, he'd regretted allowing his desire to spur him on. Despite Caro's enthusiastic participation, he knew it could have been better. *He* could have been better for her. Now, he would be.

He took his time kissing her, tasting her. He learned her all over again and he encouraged her to do the same. They knelt together on the bed, hands roaming and exploring, relearning the planes and dips and hollows of one another's bodies. His teeth teased the sensitive lobe of her ear; his tongue sampled the hollow of her collarbone; his hands slowly, deftly untied her nightshift and began to separate the panels.

Caro's hands were performing a survey of their own and sent chills of awareness rippling back and forth across every inch of his body. "Take off your sodding shirt," she growled against his mouth before giving his lower lip a little nip.

Anything for you… his mind purred.

It took him less than half a second to break their kiss and rip the garment off over his head. He would have swooped back in to reclaim her mouth, but she stopped him with a gentle palm to the center of his naked chest.

"Now…the breeches."

Gideon lifted a brow. Though her nightshift was undone, it still provided her a measure of modesty despite the filmy fabric clinging to her dark, erect nipples. She wanted him quite literally laid bare before her, and he would gladly comply. He would do anything she required of him. It mattered not if the request was made out of desire or if it was to help her feel more comfortable placing her trust in him, Gideon was long past the point of denying her anything.

It wasn't graceful—he was too aroused for that—but he shucked his breeches and resumed his kneeling position. Caroline leaned back, her feline green eyes raking him up and down, lingering on the bulging curves of his arms honed from regular pugilism practice, the swells of his chest and carved ladder of his abdomen, the vee of his pelvis and the muscular thighs honed from years of riding hard and fast, the thick, ruddy column of his sex jutting from the nest of dark curls between his legs. Ah, yes, that bit appeared to interest her a great deal.

"I did not have the opportunity to see all of you the last time we…"

"The last time we made love?" Color crested Caro's cheeks as she nodded. They'd been practically frantic with need that night, only taking the time to remove half their clothing before they collapsed into a writhing heap upon the bed. "You may touch me anywhere that pleases you," Gideon added hoarsely. He prayed she would. He saw her fingers flex in indecision, and he gently took her hand in his and guided it to the center of his chest. He held her loosely enough that she could have pulled away if she'd wanted, but she did not—thank God. He helped her trace the lines of his pectoral muscles, his breath hissing through his teeth as she grazed his hard nipple again and again. His cock bobbed between them and begged for her attention as her nails tickled the ridges of his abdomen. He could read in her eyes how badly she desired to hold him, but she didn't take him in hand. "Caro, please..." he groaned, more vulnerable than he could ever remember being in his life.

"Please, what?" she whispered with a mixture of curiosity and hope—could he be asking her what she thought he was?

"Please touch my cock if that is what you wish. I have waited for months and I can stand it no longer." Bolstered by his plaintive tone, Caro finally wrapped her fingers around his girth. "God, yes," he hissed and tilted his head back. "Your hand is so soft."

Caro explored its weight and girth, testing to see whether she could wrap her fingers around it fully and coming up just shy. She gave his length a tentative stroke and Gideon saw stars. "It is so hard," she murmured.

"For you," he groaned. "Only for you."

"I enjoy that—hearing you say it is only for me."

"Because it is the truth." The last word was said as a gasp when she brushed her thumb over the swollen head, swirling a peal of moisture from the slit around and beneath the edge of his sensitive foreskin. "Mmm. Like that." His head dropped back in utter abandon as each of her gentle strokes unleashed a wave of sensation to lap at him like the ceaseless tide. It would carry him away if she continued on as she was for much longer.

But he could handle a little more.

He covered her small hand with his and encouraged her to grip him more tightly, stroke him more firmly. He rocked into her touch, his hips rolling to meet her. Gideon was enraptured by the sight of their hands working together to bring him pleasure, the bob and sway of her full breasts as she concentrated on her task, the flush spreading from her cheeks to her throat to the expanse of her breasts as more of them was gradually revealed by her movements.

This would send him over the edge. And he was not ready for this to be over.

He stalled her ministrations, and she looked up at him questioningly. "If you keep doing that, then this will end before it begins." His voice was raw and rough.

Caro's brows rose, but she released him slowly, as if she did not want to stop touching him.

"May I see all of you now?" he asked, surprised to realize that his voice was unsteady. He nearly lost all control when she bit her lip and cast down her eyes. So shy and innocent when he knew her to be a woman who could enjoy carnal pleasures as much as he.

"I would like that, but know that my body is different than the last time you saw it."

"Different? Because of your pregnancy?" Gideon almost laughed at the absurdity of it—of course, her body would be different—but he recognized just in time that it would have been precisely the wrong thing to do. Instead, he took her hands in his until she met his eyes. "I must have done a piss-poor job of showing you how bloody attractive I find you if you have such concerns."

"But my body—"

"Is stunning. Drives me mad. Makes me ache just thinking about it." He flicked his gaze to his heavy erection as evidence.

She giggled and he watched her tension melt away. Rolling her lower lip between her teeth, she stared into his eyes, never breaking contact as she shrugged her gaping nightshift from her body.

Gideon followed its trail with ravenous eyes. The perfect globes of her pearlescent breasts were fuller and rounder than before, the nipples a deep red and proudly erect. Her waist was still slim, but the curve of her lower belly was undeniable now that she was bare before him. Her pale flesh was smooth and taut as if she'd been carved from marble by the most skilled of sculptors. The curls guarding her sex were already glistening with her arousal.

An enraptured growl rumbled from deep in his chest. She was glorious.

He pulled her into his arms, crushing every curve and plane of their bodies together, and claimed her mouth as his.

Gently, he maneuvered them to the mattress. Their legs tangled together and he raised his thigh to her damp heat, losing his breath when she rocked against the pressure. She was so swollen, so wet for him already. Her hands coasted across his back and buttocks, gripping and squeezing with increasing boldness as she went.

With great difficulty, Gideon broke away from her lips and trailed his mouth down her throat. He braced his arms on either side of her head, hovering above her as he licked and tasted the delicate skin of her throat. He gradually made his way down her body, pressing hot, open-mouthed kisses to her sternum while cupping the weights of her breasts. He closed his lips over one of her ripe-berry nipples and might have thought he'd caused her pain for the strength of her cry, but, rather than push him away, she held him in place with her hands tangled in his hair.

He lavished attention on one and then the other until she undulated beneath him, seeking the contact her body craved. As he prowled down her body, Gideon sliced open his heart and allowed every word he held inside to pour forth. He spoke against the alabaster perfection of her stomach, the perfect divot of her navel. "To see your body swelling with *my* child...to witness the undeniable evidence that you are *mine*...there is nothing in this world that makes me harder or arouses me more." He palmed her stomach, marveled at the life growing within and the woman who nurtured the miracle. "Not a day has gone by that my cock hasn't begged for you; my mouth hasn't watered with the memory of tasting you. I want you again and again, Caro—as many times as you will allow me. You are everything I've always wanted and everything I never realized I needed. I ache every time I hear your laughter, I throb each time your eyes meet mine. Even if I do not show it in the moment, know you do that to me and I have no control over it."

She whimpered and mewled as his warm breath tickled the

curls at the juncture of her thighs. He inhaled deeply, scenting the sweet aroma of her arousal. It struck him so powerfully that his hips made an involuntary thrust against the mattress. He couldn't wait to sink into her, to feel the pulsations of her climax as it mercilessly ripped his own release from his body.

He pressed her thighs wide and gazed his fill of the pink dripping petals of her sex. "If anyone believes me to be in control in this marriage, they would be wrong," he breathed and felt her lift her head to watch him. He met her eyes over the gentle curve of her ripening stomach. "You are the one with the power; you can break me so badly I would never be whole again."

With that, Gideon dipped his head and pressed his mouth to her. Caro's cries as he stroked her with long, slow licks turned into sobs of pleasure and nonsensical praise as he swirled around the nubbin at the crux of her sex. Quickly finding a rhythm she preferred, he continued his onslaught of her body, spreading her wide with his thumbs and palming her inner thighs as wide as they would go. The wet sounds they made were obscene and incredibly arousing. She moaned and pulsed around his tongue as it speared into her as deeply as it could. She tasted of late summer peaches and honey, impossibly sweet and slightly earthy. She was heaven.

He groaned his pleasure as she locked her fingers in his hair and held him still as she rocked against his lips. He let her use him and loved every second of it. He realized how close she was already when he dipped the tip of one thumb into her tight, wet sheath. She was so damned tight and dripped with need.

He listened as her breathing caught and the pitch of her vocalizations changed. Just when the time was right, Gideon pulled back, growling in delight at the stinging tug of her fingers in his hair when he did so.

"No!" Caroline sobbed. "Don't! Don't stop—don't—" Her words died on a scream of relief as he shoved inside of her to the hilt, filling and stretching her to her limit. She was so ready, so slick, so primed, her body offered no resistance other than to welcome him with the most sinfully delicious embrace.

Immediately, he began to pump his hips in deep, claiming thrusts. He held her thighs wide, offering him an uninhibited view of his body claiming hers again and again. It took only three strokes and Caroline was clawing at the bedsheets and tossing her rose-gold head, her body clamping down on his.

"Yes, Gideon!" she screamed over and over until she could only mouth the words, too overcome by the blinding pleasure of her climax to continue.

It took everything in him not to spill as her body tightened and tensed around his. He continued pounding into her, never breaking his rhythm, continuing to drag out wave after wave of her release. Every smack of his thighs on her bottom, every trembling breath drove him higher. Her arms alternated between pushing him away from her highly sensitized body and clutching him close for more, more, more. He was only too happy to oblige, continuing until they were both slick with sweat.

Finally, Caro raked her nails along his ribs and he was lost. His orgasm built from the base of his spine, humming with white-hot ferocity, climbing higher and higher until he was consumed by it. Unleashing a curse, his hips gave a few more deep, grinding thrusts until every muscle seized. Their bodies pressed flush together, his climax ripped through him with a roar. The knowledge that each pulse filled her with more of his seed, marked her further as his, dragged out the pulsations until he was too weak to hold himself aloft.

He dropped to the mattress as a sweating, panting mess, but he'd never been happier than when Caroline took no coaxing to wrap herself around him. They held each other tightly, reveling in the warmth and comfort of one another's arms, and were lulled to sleep by the gentle metronome of their heartbeats.

Chapter Thirteen

ANOTHER WEEK PASSED, and the morning of Gideon's surprise birthday party dawned sunny and warm, promising a fortuitous day of gorgeous summer weather. Caroline was proud of herself for having made it this far without alerting Gideon to any of their preparations. Disaster had nearly occurred when a vase was knocked over in the process of the floral delivery, but she'd quickly explained the sound away and challenged Gideon to a game of cards rather than investigate. Having prepared extensive checklists and met countless times with the butler, housekeeper, and cook over the course of her planning, she was confident that they would be able to pull this off without Gideon knowing.

One thing, however, remained solidly on her mind.

She had yet to receive a definite answer regarding Emily and Oliver's attendance at the party. She'd sent a note along with the formal engraved invitation offering them a room at Bray Castle should they be able to make the journey. Emily had sent an immediate reply indicating that she would try her best, but there had been no word since then. Caroline remained determinedly optimistic and hoped for a surprise appearance of Emily and her husband. She desired little above forming a bridge between the half brothers and granting Gideon the relationship she knew he longed for.

The hours ticked on, and Caroline kept a mental tally of all the things that, according to her carefully crafted timetable, had been completed, were still in progress, and were left to do. Food preparations had begun the day before, but the kitchens were still overflowing with organized chaos. She did her best to keep Gideon from the areas in which most of the party would take place—the front of the house and great hall, the long formal dining room, and a few smaller chambers that had been requisitioned as retiring rooms or filled with gaming tables (because it most certainly could not be a party for Gideon without a bit of gambling). She did what she could to periodically slip away and receive updates from the staff. All seemed to be going relatively well, but her task became more difficult as the evening approached.

"Supper is delayed this evening," she sighed, injecting as much regret into her tone as might be believable.

"Oh?" Gideon looked at her over the edge of his book. It surprised her to no end how content he seemed to waste quiet hours in her presence. She'd never witnessed him so sedentary. Of course, he went on long, hard rides almost daily, but, other than that, he displayed not so much as a hint of restlessness. This Gideon—the new husband, expectant father, Gideon of Bray Castle—was unlike anything she'd ever encountered. In town, he was normally flitting from one engagement to the next, almost constantly surrounded by one or more of his friends and eager to sniff out excitement. It was not uncommon for him to spend the afternoon at the races and then participate in races of his own, where the wager involved one participant to perform some absurd or mortifying act. His evenings were spent drinking and flirting, cutting a swath through London's Society, returning home just as the sun rose from a night of dancing, carousing, or gambling. Why, then, did he seem so content? She was perplexed by his complacency—this new, domestic side of him—not because it concerned her, but because it was so unexpected. She'd known her own lifestyle would need to change, but she'd never really asked it of Gideon. The fact that he'd done so without question and merely stepped into the role of doting husband and present partner…it unleashed butterflies in her stomach. Not once had he ever seemed put out by her requests; in fact, he often sought her out wherever she was enjoying a few quiet moments. For a man who'd had no model for marriage, his instincts were impeccable.

He hadn't questioned it when she invited him to join her in her private sitting room while she worked on the pillow cover she'd been embroidering (purely out of necessity because it was one of the farthest rooms from the great hall without a view of the front drive). She'd been concerned that he might decline, but he'd merely pressed his lips to the back of her hand, retrieved his book from the library, and escorted her up the stairs.

Caroline flinched at every small sound from below. If he noticed that she'd made little progress with her sewing thanks to her preoccupation, then he said nothing.

"Indeed," she answered. "Something about the venison being off."

"Well, that's rather disappointing." She almost felt guilty for the deep frown knitting his brows together. Venison was one of his favorite dishes, and she'd specifically planned for it to take a place of prominence as the main course that evening. She had to bite her lip and turn her face to hide her smile. All her weeks of planning were nearly ready to pay off; she buzzed with excitement to see his reaction. She longed to bring him joy, to let him know that she saw him and he saw her. If anyone deserved it, it was this man who consistently went out of his way to bring her joy, show her acceptance, and lend support.

Suddenly, the screech of a horse and loud jangle of tack was abruptly followed by a man's shout. The noise instantly drew Gideon's attention.

"What in God's name was that?"

Before he could stand, however, Caroline threw her sewing aside and closed the gap between them. As predicted, Gideon relaxed as soon as she lifted her skirts and straddled his narrow hips, resting her bottom on his strong thighs. His book fell to the floor with a soft thud; his concern for the sounds outside melted away. He made a low, appreciative sound deep in his throat.

"I am certain it was nothing," Caroline said lightly, slightly breathless as her body instantly came alive with the feel of him beneath her and the sensation of his wide palms running along her hips and thighs. She wrapped her arms around his neck and kissed the tip of his nose. "Unless...you wish me to stop so you might investigate."

"Not a chance," Gideon murmured as he leaned his head against the back of the sofa to gaze up at her. "Not when my gorgeous wife is on top of me."

They'd not spent a single night apart since she'd gone to him in his bedchamber following their failed cribbage game. Beyond the blinding pleasure and the deep, sated sleep they enjoyed after their bouts of lovemaking and draining climaxes, they learned and explored. Gideon showed her that she could be comfortable asking for what she desired; he gave her the space and the confidence to test her limitations in the face of her traumatic past. Patiently, he guided her in overcoming her insecurities, taking great pains to let her know that she had her own agency. He did all of this while showing her new pinnacles of pleasure she'd never imagined. For the past two weeks, Caroline had been existing in a near-constant state of bliss. Now, it was her turn to reciprocate.

"Then I wonder how we shall pass the time," she murmured as she ran her hands up the hard expanse of his chest. Already, she could feel the rapid thunder of his heartbeat, the insistent ridge of his burgeoning arousal pressing up into the cradle of her sex.

"I wonder..." he echoed suggestively. His hands trailed up her sides and cupped her breasts through her gown. His thumbs rubbed the taut buds of her nipples, and she moaned in response. He knew precisely how to stroke her there to take advantage of her newfound sensitivity. Her breasts had become so responsive since her pregnancy that he'd even managed to bring her to climax by teasing them, alone. It had been glorious. And his touch was igniting that same spark inside of her all over again. "You like that?" he purred, and Caroline nearly shuddered from his velvet voice.

"You know I do." The rumble low in his throat could only be described as appreciative. "And you like it, too." A wicked smile curled her lips. "But I believe I know something you might enjoy even more." Without giving Gideon time to respond, she reached beneath her skirts and blindly located the falls of his breeches; they were already strained taut against his impressive arousal. With a few flicks of her fingers—a task she'd practiced several times over the preceding days—his cock was freed from the confines of his clothing.

He gasped her name as she took him in hand, running the broad, blunt head into the slit in her drawers and through her folds already slick with desire. These days, it took very little for her to reach such a state, but neither of them would ever dream of complaining. She didn't hesitate to notch him in place and slowly sink onto his length, savoring the stretch as her body strove to accommodate his girth. She moaned at the pressure, the hot, hard heat of him inside of her as he filled her to the lips of her womb.

"This is heaven," Gideon gasped. "You are heaven." He grasped her hips once more and began to rock her. The position took some adjustments to account for her growing belly, but they managed.

Oh, how they managed.

The combination of grinding rolls and small, bouncing thrusts quickly worked them into a frenzy. Their bodies met with wet smacks of flesh on flesh, sucking and sliding, stoking their desire to unholy heights. Caroline leaned forward and pressed her mouth to his. Their tongues stroked in time to their thrusts, overwhelming her with the layers of sensations unleashed within her body. Everything shimmered and throbbed. Her every nerve felt raw and exposed. The chafing of the cups of her stays against her sensitive nipples, the way the pearl of her sex rubbed against

Gideon's pelvis, the sensation of his strong hands gripping her bottom with deliciously bruising force, his unique flavor of sweetened tea and something indescribably masculine... She loved this. She loved him. She loved knowing he cared for her, desired her, trusted her, believed in her.

She sobbed against his lips, the myriad sensations becoming too much for her sensitized body. Her muscles began to quake, her hands clamped down on his broad shoulders for purchase; she held him deep, deep inside of her as the ripples of blinding pleasure spread throughout her body. Her thighs gripped his narrow hips and she arched into him as her orgasm broke over her in shocks of delight. Gideon held perfectly still beneath her, allowing the rhythmic pulsations of her climax to milk his own from his body. The liquid fire of his seed filled her as his head dropped back and he groaned, deep and guttural, as if he'd relinquished a part of his very soul to her.

Caroline collapsed onto him, her forehead resting against the curve where his neck met his shoulder. Her racing heartbeat slowed as she gradually floated down from where she'd soared amongst the clouds. Gideon's fingers were trailing a gentle path up and down her spine.

"Is this how all of my birthdays will be from here on out?" Gideon asked, still slightly breathless. His deep voice sent a pleasant rumble through her chest. "Because I will gladly accept this."

Caroline chuckled and lifted her head to gaze down into his face. His molten gray eyes were so soft. The tilt of his mouth was so charming. The heavy brows and high cheekbones, the lock of dark hair that had fallen onto his forehead, the hard line of his jaw with its barest hint of evening shadow, all of it together made her heart flip in her chest. She pressed a soft, lingering kiss to his forehead and said, "It does not need to be your birthday for such treatment." His lips curled into a broad, wolfish grin. She didn't hear the words he'd been about to say because she caught sight of the clock placed atop the nearby writing desk. How had they managed to pass that much time?

"We should prepare for supper!" she said quickly, raising herself off of Gideon's lap, heedless of the warm trickle now spreading down her inner thighs. She'd have to bathe now, which left her even less time to prepare.

"Why the rush?" Gideon asked as he tucked himself back into his breeches and fastened them. "I thought you said supper would be delayed?"

"Because we agreed that we would treat tonight with some pomp and circumstance—wear fancy dress for dinner and such; treat it as the special occasion it is. That takes time to accomplish." Their bedchambers were located in the newer wing of the house, relatively far from the bustle of the party preparations and arriving guests. Gideon's valet had been enlisted to provide distractions if there were any suspicious sounds, and Caroline hoped that would be sufficient.

"But it is just us two." He tried to pull her back down to sit with him, but she danced just outside of his reach.

"Supper is already going to be later than usual, and I do not wish to delay it further by being tardy. You know how grumpy I can become when I am deprived of food."

"Do I ever," he said in mock horror.

"Go on, you insufferable man. I shall see you in two hours." She playfully swatted his arm and would have turned to go to her bedchamber had he not pulled her into his arms and planted the most toe-curling, erotic kiss upon her mouth.

"As long as you promise I can unwrap my present later," he growled into her ear before stepping away and quitting with a bow that left her head spinning.

Chapter Fourteen

"I AM TOLD Lady Swanleigh is already belowstairs," said Gideon's valet, Walters.

Odd, thought Gideon. He normally retrieved her from her chamber and they descended together to dine. Perhaps she had some last-minute preparations to complete—a small gift or a special dessert. He was not one who normally enjoyed celebrating his birthdays; his childhood had largely been absent of such frivolity. Caro, on the other hand, enjoyed life so much that she looked forward to any opportunity to celebrate it. He could humor her in any way she liked, so long as she continued to smile at him as if he'd hung the stars. A man could become addicted to a woman who saw him that way.

Gideon strongly suspected he already was.

Striding out into the hallway, he was so busy adjusting the cuffs of his black formal coat that he did not become aware of a low din and the glowing of hundreds of candles until he'd already turned the corner to the top of the stairs leading from the east wing to the great hall. He froze immediately, caught between a mixture of awe and disbelief. Assembled below were dozens of guests dressed in evening kits, glittering gems, and opulent gowns. Standing front and center was his wife.

Caro beamed up at him, joy and pride so gloriously evident in her expression. She'd donned an elegant silk gown in hunter green. It displayed the expanse of her pale collarbone to perfection and hinted at her increasing bosom. The clever draping of the fabric helped mask her pregnancy, but it wouldn't be long before she required new gowns to accommodate her growing body. Her rose-gold hair glittered in the warm candlelight, even more so from the pearl-tipped pins woven into the curls and plaits. She held her gloved hand aloft, toasting him with a crystal glass. The rest of the party followed suit.

"Happy birthday, Swanleigh," she said, her voice ringing clear. "One year older, but never one year wiser." It was followed by a chorus of "hear, hear" and laughter as everyone toasted to his birthday, his health, and his longevity. Familiar faces filled the room; friends, former classmates, neighboring lords and gentry. Gideon had eyes only for his wife. Never before had he experienced such an outpouring of love, and he knew Caroline was the catalyst of it all.

He descended the stairs and immediately walked up to his wife. Taking her hand in his, he pressed his lips to her knuckles. "However did you manage to plan this beneath my nose?" he asked, utterly astonished.

"I have my ways," she said, unable to mask her pleasure at his surprise.

"I am impressed, Lady Swanleigh," he murmured and accepted a glass from a servant.

The entire evening rang of Caroline's touches. From the local flowers to the guest list, the menu to the entertainment, all of it was perfectly catered to Gideon's preferences. She truly seemed to have thought of everything. As he moved through the crowd with Caro on his arm, Gideon simply could not have been prouder, or more in love with her.

He was in conversation with Blackwood, the man's latest stunning paramour by his side, when he felt Caro's fingers tighten around his arm. He turned to see what had grabbed her attention and, on the far side of the room, he caught sight of a tall, dark-haired man dressed smartly in a well-tailored black evening kit. Beside him, his angelic wife glittered in an ice-blue gown that made her eyes appear to glow.

Oliver and Emily.

Gideon glanced between them and his wife. Not only had she thought to invite them, but she'd convinced them to attend. He could hardly believe his eyes. She was a bloody brilliant little mastermind, his wife. A powerful emotion washed over Gideon—some tenderness he could not name. Gratitude? Relief? Whatever it was, he knew Caro would remain by his side while he sorted it out.

He and Caroline excused themselves from Blackwood and traversed the room to where Oliver and Emily stood, looking elegant, if slightly uncomfortable. Curious glances were being cast their way. Other guests were beginning to wonder who they were and, likely, to marvel at the similarities between Oliver and the guest of honor. He couldn't blame them. It was only the second time he'd seen his half brother in person. The resemblance was uncanny, especially when they were dressed nearly identically.

"Mr. and Mrs. Black," Gideon said in cheerful greeting. "I am so pleased to see you made the journey from London." He bowed over Emily's gloved hand before extending his hand to Oliver. The other man eyed the appendage—likely unused to the gesture, Gideon thought—before taking it.

"Happy birthday," Oliver said in his no-nonsense tone. "Though I will admit that I was transported here under false pretenses." He shot Emily a loaded look out of the corner of his eye. "My wife convinced me we were to look at a small country cottage."

Emily had the good grace to appear slightly bashful. "Sometimes it is easier to lie a little and deal with the consequences later."

"I should have known better when you insisted upon packing my good clothing," Oliver grumbled, though even Gideon could tell he was far less put out than he was pretending.

"A country cottage sounds so lovely!" Caro piped up, her face split into a glorious smile.

"Indeed. May I introduce my wife, Lady Caroline?"

Oliver proceeded to execute a flawless bow over Caroline's hand. "I will admit, this part of the country is tempting. I might be amenable to investing in a small cottage were I not married to such a duplicitous woman."

"Hardly," Emily snorted. "You enjoyed a foray outside of London, fresh air, and now a party in a gorgeous castle. I see only benefits to my behavior."

"Well," Gideon chimed in, looking at Oliver, "it seems we are both drawn to beautiful, scheming women too cunning for their own good. I, myself, believed I'd be enjoying a quiet dinner, and now I must play host to several dozen guests."

Caro jabbed him in the ribs with her elbow. "Do not lie—you are reveling in every moment of this."

Gideon laughed heartily and was cheered to see even the corner of Oliver's lips tilt into the beginnings of a smile.

It was then that he noticed an increase in the whispers and glances around them. With him and Oliver standing together in their formal clothing…why, they must have looked like a pair of matched bookends. He'd be surprised if speculation about their filial ties hadn't already begun in earnest. He made a silent vow that Oliver would not experience any prejudice amongst these people. These guests were people who mattered to him, but Oliver was blood. Anyone who thought to speak ill of him would have to answer to Gideon.

He and Caroline kept Oliver and Emily near their sides for the rest of the evening, introducing them to the rest of their close circle. As he'd anticipated, Blackwood and the rest were only too happy to absorb them into their fold. The sight of these men with his brother actually made Gideon's throat tighten. They were good men who deserved more than the caricatures Society had boiled them down to. Hell-raisers and lovers of beautiful women they may be, but they were not as shallow or dim-witted or without morals as the tabloids would purport. This combination of Gideon's worlds—the brother he'd always hoped to find and the friends who'd stood in for the family he lacked—was enough to make his throat tighten with emotion.

"Are you ready for one of your gifts?" Caro asked, snapping Gideon from his mental meandering. He'd been so lost in thought that he hadn't realized the assemblage had begun to migrate outside toward the west lawn.

"This party was not my gift?" he asked, delight welling up in his chest as he allowed Caroline to guide him along with the flow of the crowd.

"Part of it," she replied with a mischievous smile.

"What have you planned, Lady Swanleigh?" he murmured in her ear, savoring the delighted chill that elicited from her.

"You will see soon enough!"

The early evening sky was painted in broad strokes of goldenrod, unnatural orange, shades of pink, and clouds of lilac. The air was sweet with the scent of freshly shorn grass and warm earth. The night-blooming flowers growing against the west side of the castle were beginning to open, adding an exotic note to the atmosphere.

One excited yip was quickly followed by another. Gideon was confused until the crowd parted and he saw what Caroline had done. The lawn had been cleared, and a long, narrow course had been roped off to create a straight track the length of the gardens. Handlers managed their greyhounds as the lean, angular dogs leapt, snuffled, barked, and paced, ready to do what they had been born and bred to do.

"You organized dog races?" Gideon could not mask his astonishment at the scene laid out before the party. Wagers were already being placed as the dogs with numbers one through five painted on their flanks were paraded before the partygoers.

Having dogs run a track was not the usual format for dog racing, but Gideon knew Caro had always disliked watching coursing, where greyhounds were sent in to chase a loose hare. Though the complex points system was not solely based on which animal captured the hare, the capture and death of the lure was not improbable. This was why Gideon had so diligently sought out other versions of the sport to satisfy everyone's desire to gamble, the thrill of racing, and the preservation of life. Caro must have contacted the kennels responsible for this format of racing to have them present for this party. The lengths to which this woman had gone through for him…they were humbling.

"I did, indeed," Caro replied with a smile so bright Gideon thought he might be blinded from its brilliance. She held out her hand and, rather than taking his when he offered it in return, she dropped into his palm a heavy velvet pouch filled with coins. "Go select your winner."

"I am in awe of you, Caroline," he breathed, his eyes dancing over her face and delighting in the beauty and warmth there.

"I feel the same." Her words were soft and intimate, as chaste as a peck on the lips, yet as incendiary as what she'd done to him in her sitting room earlier that day. "Let us go," she said, giving his hand a little tug. "There are only so many races that can be run before it is fully dark, and I have a good feeling about the brindle number three."

FOLLOWING THE DOG races (during which Caroline had soundly trounced every member of their group with her race selections), Gideon and Oliver were drafted into a game of cards in the room set up for that purpose.

"Caro *must* love you," Kempton said, leaning back in his chair and gesturing appreciatively to the room with his unlit cheroot. The sitting room had been cleared out and reset with tables for cards, roulette, and dice. Servants meandered through, offering an impeccable variety of drinks and cigars. "She went to a great deal of trouble to put all this together."

Gideon only smiled as he shuffled the cards.

She hadn't said as much, but Kempton was correct. Everything around them—the weeks of planning, the thought and care that went into every little detail—it smacked of love. His chest constricted. Could she love him?

Could she know he felt that way about her?

He certainly adored her, looked forward to spending time with her, and wanted her with a fierce need the likes of which he'd never experienced. He was proud to have her as his wife and his partner, and the thought of seeing her as the mother of his child someday soon gave him the most peacefully elated sensation he'd ever experienced. Was all of that love? He was beginning to think it was the deepest version of it.

"Are we shuffling all night or are we playing?" asked Brinley with his characteristic sarcasm.

Gideon chuckled and began to deal.

All the men learned in short order that Oliver was quite talented at cards—nearly as much as Gideon was.

Blackwood made a disgusted sound as he tossed his hand of cards to the table. "My pocketbook will never survive attempting to keep up with the two of you."

Gideon chuckled and caught Oliver's eye across the table. Was it his imagination, or did they share a moment of—not necessarily brotherly affection—a warm kinship? The seedling of a bond?

Gideon fervently hoped that night was the grafting of yet another branch onto his woefully slim family tree. His heart felt fuller than it had in recent memory.

TWO LONG TABLES had been set up in the dining room, laid with pristine white cloths, the fine china usually kept in the storeroom at Bray Castle, and silverware so polished that it glittered in the glow of the shining chandeliers and candelabras. Everything about it was perfection.

Gideon looked over to Caro on his right; she was busy chatting animatedly with Kempton. He couldn't help but stare at her, his amazing, beautiful, brilliant wife. The smiling faces, all the joyful chatter…it was all thanks to her.

Unable to contain himself any longer, Gideon stood and tapped on his wine glass with a spoon until the room quieted and he had their attention. He opened his mouth to speak, but no sound came out. There was a soft brush on the smallest finger of his right hand. He looked down to see Caro's hand had inched close enough to graze his—to provide him strength and support. This was everything he needed.

"I wanted to thank everyone for being complicit in this plot to celebrate my birthday—a lost cause, if ever there was one," he began, earning a hearty chuckle from the assemblage. "Walking into this party and having all of you here to partake in this night's entertainment will forever be one of the highlights of my life." His eyes tracked around the tables, finally locating Oliver and Emily, seated opposite one another a little way down. "And thank you for welcoming my brother, Mr. Oliver Black, and his lovely wife," he added, lifting his glass in Oliver's direction. Heads whipped around and there were murmurs as people's suspicions were confirmed. "He has not received the recognition he deserved in life, and I am determined to change that. Beginning tonight, they are acknowledged parts of the Bray family." Emily made a surreptitious swipe at her eyes and Oliver offered him a slight inclination of his head.

"Most of all," Gideon continued more loudly over the smattering of chatter in the wake of his revelation, "thank you to my wife, Caroline." He looked down at her again and saw tears glittering in her verdant eyes, a soft smile playing upon her shapely mouth. "Nearly two months of marriage and she's made me happier than I ever deserved." He took her hand in his and guided her to stand. "I love you," he said. Her lips parted in surprise and he took immediate advantage, leaning in and kissing her soundly, passionately, before the entire party. Dimly, he could hear his friends cheering and whistling above a few scandalized murmurs.

Caroline's face was bright red when he finally broke the kiss. "May I?" he whispered, his eyes flicking down to her abdomen and back up. After Caro's distress following the revelation that the staff were likely aware of the baby, they'd discussed announcing the pregnancy upon their return to London. However, Gideon did not care about London; he cared about Caro and the people in that dining room. He wanted to add to the joy of the evening.

She nibbled the corner of her lip and gave a little nod.

Grinning wide as a fool, Gideon held his glass even higher and turned back to the party. "Tonight, we drink to friends, family, reckless behavior, overindulgence, and…to a soon-to-be-born addition to the Swanleigh line. Thus far, my third decade is shaping up to be an interesting one."

The room erupted into cheers and well-wishes, the clinking of glasses and excited chatter. Gideon sipped his drink before placing a quick peck upon Caro's lips and relinquishing her back to her chair, where she was immediately accosted with Kempton's congratulations. Gideon reclaimed his seat and the meal began.

Chapter Fifteen

FOLLOWING SUPPER, THE men broke off for smoking and more cards; Caroline led the women outside to enjoy the warm night in the courtyard gardens lit by romantic torchlight. Chairs had been set in alcoves of fragrant blooms growing around the tinkling three-tiered fountain. Contrary to convention, after-dinner drinks were served to the women as well. Some sipped claret as they walked the perimeter, while others examined the variety of flowers. After spending time making her rounds of the guests, Caroline discovered Emily sitting on one of the benches, watching the torchlight sparkle in the fountain's rivulets.

"May I join you?" Caroline asked her.

"Oh, yes!" she replied animatedly. A brilliant smile lit up her angelic face and she slipped her gloved hand into Caroline's. "Congratulations are in order for you as well!" she said with a grin. "How wonderful about the baby."

"Thank you!" Caroline nearly rested her hands on her belly and then remembered herself. The gown helped to hide how far along she was, but to do so would make it obvious. She'd been doing it more and more often lately, loving the idea of cradling the babe whose tiny movements she was feeling with increasing frequency.

Emily leaned in conspiratorially and cast her eyes about as if watching for eavesdroppers. "I have something to confess." Caroline adopted a similar position and nodded for her to continue. "I am expecting as well."

"Oh, that is wonderful!" Caroline pulled Emily into a hug. It mattered not that they'd only met twice and corresponded as many times, but she felt a kinship there. Neither Caroline nor Gideon had family; she wanted to embrace these people with both arms wide open and welcome them into their lives. The fact that she and Emily would be navigating pregnancy and all four of them would be learning parenthood at the same time felt like a fated bond.

"I have not told Oliver yet, so…" Emily made a motion of buttoning her lips.

Caroline nodded in agreement. "Of course! I will say nothing."

"Our pregnancies must be close in terms," Emily added excitedly. Caro did not correct the assumption. "Won't it be wonderful for our husbands? Give them something over which they can bond?"

"I hope so. Speaking of which, I am ever so grateful that you were able to attend tonight. I hope it was not inconvenient for you to leave London and travel all this way."

"I have been out of the city only once before, so I was excited to visit Kent. My world has been expanding a bit since I met my husband, but there is still so much to see."

"Did he say you lured him under the pretense of visiting a cottage for purchase?" Caroline asked, recalling their earlier conversation.

"It is something we have discussed, and I think he will be even more supportive of it once he learns of my delicate condition."

"Will you be vacating London entirely, then?" Caroline hoped not; she'd liked the thought of being able to visit with them regularly.

"No. At least not right away. I still help from time to time with my mother's business, and there is no one to replace me at the moment."

"May I ask what it is you do there?" Her curiosity won out

with that question. Caroline hadn't met any prostitutes, but her mind's image was not this composed, educated woman before her.

"The books," Emily replied, smiling kindly as if she'd anticipated the question. "I balance the accounts and manage the orders."

"Fascinating," she said, not a hint of sarcasm in her tone. "And your husband? Is he also employed there?"

She hadn't expected the shuttering of Emily's expression. "Occasionally. He recently retired from a position, and he is trying to decide upon a new industry."

Whatever it had been, Caroline thought it must have been a lucrative business for them to now manage on Emily's income alone, maintain a residence in a respectable neighborhood, and have the flexibility to consider purchasing a cottage in the country. The mysteries abounded.

"Well, I wish him luck in his endeavors; though I will say I rather selfishly hope you stay close so we might see more of one another."

Emily giggled brightly. "Do not fret about that. I can tell your husband is growing on Oliver; the speech he made went a long way toward that. And, I must say, that kiss!" Emily fanned her face dramatically, causing Caroline's cheeks to burn anew. "It is clear you will be quite preoccupied with your marriage even after you return to town. Swanleigh adores you."

I love you.

He *loved* her. He'd said so in front of everyone; even if he'd said it softly, he'd done it.

"I think he might."

"I know he does. Even if he hadn't proclaimed it, everyone can see it."

She was basking in the glow of this knowledge as Gideon and Oliver led the rest of the men out to the courtyard. Their expressions were eerily similar in the flickering light, both pairs of unique, silver eyes darkening as they spotted their respective wives. There was dark, sensual promise in those gazes.

Caroline leaned over and whispered to Emily, "It would seem that you are a recipient of adoration of your own."

"I most certainly am," she replied dreamily.

"I don't believe I have ever danced this much in my life," Emily said a little breathlessly as she dropped onto a chair positioned at the periphery of the great hall. A slight flush of exertion colored her cheeks and made her eyes flicker with joy. "It will be a wonder if I am able to walk at all tomorrow."

"I learned the hard way to plan a day of rest after any balls I attend." Caroline sighed with relief as she sat beside Emily.

"I don't know how many balls we will be attending."

"Nonsense! You will surely be attending all of ours, and I plan on hosting many."

"Do you?"

"Oh, yes! I think for my first event as Marchioness of Swanleigh this one turned out quite fine. I can only improve with practice."

"Then I am sure everything will be utterly magical. Tonight has already been such a smashing success."

Caroline smiled in gratitude. "Are you staying in the village?"

Emily nodded in response and sipped from the glass a servant had offered her. "We have a room at the Sword and Lion Inn."

"That is nearly an hour's carriage ride from here, is it not?" She remembered seeing the inn's carved sign on their way to Bray Castle.

"I didn't know how else to perpetuate the ruse I'd presented to Oliver. We couldn't very well arrive on your doorstep yesterday, but I knew as soon as he saw me in my gown, he'd never say no to attending the party."

Caroline smiled; she could well picture the stoic Oliver melting at the sight of his angelic wife in her finery. "Now that the secret is out, perhaps you might move your things here? There are more than enough bedchambers prepared. We have some guests staying the night, but they will be leaving tomorrow." She took Emily's hand. "Stay another few days if you can; we have only one more week before we return to London. It will be such fun!"

Emily looked thoughtful. "It will take some convincing, but I think I can manage it."

Caroline gave a little bounce of excitement. "Splendid! It is settled. You will return in the morning."

"Pardon the interruption," Lord Trenholm said with a flourishing bow. His kind hazel eyes danced with just the right mixture of mirth and brandy. "I believe this next dance is mine?"

"Indeed, it is," Caroline said with a gracious smile. She excused herself from Emily and allowed Trenholm to guide her to the dance floor for a spirited reel.

As she bobbed and spun, she caught sight of a tall, dark-haired man watching her with smoldering intensity. Gideon had done his fair share of dancing that evening as well, but, more often than not, he'd been pulled into conversation or games of chance with his guests—everyone vying for time with the man of honor. Now, however, he was alone and staring at her as if no one else in the world existed. It was so exciting that she nearly missed her steps a time or two. It was almost a relief when the dance finished and she curtseyed to her partner. That was, until her heart began racing at a furious pace when her husband cut across the room and headed in her direction. His long legs ate up the distance with startling speed until he was suddenly standing before her, looking sinfully, darkly handsome.

"I believe the next dance is a waltz," he murmured and held his hand out to Caroline. "And I would very much like to share it with my wife."

A few years earlier, at Lord and Lady Underhill's fete, when the fall crispness had just begun to set in and the leaves were changing to brilliant shades of red and orange, making Hyde Park look like one giant sunset, Gideon had shown her how to be her authentic self in public. For so long, she'd been trained only to do what was expected of her, to smother any "otherness" that might make her stand out in a bad way. She'd received an invitation, though she knew Lady Underhill cared little for her. Fortunately, her husband had once been close to Kempton and Brinley, and their little group attending en masse had become a foregone conclusion. Caroline had nothing against the woman, other than the bitter downturn of her lips each time Caroline spoke.

True to form, Gideon reassured her that he would pull the same face right back at Lady Underhill each time she made it, regardless of how insane it made him appear. Of course, Caroline could not decline witnessing such a thing, so she donned her best persimmon-colored gown with ivory lace trim, as well as the pearls she'd received for her sixteenth birthday. She'd felt beautiful and confident, and she'd also had the best night of her life—up to that point.

She and Gideon had danced several times despite Society's dictates regarding the number of occasions an unmarried couple might visit the dance floor. He'd twirled her about, made her laugh until she could hardly breathe, and, true to his word, pulled hideous faces at her each time Lady Underhill made one of her own. It had been a brilliant night. Her feet had ached, as had her sides and cheeks from laughing and smiling as much as she did. Never before had she been so uninhibited, so free. And Gideon had given her those wings.

They'd danced together many times over the years, both before and after the Underhill gathering, but nothing compared to this first time…as his wife.

Caroline swallowed hard and placed her hand in his. The warmth of his palm was searing and her nipples pebbled with the memory of those hands on her only a short time ago.

The first notes we played and, as the dance began, it became apparent that Gideon's mind was on a similar vein.

"I remember with burning intensity the last time we danced together," he purred into her ear, low enough that he could not be overheard by any of the other dancers. She felt the rumble of his words in every part of her body as he held her indecently close for the dance and guided her with expert care.

"Oh?" she asked, though she recalled precisely the occasion he was referencing.

"Yes. You asked me for a favor…and I agreed." A shiver of pleasure tickled her spine at the memory. That was the night she'd asked Gideon to take her to bed. "We danced a waltz much like this one. When it was over, you leaned in and asked me to take you outside for some air. You looked a little piqued, so it seemed an entirely plausible request. Little did I know what you were working up the nerve to ask.

"You smelled of sugar and cinnamon from dessert and it made my mouth water. You told me that you'd given it a great deal of thought—that we'd known one another for many years and you trusted me with your life—and you wanted to know if I would grant you a night of pleasure." He leaned in and his hot breath tickled her ear. "What else could I do but say yes when you'd just offered to make all my fantasies come true?"

He went on to detail their escape from the event and the mad dash to his townhouse. They hadn't been able to wait long enough to make it to his bedchamber, so they collapsed together on the chaise in the parlor. He told her how hard he'd been, how long he'd secretly desired her, how much he'd wanted to make it good for her. He remembered the sounds she made when he freed her perfect breasts from her gown and suckled her sweet nipples, how tight she'd been around his fingers and convinced him he'd surely die on the spot the second he sank into her, how good she'd tasted when he'd licked every last drop of her first orgasm from his fingers. "I knew from the first moment I touched you that there would be no going back for me. As much as I tried to tell myself that this would be a one-time occurrence just as you said it would be, I knew in my soul that I could never live like that. As soon as you parted your beautiful legs for me and guided me inside of you, I was lost."

Caroline was practically panting by the time he'd finished,

and it took several heartbeats for her to realize that they'd stopped moving and the other dancers were forced to avoid them.

"Gideon," she croaked, "the dance."

"To hell with the dance," he growled and then guided her from the dance floor and through the crowd. He pulled her into the hallway and led her up a smaller set of stairs that would eventually bring them to the proper wing. She was at first confused by the circuitous route, but then she realized it made the aim of their retreat less obvious to anyone who might have seen them.

"We cannot abandon the party," Caroline protested weakly, her mind and her body at war with one another.

"We most certainly can," he shot over his shoulder. "We are newlyweds, and it is expected of us; besides, we are technically still on our honeymoon trip."

GIDEON DIDN'T THINK he'd ever undressed so quickly. For that matter, he wasn't sure he'd ever undressed a woman with as much speed and skill before. It wasn't but five minutes before they were falling on the bed together in a tangle of limbs. There had always been a spark between them but never was that more evident than in the bedroom. They'd formed a level of trust through their years of friendship rarely seen in married couples of the *ton*—let alone recently wed ones.

Despite Caroline's unfortunate past with the male persuasion, she did not demonstrate the slightest bit of fear where Gideon was concerned. He assured her time and time again that she was the one in charge—could say no at any moment or change anything she did not care for—and merely knowing that seemed to be enough encouragement for her. She was easy to please, but that didn't mean he would ever stop finding new ways to make her scream his name in delight.

Her nipples were highly sensitive, so he lavished them with extraordinary attention. He suckled and nipped, licked and stroked until she writhed beneath him. He didn't stop until every inch of her had been covered in his kisses, from the pounding pulse in her throat to the virgin undersides of her breasts.

He wanted to taste her to see if there was any lingering evidence of their earlier coupling left between her thighs, but she gripped his shoulder before he could sink too low on the bed.

"I want a turn," Caroline breathed, and Gideon's heart skipped a beat. He was so caught off guard by her statement that it took a moment for his body to catch up with his brain. Eventually, he placed a kiss on her round belly and rolled off of her.

Immediately, Caroline turned to him and pressed her mouth to his in a sweet, tender kiss. Her hands gently raked through the light dusting of dark hair on his chest, trailed lower to the clenching muscles of his abdomen, and found the hard curve of his cock. He groaned when her nails tickled the pulsing vein on the underside of his shaft, shuddered when she took him in hand and gave him a few testing pumps.

"I love how you feel," she said, a note of wonder in her voice. He was too lost to the sensations she was unleashing within him to do anything but stare unseeingly at the ceiling and listen to the melodic tones of her voice. Each slow glide of her hand was sheer torture of the most fantastical variety. He was already aching with the need for release, but he managed to stave it off. This woman drove him wild, but if she wanted to explore his body, then by God, he would let her even if it killed him. "So soft and hard at the same time." Several more strokes. "May I taste you as you taste me? Would that bring you pleasure?"

"Yes!" he said almost before she was done asking her question. "Yes…if that is something you desire."

"I do desire it," purred the little minx as she slid down his body. "I desire it a great deal." He watched unblinkingly as the tip of her tiny pink tongue darted out to lick the weeping head. "You taste salty…I like it."

"Holy hell," he gasped. "Again." The word came out more

plaintive than demanding.

She did as he asked, this time following the lick with an open-mouthed kiss. Gideon's breath hissed through his teeth and then died away entirely as she took just the tip into her mouth, swirling her tongue along the soft skin edging the rim. He didn't know how long he held his breath as she began her tentative experimentation, but he felt lightheaded as she sank a little lower and took him more deeply into her hot, wet mouth. His thighs trembled with his restraint; it took everything in him not to buck up off the bed and press himself down her throat. He had to remember that she'd never done this before and they had a lifetime together for new, pleasurable adventures.

His breathing was labored and hitching as Caroline continued her ministrations. She licked and sucked her way down the considerable length of his shaft, kissed the tender sac beneath, and ripped a groan of pleasure from his chest. When she sank her mouth onto him as far as she could, Gideon saw stars.

"Bloody hell, Caroline," he choked, watching her rose-gold head bob over his lap, her hand working in tandem with her mouth when she realized she could not take as much of him into her as she would have liked. His eyes trailed down the curve of her back to the perfect globes of her bottom where they wiggled in the air. "Touch yourself," he growled through his teeth. "Touch your dripping cunny while you suck me."

She whimpered around his head, but did as she was instructed. Her free hand snaked down between her body and the bed.

"Are you wet?" he demanded. She nodded in response, her eyes fluttering closed. "Mmmm. I love that you're wet from just tasting me." Everything tingled from his head to his toes. She was a serious threat to his sanity. Her body rocked against her fingers; her mouth and hand were less controlled as she, too, began to give herself over to the pleasure. Gideon didn't mind, however, because watching her eyes flutter in rapture was one of the most glorious sights he'd ever beheld. "I want you to come with me inside of you. Will you do that for me?"

Caroline nodded heavily and, in the space of a heartbeat, Gideon clambered out from beneath her and knelt behind her delectable bottom. "God, what a sight," he moaned, caressing the muscles smooth and toned from riding. He spread them and leaned back, watching as she worked her glistening fingers through her folds, collecting the moisture and furiously rubbing it against her swollen clitoris. "Are you ready for me, darling?" She whimpered and nodded again, pressing her hips back. It was all the encouragement Gideon needed to notch himself into place and thrust home in one strong, relentless movement. Neither had time to catch their breath before he began pistoning his hips. They rocked together, his hands gripping her hips so hard she'd likely have bruises in the shape of his fingertips in the morning. He couldn't wait to kiss each one of the marks.

Caroline did not complain, however; she dropped her chest to the bed and changed the angle of his penetration, sobbing, "Yes! More! Like that!" as she did so. Her fingers continued to delve through the petals of her sex, rubbing and pinching and gliding. Fuck, he loved how tight she was. Her body rippled around his, demanding more from him. His balls slapped her sex with every thrust, his pelvis ground hard against the soft roundness of her rear each time he bottomed out.

"So good," he growled. "My darling. My love."

Caroline's orgasm rippled down her spine, beginning in her neck and bringing with it contractions of her muscles all the way down her legs. She clenched around him and screamed his name again and again as he pumped into her, relentlessly coaxing more and more pleasure from her and seeking his own.

Finally, when he could take it no more, Gideon wrapped an arm beneath her breasts and hauled her upright. He never broke his pace as they knelt together, his teeth sinking into the curve of her collarbone, his other hand cupping her breast and pinching the ripe red nipple. Her cries as she crested once again sent Gideon over the edge. He held himself deep inside of her as his climax slammed through him. He was blinded by it, rendered deaf and speechless as pulse after pulse of white-hot ecstasy was wrung from him by her perfect body.

Their bodies hummed and trembled in the aftermath. She would have collapsed bonelessly to the bed had he not continued to hold her with the arm banded beneath her breasts; her head lolled back to his shoulder in surrender. Slowly, his hands coasted down to cup the firm curve of her belly. His fingers spanned the width and he marveled at the life growing within—the life they had created. He closed his eyes and simply breathed the moment in.

Then, there was a slight bump against his palm, like the popping of a bubble. Caroline's hand immediately covered his.

"Did you feel that?" she asked excitedly.

"Was that—"

"The baby!" she squealed. "You did feel it!" She looked over her shoulder at him, and Gideon was helpless to do anything but dip his head and kiss her.

CAROLINE AWOKE TO Gideon slipping back into the bedchamber. The room was dark save for the low-burning hearth, so she hadn't slept through the night. She sat up in bed; the coverlet slipped to her waist, but she wasn't the least bit self-conscious— especially when he eyed her with such naked appreciation.

"Where did you disappear to?" she asked, her voice husky with sleep. He'd dressed once more in his formal evening kit and began to remove it all over again. Even if the effect hadn't been entirely immaculate, it made him presentable while there were guests in the castle.

"I made your excuses and saw the guests off; left Blackwood and Kempton drinking in the study."

She could hardly bring herself to care that she'd abandoned the party, not when Gideon had so sweetly handled things for her...and most certainly not when she was still so sleepy and sated from their explosive lovemaking. Caroline lay back down and gave a languid stretch, her husband's eyes following her every movement. Figuring it was only fair, she watched him intently as he stripped himself bare once more, padded over to the bed, slipped beneath the coverlet, and curled his body around hers. She snuggled into his warmth with a sigh.

"Oliver and Emily told me they would be returning in the morning with their belongings," Gideon murmured into her hair.

"Yes," she yawned. "I asked them to do so; I hope you are not displeased. We have the room—"

"Not at all," he hastened to reassure her. "I believe it to be a splendid idea." Gideon pressed his lips to her neck and palmed the weight of her breast. The hard heat of his increasing arousal nudged against her rear.

"Again?" she laughed a little breathlessly as a zing of awareness spiked from her nipple in his palm down to her core.

"Darling, I will never have enough of you…"

Chapter Sixteen

OLIVER AND EMILY'S return to Bray Castle was met with no small amount of warmth. Caroline had arranged for them to reside in the best guest room overlooking the manicured part of the grounds. "You can smell the ocean if you open the windows and the breeze is just right," she explained excitedly as their single trunk was hauled into the room. Emily wore a blue-gray morning dress, elegant in its simplicity, while her husband had opted for buff breeches, a black coat over a crisp white shirt, and a simple knot in his cravat. They looked the part of English country gentry, and Caroline said as much.

"Then the disguise worked," Oliver surprised her by replying, a wink directed at his wife. Caroline could only blink at the uncharacteristic show of levity. She hadn't known Gideon's half brother long, but she already knew that he was far more serious than her husband. The gesture went over Gideon's head, of course.

"Caro confirmed you are indeed looking to purchase a small country property," he chimed in.

"Yes," Emily replied with a smile. "We have enjoyed the fresh air immensely."

"I would be more than happy to give you a tour of the area. I've lands in Gloucestershire, Cheshire, Northumberland, and Norfolk if you would prefer somewhere other than Kent. I can put you in touch with the right people as well."

"That would be appreciated," Emily beamed. "Though Oliver

has owned properties before, nothing has been outside of London."

"Any insight into the areas would be beneficial, thank you," Oliver added quickly, clearly not wishing to discuss any of the properties Emily had mentioned. It was becoming more and more apparent to Caroline that the man was much more guarded than his wife, especially when it came to his past and his former profession. This, of course, piqued Caroline's interest tremendously. Was he hiding something?

Seeming to recognize her misstep, Emily quickly requested a tour of the grounds. "The party was so lovely, but I saw so little of the castle. I have never been inside such a grand and ancient home before."

"She enjoys historical accounts," Oliver explained. "The bookshelves at home are filled with them."

"Well, then you are in luck!" Gideon chirped. "These halls are dripping with history—Bray family history." He looked at Oliver, and Caroline watched the unspoken moment that passed between them.

"Why don't I show Emily around while you gentlemen have some time to yourselves, hm?" She quickly ushered Emily out of the room and launched into a dramatic retelling of the castle's history. It was, perhaps, a bit more elaborate than the one Gideon had shared with her upon their arrival at Bray Castle, but where was the fun in dry recitations of names and dates?

"I truly am so pleased you both decided to join us," Caroline said once they'd reached the peaceful sanctity of the library. At one time, the room must have served as a dining hall with its long, narrow dimensions, high ceiling, and elaborate chandeliers. It served the purpose of a country library quite well and, as Caroline had discovered during her own tour of the grounds, it possessed a more than passable collection.

"The invitation was much appreciated," Emily said, her voice a little breathless as she took in her surroundings. Her fingers twitched with the need to explore.

"Go on," Caroline urged with a smile. "Browse to your heart's content."

Emily did not require any further urging, and she immediately dashed over to the nearest shelf and began running her fingers along the spines as she read the titles. Her unabashed joy was infectious. Caroline allowed her as much time as she pleased to peruse the rows, periodically reassuring her that it was, indeed, fine that she selected more than one she desired to read.

Her feet weary from all the walking and the dancing the evening before, Caroline lowered herself onto a settee. "I think I will rest for a little while, if you don't mind," she sighed and rested her legs on a cushion.

"Oh, you are exhausted." Emily's sapphire eyes were wide with regret. "I shouldn't have kept you so long."

"No, no!" Caroline waved away her concern. "You continue what you are doing while I put up my feet. I enjoy your company and the sunlight in this room is so nice this time of day." And she was not lying about any of it. She enjoyed getting to know Emily and her husband, and the warm glow slanting through the windows was undeniably pleasant.

"If you are certain…"

"I am."

That seemed to put an end to Emily's protests, and she turned back to her task. "I do not believe I ever learned how you and the marquess met," Emily commented.

"We have been friends for a very long while." Caroline paused as she did the math. "A little more than a decade, if memory serves."

"That long?" Emily sounded impressed.

"I don't believe I even realized it had been that long until now," Caroline chuckled and shifted her position.

"And you two were fast friends? You do seem to have a great deal in common."

"Not immediately, no. We met several times at Society events during my first London Season when I was seventeen. It was not until—" Caroline's words died.

"Until?" Emily looked over her shoulder at Caroline.

Her heart thudded a little harder within her breast. "Until the scandal," she finally said, simultaneously appalled and relieved to have the words in the open.

"A scandal?" Emily's voice rose, but not with salacious glee. She added the book she held to her accumulated stack and turned her full attention to Caroline. "I did not realize there was a scandal."

Caroline nodded, willing the flashes of memory to stay away as she turned her gaze to the ceiling. She did not wish to cry in front of Emily.

"You do not need to discuss it if you do not wish to," Emily rushed to reassure her, astutely reading Caroline's distress, but Caroline was already shaking her head before the sentence was complete.

"You will hear of it soon enough if you spend enough time in Society; I would much rather you learn the truth from me." She took a slow, bracing breath and then continued. "I was…assaulted by a man who I believed to be a worthy suitor." Emily said nothing in response, merely taking Caroline's hand in hers and holding it firmly, reassuringly. "We were discovered, and I was blamed for the circumstances, while Lord Fitzwilliam Callbeck received an apology and continued his life as normal."

"An apology?" Emily squeaked indignantly.

Caroline nodded and swiped at the single tear that had managed to escape and run down her cheek. "I have spent many years sick with frustration over the unfairness of it all, but I have made a life for myself. With Gideon's help, of course. He was one of the few who were not scared off by the scandal and my new title of 'the Disgraced Debutante.' He was the reason I had friends and a social calendar."

"I am glad you had him, but forgive me for saying I wish someone had seen to the punishment of that Lord Fitz-whatever-you-call-him." Emily's eyes flashed with fierce indignation on

Caroline's behalf. It was really quite touching.

"Maybe not to the degree he deserved, but he did not escape entirely unscathed."

"Good. Do tell."

"Once again, Gideon came to the rescue," Caroline began, a smile on her face as the memories started to overtake her sorrow. "He never did directly ask me what had happened during that evening years earlier when Callbeck and I were discovered in my family's garden, but he'd gleaned enough information to understand that I had been the victim in the scenario. I was certainly no seducer—I could hardly look Gideon in the eye when we first became friends!—and, in fact, it was suspected that I was not the first woman whom Callbeck had injured in such a way."

"And he was still allowed to become your suitor?" Emily asked, appalled.

"At the time, I had been sheltered from the gossip by my parents. In doing so, they cursed me. They overlooked Callbeck's obvious flaws in favor of encouraging a match with a man who stood to inherit a title and decent holdings. His character mattered not one bit to them. Gideon, on the other hand, saw things differently... Are you familiar with the Golden Hell, Duke's?"

Emily's brows rose, and she nodded after a brief hesitation.

"Gideon received his invitation to apply for membership there. He and our friends, Lords Trenholm, Kempton, and Brinley, coordinated their first foray. Blackwood had yet to receive his invitation and was quite sulky about being left out. I believe you met all of them at Gideon's birthday party."

"What a lively lot they all must have been at Duke's," Emily giggled. She'd certainly read them properly after meeting them only once.

"I am certain the proprietor regretted their admission almost immediately. That visit was cut short, to say the least, after there was a bit of a brawl."

"A brawl!"

"It took me some time to learn of the events and piece them together from various sources, but, from what I understand, Callbeck approached Gideon at one of the tables. He, like the rest of Society, misjudged the nature of my relationship with Gideon—we hadn't so much as shared a kiss at that time. Lewd comments were made. Gideon snapped. Lord Kempton said he'd never seen a man move so quickly and inflict so much damage in the blink of an eye."

Emily gasped and covered her mouth, but not from disgust. She seemed almost thrilled by the prospect of Callbeck receiving a spot of justice at Gideon's hands.

"Apparently, it took four men to pull Gideon off Callbeck. They were both nearly banned from the premises when Duke, himself, became involved. Upon learning why Gideon had attacked him, however, Duke turned his ire upon the bloodied and broken Callbeck. He was stripped of his membership, which Callbeck did not appreciate in the least, and he rashly threatened to exact revenge upon the business. I was told Duke said he would publish a statement that any man found to be abusive toward women would no longer be granted access to the club. A list of offenders would be included, with Callbeck's name at the top…and Duke even offered house credit to those who put men such as Callbeck in their places. Naturally, news of the altercation spread like fire jumping from one Mayfair house to the next."

"So, not only was he beaten, but he also experienced a taste of shame. How appropriate." Emily said that last bit with such malicious glee that Caroline couldn't help but laugh. "I am grateful that you had him."

"I am, as well," Caroline replied, squeezing Emily's hand in return.

Even after Callbeck's disgrace and banishment to Essex by his incensed father, Caroline's parents never reached out. They never apologized for their belief in a man who was as vile and duplicitous as Callbeck, not so much as a simple note. She had, however, received a visit from Gideon.

His lip had been split, but he seemed otherwise no worse for wear. It had been on the tip of Caroline's tongue to thank him for standing up for her, for defeating the monster that haunted her nightmares, but no words came. Instead, she'd only been able to fall against Gideon in relief, and he held her so securely she never wanted it to end.

"A MORE CURRENT portrait is hanging in the library of Swanleigh House in London, but I think you will still see some marked resemblances in this one." Gideon led Oliver through the cavernous portrait gallery, passing centuries of faces until they reached the one he sought. Hanging in the center of the wall was the portrait of a lad about fourteen years of age. He was slim with disproportionately broad shoulders. A shock of dark hair was curled and sculpted around his ears. His mouth was a harsh, unforgiving line beneath a straight nose. His eyes were piercingly silver and stared with unnerving directness at the painting's viewer. He wore a bright-blue coat in the style of the previous century. A gold-patterned waistcoat, thickly ruffled cravat, white breeches and stockings, and black buckled shoes completed the ensemble. A saber hung from a belt at his waist as he stood with the affected confidence of a man twice his age. The bulk of Bray Castle was an unmistakable shape in the background, standing out against the mostly cloudless sky.

Oliver simply stared in silence. His silver eyes, so like the portrait's subject, focused unblinkingly. Gideon had the distinct impression that a silent conversation was taking place and, out of respect, he stepped back and allowed it to occur. It was clear that Oliver, like Gideon, had his demons to fight; the portrait of their scoundrel of a father was one of them.

"Am I the only one?" Oliver finally asked.

"I do not know," Gideon replied truthfully. "You are the only one I knew of—the only one my mother discovered." Oliver gave a curt nod of understanding. "You see now why I knew you were that boy with such certainty?" Oliver nodded again after a brief hesitation.

"My life has had very few certainties in it, one of which was knowing who my parents were. This portrait has thrown that knowledge on the fire like scraps."

"I understand this information is difficult to come to terms with, but I believe, together, we can make the bastard spin in his grave. He never wanted us to know one another, but here we are." Gideon took a chance and squeezed Oliver's shoulder in a show of brotherly affection. "It might take time, but I will be here whenever you are ready. Caroline and I are going nowhere."

Oliver chuffed. "Our wives, it seems, have become fast friends. I do not believe I could carve you out of my life now even if I wished it."

"Is THIS REALLY necessary?" Caroline groused, frustrated that men could be such boorish creatures.

"It is all in good fun, my love," Gideon replied good-naturedly and planted a placating kiss on her temple. Three days of peace had passed, and now it had come to this.

"Rolling around on the ground with your brother is not something I would consider fun." She wrinkled her nose.

"Making up for lost bonding time. Isn't it supposed to be a rite of passage, fighting one's sibling?"

"I wouldn't know; I have no siblings," Emily said with a shrug, looking every bit as skeptical as Caroline felt.

"And I cannot say my sister and I ever came to blows," Caroline grumbled and watched as Gideon and Oliver removed their coats and unwound their cravats. "This seems barbaric."

The topic of physical activities had come up in conversation during a stroll through the fields. Both Caroline and Gideon were accomplished riders. Emily had never mounted a horse and Oliver said he'd done it "a time or two." Caroline had always enjoyed walks, but more so in the Kentish countryside now that riding was out of the question due to her condition. Hunting was not something Oliver had an interest in, though his wife mentioned he was a brilliant shot. It was Gideon who mentioned how exhilarating an exercise fighting could be. As that conversation progressed, it almost seemed that a dam had been opened up within the normally staid Oliver. As it happened, his childhood in London's slums had gone a long way toward teaching him how to defend himself. For his part, one of Gideon's favorite pastimes was spending a few hours at Gentleman Jack's.

Caroline could still remember the first time he'd mentioned to her he'd begun attending pugilism lessons. After twelve months of instruction, he'd finally admitted that he had aimed to participate in an exhibition. It was scandalous that a marquess would fight before a crowd. Though Caroline had seen his strength and he'd assured her he felt quite well prepared, she still wondered at his sanity. Besides, she would have hated to see him injured. His face was so beautiful that it would have been a shame to see it ruined…though she'd suspected he would look quite dashing with a blackened eye.

Gideon had wisely waited until the day of the event to tell her of his plans because, as he'd put it, she was one of the only people who might be capable of talking him out of following through. At that point, his attendance had been announced, and his honor was at stake.

Caroline had been determined to find a way to attend the fight. Blackwood, ever the loyal friend and game for anything, insisted he would accompany her and find her some boy's clothing if she required a disguise. In the end, it hadn't been necessary. She'd gone as herself, her friends flanking her on either side to protect her from the rowdy crowd, and they'd watched Gideon's bare-knuckled brawl.

The fight had lasted two rounds before Gideon won. The speed and strength of his movements had left her breathless, but it had still been difficult to watch the few good blows his opponent had landed.

Gideon had wound up sporting quite the bruise on his jaw, but he seemed to enjoy playing up his injury to have her fawn over him. Despite insisting that he was mad if he believed she was that type of woman, she'd secretly longed to hold a compress to his jaw and kiss his split knuckles like the besotted ninny she was.

As she watched the brothers converse, Caroline could see the direction their conversation was taking from the glitter in Gideon's eyes—it was an expression she'd witnessed more than once within their group. One man mentioned something that sparked an idea, which then spread like wildfire through the shortsighted minds of the men. Caroline could usually act as an effective voice of reason, but she hesitated in that instance. Gideon and Oliver were speaking more animatedly, more relaxed than she'd seen them do so before. The last thing she wished to do was stop whatever bonding was beginning to take place between them.

"Wrestling is one of the oldest forms of combat. It is highly respected," Gideon insisted.

"And Emily wouldn't allow us to fight with fists," Oliver added matter-of-factly.

She glared at her husband. "Excuse me if I do not wish to see anyone's face battered beyond recognition."

Caroline had been relieved when a pugilism exhibition had been removed from the table. Gideon belonged to a pugilist club in London and she'd witnessed his fights a time or two. The last thing she wanted to see was Oliver beaten to a pulp. However, she'd been confident up until the point she overheard Emily whisper, "Go easy," to her husband. Caroline's stomach flipped.

The men stripped off their boots and stockings, and then their shirts. "Oh my," Caroline whispered. The pair of them together were like marble statues of the Greek gods of antiquity. Their pairs of broad shoulders and leanly muscled torsos, tapered waists and strong legs were a sight to behold.

"Oh my, indeed..." murmured Emily, nearly missing the bench as she sat down. Caroline dropped beside her, both women staring in awe at the specimens of masculinity. "Do you suppose their children will be quite so large," Emily suddenly asked, sounding slightly concerned.

"That was not something I'd considered," Caroline replied with a grimace, "though I probably should have, given how strong the paternal bloodlines are." She rested a hand on her stomach, silently begging the babe within to grow to a manageable size before he made his appearance.

"My thoughts precisely."

"Three rounds—"

"One!" Caroline interrupted Gideon. "One round, only. Less opportunity for injury."

"One round," Gideon agreed begrudgingly. "Winner announced by submission or rendering his opponent unable to continue."

"Unable to continue?" Emily squealed.

"Unconscious—not death," Oliver clarified for her.

"That does *not* reassure me."

"It will be fine, Angel," he said to Emily.

Gnawing on her lip, Emily finally nodded in agreement.

"Ready?" asked Gideon.

The men began to crouch and circle, arms raised in similar fashions, intelligent eyes darting for openings. Then, with explosive speed and force, the men began to grapple. Caroline's heart nearly burst through her ribcage as the men grunted and strained. Powerful muscles bunched and flexed. Chunks of grass and dirt were torn up beneath their bare feet. She fought the urge to cover her eyes; the sight was as beautiful as it was terrifying. These were men of warrior stock. She could well imagine them fighting alongside their ancestors as they guarded this very castle from invaders. Hands slipped on sweat-slicked flesh. Gritted teeth gnashed as limits were pressed. Gideon's heel slipped, and the men went down in a rolling, tumbling heap.

Caroline clapped her hand over her mouth as the men flipped positions. Oliver was on top, then Gideon, then Oliver again. Legs lashed about a torso and, with the dirt flying, it was nearly impossible to discern who was who until they stilled. Eventually, Oliver held Gideon's arm pinned behind his back. Caroline thought the match would be declared over, but Gideon never conceded. He fought with all his might until he was able to gain enough purchase to wrench his arm free and roll beneath his brother. Exhibiting surprising flexibility, Gideon flung up a leg and twisted, catching Oliver about the middle and dropping him to his back. They were locked together in combat, these two men with near identical physical builds and capabilities; however, the match went to Gideon when he began to bend Oliver's leg at an awkward angle. He tapped Gideon's shoulder and was immediately released. Both men collapsed to the ground, chests heaving, skin glistening in the afternoon light as they stared up at the blazing summer sun.

The women rushed over to them. "Any injuries?" Caroline asked, half afraid of the answer. Both dark heads shook.

"None," panted Gideon.

"Then what do you call this?" she asked, touching a long red scrape on her husband's arm.

"A minor flesh wound."

"Indeed," she replied. She was close enough now that she could see the pale marks on Oliver's torso from injuries long healed. Were all of them earned in his youth on the streets? What hell must he have lived through?

Emily knelt beside her husband and pushed his damp hair back from his face. "You did well."

"I feel brilliant," he replied, chest heaving, but already beginning to slow to a more normal pace. His eyes glittered with excitement. "I haven't experienced that type of exertion in ages."

She gave him a small smile. "And you will be sore tomorrow to prove it. Come on, let's get you standing and into a bath."

"I'll send some liniment to your bedchamber," said Gideon as he sat up. "It will help with any soreness."

Oliver inclined his head in thanks and he held his hand out to Gideon. After a moment, he allowed Oliver to pull him to his feet. A moment of mutual respect and understanding passed between them before Oliver allowed Emily to guide him away to gather his clothing and wash.

"I still do not see how that was necessary," Caroline groused as she, too, began to retrieve her husband's discarded clothing.

"No congratulations for the conquering hero, then?" Gideon asked, arms held out as if waiting for her to rain kisses and praise upon his person. She decided not to share her suspicions that Oliver had allowed Gideon to triumph.

"You wish for me to congratulate you for behaving like a child?" she scoffed. Gideon caught her about the waist and she fought half-heartedly to free herself. "Leave off! You smell horrendous."

"Does that mean you will not join me for a bath?" He raised a suggestive brow that melted her insides and halted her protests.

"We will see about that..." she trailed off and slipped free from his arms to retrieve his cravat from where it had been draped over a bush. "Was your wrestling everything you'd hoped for?" She hadn't expected the somewhat wistful look she saw on his face when she turned back to him.

"Actually, it was. I never had a playmate growing up; I was never able to form that bond with anyone. By the time I met Kempton and the others at school, our lives were too regimented. We found our fair share of trouble, but never anything brothers might when they grew up together. Imagine how different my life might have been had Oliver and I been children together— especially as close in age as we are. For the first time, I feel like I have family—or at least what I'd always imagined having one might be." It made an odd sort of sense to Caroline. She may not have understood the act of wrestling itself, but the process—the bonding it symbolized—had a much deeper meaning than proving who was stronger or faster or the better fighter.

She took Gideon's hand and brought his scraped knuckles to her cheek and pressed them there, not caring if it left her streaked in filth. "I am happy you have had this time to get to know Oliver, and I am even happier that you two are beginning to develop a relationship. He is your family."

"As are you," he said and pulled her close once more. "As is this baby," he added, placing a protective hand over her abdomen that appeared to be expanding by the day.

"And you will always have us." Caroline stood on her toes and pressed her lips to his.

Chapter Seventeen

I T WAS ONLY their second day back in London when a demon from Caroline's past called at her doorstep. Gideon was out of the house on business, so she spent a lazy morning abed before dressing in a simple morning gown of dyed teal muslin and delicate rosettes and wandering the expansive halls of her new home. Of course, she'd spent a great deal of time there, but this was different. Now, this was her home.

Perry located her in the music room as her fingers danced playfully across the keys of the untuned pianoforte. He held out a card to her on a small silver tray.

"A caller, my lady," the butler said with a bow. "Should I tell him you are not at home?"

"For me?" Caroline asked, her confusion evident as she reached for the card. "Are you certain I am the one he seeks and not my husband?" It couldn't be one of their friends—none would have been forced through the stuffy song and dance of handing over a card and waiting to see whether they would be permitted into the house.

"Quite certain. In fact, he made it clear he wished to speak with you privately, if at all possible."

Caroline barely heard Perry's words as her eyes froze upon the name engraved upon the calling card.

Lord Fitzwilliam Callbeck.

The monster who had haunted her nightmares.

The man who had brought about her social destruction.

The fiend who had stolen her innocence in a despicable act.

She did not doubt Callbeck had waited until Gideon had finally exited their bubble of newlywedded bliss and left Caroline unguarded. But what could he want from her? Especially now?

Her heartbeat pounded almost deafeningly in her ears, and she had to brace a hand on the pianoforte to remain upright. As if sensing its mother's distress, the babe in her womb began to flutter almost frantically.

She pressed a gentle palm there over the child and knew what she must do.

"Have him shown into the front parlor. Offer no refreshments—he will not remain long enough for a pot of tea to steep."

"Are you certain, my lady?" Perry asked in an uncharacteristic balk. The man's behavior was usually above reproach, but he must have seen something in Caroline's face or heard the slight warble in her voice.

"Yes," she answered more steadily.

Though he still appeared quite skeptical, the butler turned on his heel and quit the room to do as she had instructed. Caroline closed her eyes and exhaled slowly through numb lips. She would see what that coward Callbeck wanted and then banish him from her doorstep, lest he wish to be bloodied and bruised all over again when Gideon arrived home.

What a fool she had been to allow herself to be so easily drawn into Callbeck's web during her first Season. She had been young and naïve; to her, he was impossibly handsome, in line to inherit a title, came from a family so respectable that not even Mama could object, and he'd danced with her at every event they'd both attended. The knowledge of the monster he was beneath his golden façade made her nauseous, but, back then, his smile had made her sigh and his hollow, poetic words made her wish she knew how to swoon properly. His golden hair and sapphire eyes were precisely what she'd imagined a knight would look like had he been plucked from one of Nanny's fairytales.

All of it had been a lie.

And now, years later, he'd come to darken her door once more. This time, however, Caroline would face him down. She would send him on his way and tell him in no uncertain terms that he was never to show his face there again, nor was he to ever approach her. As far as she was concerned, he was a ghost from her past, and he was meant to stay that way—an unfortunate shadow burned away by the glow of her future.

When she was reasonably sure of her composure, Caroline made her way to the appointed parlor and found Perry waiting outside the room. He was staring toward the front door and, as such, he did not immediately notice her approach. The man practically jumped out of his impeccably pressed black coat when she asked him if all was well.

"My, but aren't you a bit tense," she commented lightly.

"Apologies, my lady," Perry stammered as he straightened his lapels and cast one more longing glance at the front door. His mouth opened and closed several times, but no sound emerged.

"What is the matter?" Caroline was growing more alarmed the longer this went on. The man was usually so unflappable.

Perry's sigh was a mixture of resignation and discomfort. "I do not care for you to be in the presence of this man. It is clear that he makes you uneasy."

Caroline was taken aback by his candor—so much so that it made the backs of her eyes burn. "Oh, Perry…" She willed the tears not to come. "I appreciate your looking out for me, but this is something I must do."

"Can it not wait until the marquess returns?"

Caroline shook her head. "I will see to this and inform Lord Callbeck that a repeated appearance will be most unwelcome."

The butler's mouth narrowed into a grim line, but he nodded in agreement. "I will remain just here in the hallway should you have need of me."

She shot Perry a grateful smile as she entered the parlor.

Her unwelcome houseguest stood at her arrival, the light glinting off his golden hair, and Caroline was instantly transported back to that horrible night nearly a decade ago.

Callbeck had convinced her to steal away during an uproarious reel at a ball and took advantage of the privacy to bestow upon Caroline her very first kiss. It had been different than she expected—lots of lips and wriggling tongue and very wet—but the cad had reassured her that she would improve with time. Before they'd parted ways, he'd asked if they might meet in secret again. Even back then, Caroline knew she shouldn't have agreed, but how could she have been expected to resist when he swore he would not survive if they were parted for too long...that he would not ask something of her if he weren't so desperate for her. She'd believed it all tragically romantic, like something out of a medieval play. She could not turn him down.

She knew Mama and Papa planned to attend the theater, so she and Callbeck made their hasty arrangements. He met her at the appointed time and place, the darkest corner of the gardens behind the Fischer townhouse. The building resided on a corner, so there were fewer opportunities to be seen.

His kisses had begun immediately.

The joy she'd felt at seeing him and being once more in his arms evaporated as his touch became more forceful. The bodice of her carefully chosen gown tore and she was exposed. Her mouth was bruised against her teeth from how hard Callbeck held his hand over it when he rucked up her skirts. He claimed repeatedly that she had wanted this, how she had asked him to do this to her, because she had agreed to meet with him.

What he did to her...it hurt.

Everything he did to her hurt, and she wanted none of it.

Though she'd cried and fought and tried to scream, he held her too tightly—so tightly that she nearly fainted from lack of air. None of her efforts mattered.

She didn't understand.

She could not possibly have known what he was planning.

He took his pleasure and left her in a heap.

Mama and Papa had returned home early after the theater

performance was canceled and had brought with them the Harrows and Bartsons. She and Callbeck had been discovered after her sobs were finally overheard by the kitchen staff.

Callbeck had been unable to retreat quickly enough to avoid discovery, so the vile man had concocted a story that she had seduced him with her poor morals and illicit promises.

The result?

Caroline's parents had apologized to *him*, and he had been allowed to leave without any recourse, while Caroline had been berated for her behavior and verbally abused for shaming her parents in front of their friends. Her scrapes and bruises went ignored and untreated. As predicted, news of the situation flooded London Society the very next day, and Caroline had been removed from the Fischer household, discarded and quarantined like a pox-infected blanket.

Because of him, she was ruined.

"Caroline. How pleasant—"

"You are too familiar, Lord Callbeck," Caroline bit out, his name acidic on her tongue like a spoiled tomato.

He had the temerity to respond with a raised brow and a disarming smile. "We were once much more familiar."

"An unfortunate and grave mistake. Now, I would much rather be sick on your boots and send you on your way."

Callbeck's smile cooled ever so slightly; his eyes began to harden into icy chips of blue. It chilled her to the very marrow of her bones as she was visited by the ghost of her nightmares, but she remained steady and strong.

"Now, now, Lady Swanleigh, there is no need to be crass. You may have tumbled down in Society's estimations, but that should not give you leave to speak like a fishmonger's wife."

"I did not stumble; I was pushed. By you." A muscle in Callbeck's cheek twitched. "Now, are you going to explain your sudden appearance, or shall I have you removed now?"

"Such a hostile little kitten."

"Do you assume I am jesting?" she barked incredulously. "I

will watch with glee as you are booted out into the square."

"Why did you admit me if you were going to speak to me in such a manner?" he asked, feigning wounded feelings.

"Because you must believe you have something of significance to say if you dare show your face here. You must have waited until my husband was out because the last time you met, he rendered you unconscious with one blow. And you must be slightly mad if you thought I would greet you with even a modicum of civility." Caroline's hands fisted in her skirts, and she prayed Callbeck did not notice. Why couldn't he get on with it and leave her be? Hadn't he already caused her enough damage?

"Yes, well…" Callbeck began in a frigid tone, finally dispensing with all niceties as he plucked a porcelain swan from the nearby table and turned it in his hands. "I do believe I have an interesting proposition for you." Caroline gritted her teeth as she waited in tense silence for him to continue. "I require a sum of money, and I believe you are now in the perfect position to provide it." He set down the swan with a decisive click, not caring that it now sat at an odd angle.

"You expect me to simply hand over money?"

"Not for nothing, of course." His smile was evil. How could she have ever thought him charming?

"You already ruined my reputation. You assaulted me. What could I ever want from you?"

Callbeck was the reason her parents had disowned her when she was not yet twenty years of age; he left her life in shambles and destroyed her future. Mama and Papa no longer wished to see her or speak to her and had deposited her in a small rented flat with no knowledge or practical experience in running a household or hiring what little staff she could afford. That first night, she had sat alone in her dark home without so much as the knowledge of how to properly set and light her hearth without creating a cloud of smoke. Rather than live as the daughter of a viscount, she'd been relegated to obscurity and forced to survive off a small annual allowance that would remain intact and paid out in regular installments by her father's man of business so long as she had no contact with them, or her sister, and brought no further scandal to their doorstep.

Because of him, she'd been called every vile and vulgar name one could think of by her family, Society, and the tabloids alike. She had been branded as the Disgraced Debutante.

"There is still a reputation to protect," Callbeck replied coyly.

"Swanleigh's?" she shook her head. Gideon would care nothing for what Callbeck had to say about him. "You do not understand my husband if you think anything you could say might hurt him."

His gaze flicked to her abdomen, where the shape of her pregnancy was beginning to show, and her blood froze in her veins. She could not stop herself from placing a protective hand there, as if to shield her unborn child from this man's evil.

She swallowed hard and took a bracing breath. "I am certain all of London has heard of our marriage by special license. Regardless of whatever you might say, this child is legitimized."

Callbeck's mouth twisted wryly. "Swanleigh has been rather understanding of your sordid past. A lesser man might have allowed it to color his perception of you. Of your marriage. Of the parentage of any children you might bear…"

"What are you saying?" she demanded, her fist clenched so tightly her nails nearly drew blood from her palm.

"I am saying, Lady Swanleigh, that Society already believes the worst of you. It would not require much work to cast a stain upon a life not yet in existence. Everyone knows of your loose morals."

"Stop," Caroline hissed, but he continued.

"Even if Swanlegh believes in your fidelity, a few well-placed comments and insinuations would cast doubt upon the child's entire existence; they would follow it wherever it goes."

"Enough."

"Some may even do the work for me and assume I am the sire, given our illicit history…"

"No more!" Caroline's voice was only slightly below a scream. She caught movement out of the corner of her eye and knew Perry had moved into the doorway, no longer content with remaining uninvolved. Even that bit of support was everything Caroline needed. She swallowed back bile brought up by Callbeck's disgusting threat. "How dare you come into my house and threaten me? My family?"

He tilted his head and tempered his tone as if speaking to a petulant child. "You hopped from one bed to the other until you finally landed a title worth keeping. D'you think that should really be rewarded?"

"Of all the—"

"Five thousand pounds should suffice," Callbeck interrupted her.

"You are threatening harm to my unborn child if I do not pay you five thousand pounds…?"

"I think it's rather a fair amount. Everyone knows Swanleigh's annual income is at least double that. Eight thousand would be preferable, but I would rather not be greedy. I've some debts that need repaying and I've found it unbearable to live off the paltry monthly sum I'm afforded."

"You are a monster."

"I prefer to think of myself as enterprising."

Caroline did not think. She did not breathe. She did not pause to consider the ramifications of what she was about to do.

She merely hauled back her fist like Gideon had taught her and sent it hurtling toward Callbeck's obnoxiously perfect nose.

The man stumbled backward with a howl the precise moment Caroline yelped and shook out her smarting hand.

"You struck me!" Callbeck's words were muffled by his hands as he held his face.

Caroline hissed through her teeth. "Serves you right!"

"My lady!" Perry burst into the room, eyes so wide that Caroline was concerned the man might expire from shock.

"I am fine," she told the butler. Her hand throbbed fiercely, but she didn't think anything was broken. She looked back at Callbeck. "After what you said, you are lucky that is all I do to you. I owe you a great deal more than that." A trickle of blood seeped from between his fingers, and he shot her a vicious glare from his watering eyes. "I strongly suggest you reconsider your threats against my family. If I hear so much as a whisper of insinuation that my child's parentage is questioned, then I shall seek you out to pay in your pound of flesh. As a matter of fact, it is likely in your best interest to *discourage* such chatter. We will not be meeting your demands, and you are unworthy of a second thought." She turned back to her pale-faced butler. "See that Lord Callbeck is escorted from the house posthaste. He will not be returning, and, if he so much as sets foot on the front step of any of the Swanleigh estates, then he will have greater concerns than a broken nose." She met Callbeck's narrowed eyes. Every one of her nerves sang with adrenaline and elation. She felt triumphant.

Until Callbeck broke free from Perry's arm on his shoulder and charged toward Caroline.

"You bitch!" he snarled.

Caroline stumbled back several steps, but he was moving too quickly, and her body was too cumbersome. Just before he grabbed her, however, Callbeck was stopped dead in his approach and thrown to the ground with an impressive thud.

Caroline's shocked mind took a handful of seconds to register that her Gideon had blown into the room like a furious storm and now held her assailant pinned to the ground.

"I thought I already dealt with you," Gideon growled, jaw like granite and eyes like silver hellfire. Callbeck swung out wildly but did not once connect with more than the solid block of Gideon's shoulder. "I loathed you before, but, in coming into my house and in threatening my wife, you have made yourself an enemy."

"Go to hell," Callbeck gritted out through teeth stained pink with blood.

"I will meet you there, Callbeck. The devil has your name for all your cruelties and misdeeds, and he will drag you there screaming one day; I...I will gladly go to hell for her if it means protecting her. That is where we differ." One swift punch from Gideon's trained fist, and Callbeck fell silent and slack.

Chapter Eighteen

GIDEON ROSE TO his feet and straightened his coat. The haze of red still clouded the edge of his vision, but it felt decidedly better to have that bastard silenced. "See that he is tossed out in the alley, Perry. Throwing a few extra scraps on him wouldn't be remiss."

"Right away, my lord." The butler gestured to two of the footmen who had gathered following the ruckus. They grabbed Callbeck's limbs and rather unceremoniously carted him from the room. Immediately, Gideon went to Caroline and pulled her into his arms. He likely held her too tightly, but he could not help it.

He'd fled his meeting at his solicitor's office as soon as he'd received Perry's note. His entire body had numbed with terror, and then his senses had come alive. He knew it would take him at least half an hour to reach Mayfair, but he was determined to cut that time in half. Knowing Callbeck was in his home seeking out his wife shoved Gideon into a haze of rage.

He didn't recall the ride back through London or ripping open the front door to his home. As soon as he saw Perry's aghast expression, the alarmed footmen standing beside him, and witnessed Callbeck lunge for Caroline, Gideon acted only on instinct. He needed to protect her. He needed to protect their child. She was his, and he would shed any amount of blood required to keep her safe.

"You are trembling," he murmured into her sweet-smelling hair.

"I am relieved," she said tremulously.

"Relieved?" he leaned back to look down into her face. She clung to him so tightly, yet he did not ever want it to end.

Caroline nodded. "Relieved. Triumphant. I haven't faced him since—"

He shushed her and pressed his lips to her forehead.

But she wouldn't be still. "I need to say this. I haven't faced Callbeck since the assault. It has been years of him haunting my past, and I feel as if he has finally been eradicated."

"You were so brave, darling," Gideon said earnestly. "I wish he hadn't been admitted in the first place, and I am none too pleased with the danger you were in, but I am happy you feel freed by it." He could not resist tucking a loose lock of hair behind her ear. "What did he want?"

Caroline's eyes began to glitter, and Gideon wished he hadn't asked. "Money."

"Money? He came here asking you for money?"

"He came here trying to extort it," Caroline said with a shaky exhalation.

Gideon's rage had begun to cool slightly, but her admission caused it to roar back to life—more so when she went on to explain what Callbeck had planned. "I should call him out," he bit out through gritted teeth.

"No, Gideon," Caroline grabbed his biceps, knowing full well he was about to storm from the house, track the man down, and demand satisfaction at dawn. "No," she repeated.

"You do not believe I would win?"

"I believe you would, but he is not worth risking charges against you for dueling and murder."

He wanted to reassure her that his title was powerful enough that any charges likely would not go past a perfunctory questioning from a magistrate, but the pleading note in her voice and the desperation in her eyes made him nod his head in agreement.

"It would be too noble a death for the man, anyway," Gideon groused.

"We must wash him from our lives. For good."

"I beg your pardon, my lord, my lady." Perry seemed hesitant to interrupt them, but equally as eager to see if he could be of further assistance. "May I bring you anything? Is there anything else you require?"

Gideon chaffed Caroline's upper arms and turned back to his butler. "Thank you, Perry, for your quick thinking and your urgent message." After helping Caroline to a chair, he approached the older man and clapped him on the shoulder. "I will forever be grateful for it. I do not care to think what would have happened had I not arrived on time."

"We would have protected her, sir," Perry said, standing up straighter, narrow chest puffing out slightly. "But it was quite satisfying to watch you deliver that blackguard with his comeuppance. Attempting to assault a lady—" He made a disgusted scoff and then seemed to remember himself. He cleared his throat, inclined his head, and added with a great deal more dignity, "My lord."

"Yes, thank you, Perry," Caroline chimed in with sincerity. "Might I request a cold compress? My hands have stopped shaking and I am only now realizing just how badly my knuckles hurt."

"Right away!" The butler nearly leaped to fulfill her request. In fact, he did so with such swiftness that Gideon had hardly settled beside Caroline before the man returned with a bowl of water and toweling. Perry ducked from the room to afford them some privacy.

"When you instructed me on the proper form for throwing a punch, you neglected to inform me that it hurts," Caroline groused as Gideon held the compress over her knuckles.

Gideon chuckled. "If I had, then you might not have delivered such a successful strike." The fine bumps of her knuckles were faintly bruised, and she winced when he palpated the back of her hand, but he did not feel anything broken. "Should I send for a physician to look at your hand?" he offered.

"I would rather you did not. I will watch the swelling and address it then, if need be. I am sure the visit would prompt more interest and inquiries than I am prepared to answer at this time."

Gideon reached up and cupped the soft curve of her cheek. He expected her to lean into his touch like she usually did, but she surprised him by remaining still, her eyes downturned and shaded beneath the long fringe of her lashes.

"Caro?" he said softly, dipping his head to try to meet her gaze. "Darling?" She pulled her lower lip between her teeth so tightly that it blanched. Her demeanor had changed so abruptly from his arrival, from one of elation and indignation to introverted and contemplative. It wasn't uncommon after an emotional physical confrontation, but it was disconcerting to witness his pregnant wife experiencing such distress. "Please speak to me," he pleaded gently.

"I have...the bloody worst judge of character," she finally answered shakily. "I don't know how I can trust my instincts at all anymore."

Gideon understood. This confrontation had resurrected her ancient insecurities, her self-doubt, the unjust self-persecution he'd worked for years to help her overcome and bury.

"You cannot blame yourself for the man's duplicitousness. He is a predator disguised behind a gentile façade. Many people have fallen for it in the past, and many will continue to do so until he is revealed for the villain he is."

"I trusted him," Caroline ground out as her eyes flew to his face. "I invited this evil into my life, and now it is bleeding over into our future."

"It is done; he has been told in no uncertain terms that no further threats will be tolerated. Let us forget about him—wash him from our lives, as you said."

"My poor choices will forever be a stain upon my conscience," Caroline said, choking slightly on the tears as they spilled one after another down her pink cheeks. "I doubt myself. I doubt everything."

"Everything? Even us?"

Caroline's mouth snapped shut, and she met his eyes square-ly. "My history is quite deplorable, is it not?

Gideon's heart skipped. "You do not mean that," he said in a low tone and she looked away again.

"I do not know what I mean anymore."

"You are exhausted and overwrought." Despite the sting of her words, Gideon recognized that she needed some grace in that moment. She'd had a trying ordeal and, especially in her state, she required appropriate time to process and recuperate. "The rest of my day has been cancelled. We will spend the rest of the day in bed."

"You do not need to do that."

"I fear it is already done." He swooped in and left a peck on the tip of her nose while he smoothly scooped her into his arms. "I will even read aloud to you if you would like, so long as it isn't anything too romantic."

He knew he'd won the moment the corner of Caroline's mouth twitched, and she wound her arms around his neck. "But I was so looking forward to reading my new one from Thorpe & Son."

Gideon sighed dramatically and rolled his eyes to the sky. "I suppose if there really is nothing else that will satisfy you."

She rested her head on his shoulder, making Gideon marvel once again at how well they fit, how comfortable they were with one another. It tortured him to see her upset, but he took great pride in the knowledge that he could comfort her and provide her with a haven. He had meant what he said earlier; he would do everything to protect Caroline and do whatever she had asked of him. He'd never dared hope to experience this love, this connection, but he knew he would never let her go now that he had it.

UNFORTUNATELY, CAROLINE'S PEACE was short-lived.

The papers began trickling in the day after the altercation

with Callbeck. At first, Perry had brought them to Gideon's attention. His response had been a refusal to read whatever drivel was being written and instruct the butler to have the copies removed from the house. Caroline had been subjected to vile slander in the tabloids following the initial scandal. It had never truly died out, thanks to her close friendship with their group of rakehells. Authors hid their subjects behind flimsy nicknames (reading "the Scandalous Miss W" and "the Disgraced Debutante" always made him want to gnash his teeth), but they fooled no one. The salacious gossip was consistent fodder for those looking to sell their papers or discuss the latest tidbits over tea.

Over the years, Caroline had come a long way in overlooking the rumors, even if she couldn't be completely deaf to them. More than once, he'd heard it commented that she should have changed her behavior if she did not wish to attract so much attention. But Gideon knew the lengths to which Caroline had gone to fit into the tiny box Society allowed for a woman, and it did nothing to quell the wagging tongues. He was the greatest supporter in encouraging Caroline to live her life as she pleased— those people were going to talk about her one way or the other, so she might as well *live her life*. There was no denying she'd been much happier, much freer since she decided to do just that.

It was also quite pleasing to see their nicknames beside one another's on nearly every occasion they made the tabloids.

Gideon's attempts at shielding Caroline from the current wildfire of gossip worked for only two days before a paper slipped through the defenses by way of a sealed envelope whose only mark was an address for the new Marchioness of Swanleigh.

Gideon was enjoying a leisurely morning in Caroline's private sitting room, reclining with his head in her lap as she sifted through her post. He enjoyed resting his cheek against the firm curve of her belly and reveling in the tiny ripples and bumps of their child. When her body went rigid beneath him, Gideon was immediately alerted to something being terribly wrong with the letter she'd just opened. He bolted upright, his heart pounding with the need to address whatever had upset her.

Caroline crumpled the documents in her fists, hung her head, and sobbed. She'd done a remarkable job of piecing herself back together after Callbeck's intrusion, but that had only been two days prior. She was still fragile, still emotional, and still pregnant, which, Gideon was learning, was making her moods all that much easier to tip one way or the other.

Watching her so tortured made it feel to him like hours since Caroline had begun crying, yet she showed no signs of stopping. Gideon was at a loss. With everything in him, he wanted to take away her pain and ease her mind, but it wasn't that simple—to believe it was would diminish everything she had been through.

"What is it?" he begged her to respond. "Please, tell me what has upset you so." She fell against him, seeking his support as she pressed her tear-dampened eyes to his cravat.

"T-The tabloids," she managed to choke out. Someone had sent her a tabloid. Gideon cursed beneath his breath.

"Caro, darling," he said, stroking her hair as she shoved her face more deeply into his throat. The front of his shirt was soaked with her tears. "My love, it is just a tabloid. They are saying nothing that they have not already said a thousand times." She'd been more emotional lately, but nothing quite compared to this. Some things had changed now that she was solidly in her sixth month of pregnancy. While her queasiness had subsided some time earlier, her emotions had been a heart-wrenching swing of highs and lows. He did what he could to cheer her or give her space when these moments happened, depending upon the circumstances.

Unfortunately, everyone was at the mercy of the tabloids. Even royalty could not completely stop the gossip columns from spewing their vitriol.

"This is worse," she sobbed, clutching his shirt. "Now they are going after our child, and he is not yet born."

A well of furious rage boiled deep within Gideon's chest. He wanted to knock down the doors of these damnable publications and beat the editors and writers until they had no more working fingers with which to spread their hate. Attack him for his wild ways—he had never been a saint—but to say reprehensible things about his unborn child…that was unconscionable.

"What did they say?" he ground out.

She released the crumpled and slightly smudged print from her hand. What Gideon could make out, however, made him see red.

Across the top of the page in spidery handwriting were the words, "You should be ashamed." What was worse, news of Caroline's pregnancy had, understandably, spread since their return from Bray Castle. But the things they said…the caricatures that accompanied them…choked Gideon with fury.

They described Caro as finally having entrapped a titled man into marriage with pregnancy, hinting that it had been her only choice since she'd failed at capturing a husband during her debut. They said it was bound to happen with the way she and Gideon had carried on over the years. They portrayed her as a scheming harpy, her nipples nearly visible above her indecent gown, as she enticed a line of men toward her skirts, each of them labeled with sashes reading Lord S, Lord B, Lord K, Lord T, and Lord PB. The *ton* had never been able to wrap its simple, antiquated mind around the fact that men could be friends with a woman without sharing her bed. The insinuation that she'd shared her favors with all of them…it turned Gideon's stomach.

The next panel depicted an infant in a cradle crafted from gold and jewels, thanking his mother for choosing such a wealthy father. Another panel showed a baby shackled to Gideon's leg like a prisoner's weight, holding him back from his future as a poorly drawn Caroline rifled through his pockets.

It was easy to assume that Callbeck had had a hand in the slander, but his name was not mentioned, and this afforded just enough doubt to keep Gideon from lopping off the man's head. He and Caroline had been the subject of many a gossip rag; to unquestioningly lay blame for this drivel at Callbeck's feet was, regrettably, unfair. This could have been anyone with a vendetta against them, anyone who was righteous enough to throw stones, even a man looking to make a quick penny off an easy target.

He crumpled the parchment in his fist and threw it to the ground, wishing there was a fire in the hearth so he could watch the disgusting lies burn to ash.

"Utter filth," he growled and held Caroline closer. "You know none of that is true."

"But I did trap you in a way," she sniffed and looked up at him. The tears overflowing from her eyes split his heart in two.

"I never want you to hear you say that again. It is most certainly not true, and you know it." He watched her lips tremble as he tilted her face to his with a crooked finger beneath her chin. "I need to know that you are hearing me. Do not ever think for a second that I did not do anything I did not wish to. I love you. I love this child. I have loved you for a long while, I was just too afraid to admit it for fear of losing you forever."

Caroline's face scrunched and new tears overflowed. "And now I am crying for an entirely different reason!" she wailed and buried her face in his chest again.

A small laugh of relief welled up from his chest. "Now *that* is all the truth. Let them say what they wish; they know nothing about what happens between us. Not once have they managed to get anything right in all the times we've been mentioned in those rags. Pay no mind to their drivel."

"I know..." Caroline said with a hiccup after she managed to regain most of her composure. "And I know I am being overly sensitive about it, but I cannot help it. Our child has done nothing to deserve this, and just because of my past, he is coming into a world that is prejudiced against him."

"We won't allow that," Gideon said with all the confidence of generations of good breeding. "He will have adoring parents, a loving extended family, and the Swanleigh title behind him. No doors are closed to the Swanleigh heir." Then, he had an idea. He pulled a fresh handkerchief from his pocket and handed it to her. "Why don't you consider taking Emily and Oliver up on their offer for a visit?" Swanleigh House had already been inundated with well-wishers and curiosity seekers since their return from Kent. The streets of Mayfair were littered with gossipmongers. Everyone wanted a piece of Caroline. If he couldn't wipe out the whispers in one fell swoop, then he would find a place where Caroline could escape. "I still have a great deal of business to catch up on. You will be safe with them and somewhat removed from the evil lurking in this part of town."

She released a watery laugh. "Are you sending me away?"

"Not like that," he reassured her. "I do not want you alone right now, and, unfortunately, I need to spend most of the coming days in meetings. I set aside my duties for our honeymoon—and I don't regret a minute of it," he added the last when she seemed about to complain, "but it must be done. In the meantime, I think it might be a relief for you to spend some time with them. You are not so far away that we will not see one another, but you will be a bit farther from everything here in Mayfair."

"Won't it look odd?"

"I don't give one flea-bitten rat's arse what it looks like to anyone else; I care only for you and your wellbeing. Staying here in Mayfair is doing nothing for your nerves. *We* will know the truth and *that* is all that matters." He pressed his forehead to hers and closed his eyes, breathing her in.

Her hand cupped his cheek as she did the same. "I will go," she whispered.

A tide of relief began to flow within him. Even if it did not entirely extinguish his rage over the despicable treatment of his family, he felt better knowing Caroline would be in a place where she could be safe. In her absence, he vowed to do what he could to quash the gossip. He would tell anyone and everyone how utterly, hopelessly in love with his wife he was. He would scream it until there wasn't a single person who doubted that Gideon could not have chosen a better wife and partner for himself. And, one day, he knew they would see Caroline as the wonder she was.

ONLY TWO DAYS later, Caroline was comfortably ensconced in Oliver and Emily's townhouse. Three stories in height, the narrow brick building was cozy and tidy, and it overlooked a small, well-kept park. Upon her arrival at the address, Emily had apologized that their home was not well-equipped for hosting a marchioness. Caroline had pulled her into a hug and reassured her that she was not at all snobbish and had made do with much less for a long while.

She was utterly charmed by the floral papering and simple furniture, the elegant little paintings so lovingly chosen and carefully hung throughout the home. There was just enough decoration to make it feel like the home of someone who lived comfortably.

The home had three bedchambers, and Caroline was shown into one papered in creamy, buttery yellow with dark wood furniture and robin's-egg blue details. It was utterly delightful and she told Emily as much. Sitting on the bed, Caroline experienced a wash of relief and peace. Gideon had been right; she already felt much lighter now that she'd escaped the prying eyes of Mayfair. It pained her to be away from Gideon for such a ridiculous reason, but she saw the logic in his suggestion. The stress of it had been making her ill; she'd cried far too much, far too often. Now, she could be more herself. It wasn't long before she would enter confinement for the rest of her pregnancy; she deserved to enjoy these last few weeks of freedom. Cupping both hands beneath her belly, she gazed down at the curve in her gown. She was less than three months away from giving birth, and she needed to focus on that. The baby gave a powerful kick, and she rubbed at the spot. "Not too much longer..." she whispered.

The rest of the week was rather much the same. Emily had been worried that Caroline would be bored in their home, but it was a delight. Caroline learned how to chop carrots and stir a stew so it did not scorch or boil over. She hadn't been able to stomach preparing the beef for the stew, but Emily didn't so much as bat an eye. She gave Emily another task, plucking the herbs from their stems. It was a novel experience for a woman who had only ever stepped into a kitchen to pilfer treats.

Emily and Oliver spent their evenings reading. Caroline often joined them by the hearth and brought along her embroidery. She was working on decorating a christening gown for her baby. The project caused her an equal mixture of joy and sadness because she thought of Gideon each time she used the scissors he'd gifted to her years before. Her heart ached for him and she struggled to sleep without him holding her, but, other than that, her time with Emily and Oliver was pleasant.

Shortly before luncheon one day, Emily told Caroline she needed to make a trip to her mother's place of business, the notorious brothel of Lady Night. "I must balance the books and ensure enough supplies are ordered for the week. I should return well before supper, though."

"Oh! May I go with you?" Emily's eyes widened, clearly taken aback by Caroline's enthusiasm. "That is, if you don't mind. I shan't be in the way. I would love to be able to say I've been to a brothel."

"You are certain?"

"No one will know who I am. I will be unobtrusive and merely observe."

"It is not as exciting as you think it is—just a great deal of numbers."

"I don't mind."

"And how do you think Gideon will react when he finds out you've been to Lady Night's?" Oliver interjected flatly.

"He has been to the brothel; why shouldn't I?"

Oliver cleared his throat and averted his eyes, unwilling to touch that argument.

"Please?" She looked back at Emily and pressed her hands

together in a prayer-like gesture.

"Very well. If you are certain—"

"I have a meeting with an associate in an hour. I can escort you to Lady Night's after," Oliver said.

"That will be too late," Emily sighed. "We will be there well after dark if we have to wait for that."

Oliver's mouth was set in a grim line of displeasure. He and his wife seemed to have a silent conversation with their eyes before he released a small sigh of resignation. "I will take you to Covent Garden before my meeting, deposit you there safely, and you will be escorted home by one of Lady Night's guards."

"Guards?" Caroline reared back in surprise.

"To keep the employees safe," Oliver explained. A frisson of excitement danced down Caroline's spine. She couldn't wait.

LESS THAN TWO hours later, Caroline and Emily were seated in the room which had once been Emily's bedchamber. In the months since her marriage to Oliver, it had been cleaned out and transformed into an office complete with shelves of organized documents and books. Emily was about to begin reconciling the accounts and was busy selecting the proper book.

"Your mother is quite the most wonderfully fantastic person I've ever met," Caroline gushed. Everything about the madame was over the top, from her elaborate hairstyle to her silk kimono robe imported from the Far East; she exuded confidence and no-nonsense.

"You would be in good company," Emily replied distractedly as she continued her search. "Everyone she meets seems to find something about her they are drawn to."

"I think it is how she is unapologetically herself," she said thoughtfully.

"There it is!" Emily pulled the book from the shelf and opened it on the desk. She began setting up her quill, ink, and blotter. "Would you ask Mary to have some tea and sandwiches prepared? I'm feeling a bit peckish."

"That happens," Caroline said in commiseration. The women had shared several conversations about the symptoms of early pregnancy, the unbearable fatigue, the increase in one's appetite, and the like. Emily still had not disclosed the pregnancy to her husband, but promised she would in just a few more weeks after she missed another of her cycles. "I shall go find her." Caroline stood and shook out the skirts of her dove-gray gown. It was the simplest one she'd brought with her for her stay with Oliver and Emily; luckily, it was also the one that had the most pleating and extra fabric in the skirts. This allowed her greater freedom of movement but also reminded her that she would need to make even more adjustments to her wardrobe, and soon. A visit to the modiste would be in order since only two or three of her pieces still fit her. She'd already had to give up on stays altogether.

She found the maid to whom she'd been introduced earlier and passed along Emily's request.

"She should return with a tray soon," Caroline told Emily as they settled in. Overall, the brothel appeared relatively innocuous. Caroline had seen few of the public spaces, but what she saw was opulent and enticing. She wanted to explore more, but she thought she might have to save that for another time. The last thing she wanted to do was push things too far and never be invited back again. She was lost in a daydream of just what the pleasure rooms might look like when there was a knock at the door.

"I will go," Caroline offered, noticing Emily was hunched over her numbers and lost in deep concentration. She was somewhat surprised to notice a man standing on the other side of the door. He was built like a bull with a barrel chest, round, dark eyes, and an oversized nose. Then, she remembered that Lady Night employed men as guards. Perhaps Mary had been waylaid by a task and this man was sent in her stead; he was, after all, carrying the tray of tea and sandwiches. She stepped aside and let him in. "In the office, please, if you don't mind," she said politely and left the door unlocked as she followed the silent, hulking man.

Emily looked up as they entered the room and she froze. The quill dropped from her fingers, leaving blots of ink across her orderly rows of numbers.

"Caroline…"

"What is it dear? You've gone white as a sheet." She rushed over to Emily's side and grasped her frozen fingers. Behind her, the man set the tray on a table with a slight clatter.

"I do not know that man," she hissed beneath her breath.

"What?"

She squeezed Caroline's fingers even tighter. "I do not know that man. And I know every employee."

Ice seemed to seep from Emily's hands into Caroline's blood. "What are you saying?"

Slowly, Emily reached beneath the desktop. A small metallic click indicated something had been dislodged. "Run."

Terror clogged Caroline's throat, but she did as she was told without question. She turned and, hiking up her skirts, she bolted from the room. She was only able to avoid the bullish man because Emily threw a glinting silver blade in his direction. Unfortunately, no sooner had Caroline escaped the office than she ran into the chest of a second man so strong and solid that the collision nearly knocked the breath from her lungs.

How? The door!

She'd left the door unlocked. Caroline fought even as the man's arms closed around her in a vice-like grip. There was a shout and a bang from the office. *Emily.* Caroline continued to kick and flail, bashing her heels into the man's bony shins several times before she finally connected with a kneecap. He dropped her with a grunt and she fell to her hands and knees with a painful thud that jarred her teeth in her skull. She attempted to crawl away, but a vicious hand grabbed a fistful of her hair and yanked. She cried out in pain, reaching back to claw at the offending hand as it tugged painfully on her neck. She was opening her mouth to scream when a calloused hand clamped over her face. It covered her nose as well, making it nearly impossible to breathe, so she sank her teeth into the palm. The man bellowed and wrenched it away, but he also shoved Caroline to the side.

The front of her body collided with the low table in the parlor. Pain exploded behind her eyes and she collapsed dazedly to the ground. Acting only on instinct, she curled her body around her abdomen as the ache began to spread. Her belly was already sore and tender to the touch from the collision with the edge of the table. She was paralyzed with shock as the first cramp seized her.

Mercilessly, she was hauled up from the ground, a damp rag was shoved in her mouth, and her hands were bound so tightly that her fingers began to lose sensation. Despite flailing and scrabbling for purchase with every surface they passed, she and Emily were spirited down the back stairs of Lady Night's, down an alley, and forced onto the floor of a covered carriage where they huddled together, bruised and battered, crying silent tears of fear and pain.

Chapter Nineteen

G IDEON MISSED CARO with the furiousness of Odysseus and Penelope. He felt as if they were an ocean apart rather than in different neighborhoods of the same city. The tug on his heart was constant and undeniable, drawing him away from whatever he was attempting to accomplish and distracting him with Caroline's absence.

He gradually came to terms with the fact that he *needed* her by his side as much as he *wanted* her there. More than the physical aspect of their marriage, more than simply sharing a bed with her, he missed the sound of her voice and her laughter. He longed for her to cast him an amused look out of the corner of her eye when something ridiculous was said. He wanted to see her each day to reassure himself that she was well—that the pregnancy was not too difficult on her.

Having made up his mind, he rifled through her desk and located a note with the address for Mr. and Mrs. Oliver Black. Excellent.

Less than an hour later, Gideon arrived at their home. The narrow building was a tidy brick building with colorful blooms framing either side of the front steps. It was remarkable how somewhere so innocuous could send his pulse racing. He didn't know why he hadn't thought of it until that moment, but this was the first time he'd called upon his half brother and his wife at their home.

He and Caroline had hosted Emily and Oliver following the

birthday celebration Caroline had planned, but this was different; this was Gideon inserting himself into their life, stepping past the threshold and into their sanctuary. They'd welcomed Caroline with open arms, but he knew firsthand how it was impossible to truly know her and not love her. Gideon's presence was different. He and Oliver had formed the beginnings of a decent bond at Bray Castle, but would it carry over into their lives in London?

Oliver answered Gideon's knock with swift efficiency. When the door opened, it was like peering into a full-length looking glass. The similarities between them never failed to unnerve Gideon those first few seconds upon meeting.

"Swanleigh," Oliver greeted him, if not warmly, then at least pleasantly. Despite the progress they'd managed, Oliver seemed determined to hold Gideon at arm's length, far enough that he was outside of striking distance…as if he were some venomous creature from the jungle. Not for the first time, he wondered when the man might begin to trust him. He couldn't blame Oliver's skepticism—not after everything he'd been through—but he hoped soon he'd understand that Gideon held no ulterior motives. He wanted only to know the family he had left, to form a relationship with the sibling who had been denied him for so many years. The odds of finding one another in London were astonishing, and yet they'd managed. Shouldn't that be celebrated?

"Afternoon, Black," Gideon returned his greeting in kind. "I've come to see my wife."

Oliver stepped aside to admit him into the home. It smelled pleasantly of lemon and beeswax. "The ladies are out. Emily brought her along to Lady Night's," Oliver explained while Gideon removed his hat and gloves.

"The brothel?" His fingers tightened dangerously on the brim of his hat.

Oliver held up his hands. "Once Caroline learned of Emily's plans for the day, she would not take no for an answer."

"That sounds about right," Gideon grumbled.

"I escorted them there and one of the guards will see them home. Trust me when I say that I made sure they knew to remain out of sight and keep to the private rooms on the topmost floor, especially as the evening hours approach."

Gideon's skin tingled at the thought of his marchioness wife going to a place such as Lady Night's, but if he knew anything about Caro, it was that Oliver was telling the truth. She wouldn't have been able to resist seeing the business, exploring the rooms, even meeting some of the prostitutes. It caused him no little amount of discomfort that he was not there to serve as her companion, but the last time he'd visited had been such a horrendous disaster that it was probably for the best.

"Emily spent most of her life in that building. I trust every employee and personally interviewed everyone who works closely with my wife. The only way they'd be safer is if I were there as well."

"And why aren't you?"

"I had errands of my own," he explained unapologetically. "I offered to accompany them when I was finished, but they did not wish to wait. I saw them to Covent Garden and escorted them inside before I continued on my way." He glanced at the clock set into a carved wooden frame atop the hearth. "They should arrive within the next two hours. You are welcome to stay here and wait if you would like, or I can tell Caroline you called."

"I will wait," Gideon said gruffly, his mind spinning with all the possibilities of the trouble Caro might get into, of the things she might see at the brothel. Would she enjoy it? Would it inspire her?

Feeling his flesh begin to heat, Gideon cleared his throat and dropped into the seat Oliver had indicated. Oliver followed suit.

The men sat stiff and silent for interminable minutes, the ticking of the timepiece the only sound in the mint green room.

"This is…a lovely home," Gideon tried, feeling every bit as awkward as the words sounded.

"Thank you. Emily is to thank for any of the 'homey touches', as she calls them. There'd be bare plaster walls and naked floors were it left up to me."

Gideon chuckled. "The women do add color to our lives, do they not?"

There was a softening in Oliver's dark-silver eyes at those words, something rare enough that Gideon took note. The man adored his wife as much as Gideon did Caro.

"They do, indeed."

The corner of Gideon's lips tilted as they shared a moment of camaraderie. He turned his attention to the rest of the room. "Caro's former townhouse was not all that far from here. The area is quite nice, rather safe as far as London areas outside of Mayfair go. Is your employment near here?"

The warmth that had been in his half sibling's eyes a moment before was doused and shuttered away. "Currently, I assist when and where I am needed at Lady Night's." The reaction confused Gideon; it was a perfectly respectable inquiry, and there hadn't been so much as a speck of derision in his tone. He wasn't a man who looked down upon anyone who worked for his living, let alone his own brother. It was more admirable than those lords who sat on their fat arses collecting rents without lifting a finger to improve their tenants' lives or investigate new industries. Relying on inherited wealth could only take a man so far, and the complacency would likely result in the eventual collapse of his title and holdings. No, it was far more admirable to put one's mind and body into work.

"And before?" Gideon pressed, trying to understand what had caused this shift. "You seem to have done well for yourself, based on what Emily has told me of your history. Did you run a business? Invest?"

"I did whatever needed to be done."

That earned a frown. "Are you always this purposefully obtuse?"

Oliver's head whipped to the side, his eyes meeting Gideon's with piercing intensity. "Not everyone is willing to have his life be an open book for all to read."

Gideon opened his mouth to retort, but was cut short by a loud knock on the front door. Both men turned toward the foyer, dark brows knitting in deep frowns when they looked at one another, their blossoming disagreement forgotten.

The women would not have knocked.

Both of them stood, Gideon hanging back as Oliver went to answer the door. What he said made Gideon's blood run cold.

"What are you doing here?"

Alarmed by the greeting, Gideon stepped into the entryway to see a tall, lean man dressed all in black. He stood in stark contrast to the red-and-gold light of the sunset outside and brought with him an unnatural chill. Gideon was certain he'd never seen this man before in his life, but the grimness of his angular features, the coldness of his eyes, set him on edge and made him feel as if he were meeting Death, himself.

"You don't usually make house calls," Oliver said icily. Gideon noted the tightening of his fingers on the door handle, the clenching of the fist at his side. Whoever this man was, Oliver was blatantly uncomfortable with his arrival.

The man crossed the threshold. Every one of Gideon's muscles tensed as his eyes flicked back and forth between them.

"This *is* interesting," the man said, his voice low and clear. "A close relation?" He directed the inquiry toward Oliver, but nodded without requiring an answer. "It makes more sense now."

"What makes sense?" Oliver demanded.

"You know this man?" Gideon chimed in, feeling like the tension would suffocate him. "Who is he?" And what did he want? Why did his arrival so disconcert Oliver?

"My *former* supervisor," he replied gruffly without removing his eyes from the visitor.

The man inclined his head as if he was either fully unaware of the unease in the room, or he cared not one bit about it. Likely the latter, given his unaffected mien.

For only a moment, the man's lips twisted into the semblance of amusement before it dissipated. He reached into an inner pocket of his midnight-black coat and produced a folded letter. Gideon could see the black wax seal had already been broken. "This was dropped at Scotland Yard. No one can recall who left it, but it appeared within the last couple of hours."

Oliver accepted it and began to read. His face blanched to a sickly white, but he read it a second time, his eyes flying over the words like a kingfisher on the surface of a lake.

"What is it?" Gideon's voice was louder that time. He felt that if he did not receive some answers soon, then he might just go mad. Gideon did not miss the darkly disapproving look on the newcomer's face as Oliver silently handed the letter over. He glanced at the seal, but it was unmarked, just a lumpy splatter of dark wax. The words inside were hastily scrawled and made his blood run cold and black dots to dance in his vision.

Two women were taken from Lady Night's in Covent Garden. Their lives hinged upon a trade for the man known as Marcus Holden.

"What is this?" Gideon demanded as his heart pounded a deafening beat in his ears. It felt as if ice water had been pumped into his veins. "Two women were taken from the brothel? Who the hell is Marcus Holden?"

Stoically, the man produced a small, waxed paper envelope from his coat and handed it to Oliver. "This was placed inside the letter as well." Oliver's fingers trembled slightly as two locks of hair dropped into his palm, one white-blond and the other a shimmering rose gold.

"Dear God," Gideon breathed, knowing in his soul now, seeing the undeniable proof, that their wives were the ones in danger. His knees nearly buckled, but his rage bolstered him. "Caro," he croaked painfully. He ripped his eyes away from what lay in Oliver's palm and faced the man in black. He charged him until they were nearly toe-to-toe. "Tell me now what is going on, or I swear to God I'll—"

"I suggest you step back," he interrupted icily, not so much as blinking at Gideon's imposing voice and presence.

"Gideon," Oliver said firmly. Though Gideon tried, he refused to be shaken off as he pulled him away from the other man.

Gideon whirled on his half brother, locating a new target for his terror and anger. "Tell me! I've a right to know—this is my *pregnant wife!*" Panic nearly choked him as its fingers curled 'round his throat. Still, he did not miss the weighty look that passed between Oliver and the man who'd delivered the horrific message. "Tell me," Gideon snarled. He might just start swinging his fists if he didn't receive answers soon.

Oliver looked at him, a shadow in his familiar eyes. "I am the one these men seek."

"Why would they be after you?"

A small flicker of movement came from the man in black, a minute gesture of his hand to order silence from Oliver, but he did not comply. "Because," Oliver answered, "they know I am Marcus Holden."

"What do you mean?" Gideon's confusion was only growing.

"I've suspected there has lately been someone watching me. I should have listened to my instincts instead of brushing it aside as paranoia from old habits. They must have seen me with Emily and decided to take her as a way to flush me out."

The man in black nodded. "That would appear to be the situation. Too cowardly to approach you alone, so they devised a way to force you to surrender yourself."

"But what does this have to do with Caro?" He looked from Oliver to the other man, his stomach roiling so powerfully, he feared he might become ill. "Do they want a ransom? I will pay whatever it takes to have her back safely."

"She was likely collateral damage." Oliver's tone brimmed with regret.

"Or…she was seen with you and you were believed to be him," offered the man, gesturing between the half brothers. "The resemblance is remarkable. Perhaps they were both taken, just to be certain they had at least one woman worth bartering for."

Gideon turned on Oliver. "Why? Why the secret identity? Why would these men want you and take our wives as the means to have you?"

"Because I was a spy for the Crown."

The ensuing silence was thick and heavy, as if a woolen blanket had been draped over the room.

Surely this was a jest—a game, a prank—anything to help explain the absurdity of the situation. Oliver was having a bit of revenge on him for all he'd suffered. Gideon was dreaming. His mind grasped frantically for logic but came up with nothing.

A bubble of incredulous chuckles escaped him. "You expect me to believe the women were taken because you used to be a spy and now your enemies are seeking revenge?" Gideon couldn't stop his manic laughter as he turned in a circle and raked his fingers through his hair again and again.

"He does because it is the truth," said the man in black, making Gideon freeze in place. The seriousness in both his and Oliver's expressions made Gideon pause, his laughter dying in the air. "He never should have revealed as much, but that is the sum of it."

"No."

"Yes," Oliver answered.

"Impossible."

"Improbable, but entirely possible," said the other man.

"And you were his supervisor?" Gideon asked, his mind haltingly beginning to accept what he was being told, more out of desire to do whatever it took to see Caroline safe than true belief in what he was being told.

"For many years until his retirement."

"If I believe you…if this is truly the reason the women have been taken…then what now? What do we do?"

"You leave this to me and my men," the man said to both of them, aiming a more pointed look at Oliver. "You cannot interfere in the investigation. I only came to you as a professional courtesy."

An impossibly tense silent conversation passed between Oliver and his former boss before the man inclined his head to both of them, advised them that he would be in touch, and took his leave, slipping out the door like a shadow into the fading light.

Gideon tore around the room like a caged lion, enraged and helpless, shackled by his ignorance and all the more furious for it. "We are expected to wait while some madmen have our wives? I am to place my trust in this man whom I do not know, while Caro—fuck, *Caroline!*" He roared in impotent fury and whirled on Oliver, who stood with arms crossed over his broad chest as he watched Gideon's pacing. "How can you stand there like that?" he demanded, throwing his arms wide in disbelief. "As if our wives weren't in mortal danger."

The muscles of Oliver's jaw flexed. "Because we are *not* going to stand here doing nothing. Ramsay wouldn't have shown up in person and handed over the only pieces of information he had if he did not want me to become involved."

"But he said—"

"He knows I am the best man for this job, whether or not I am retired. He cannot expressly ask me to become involved—not when I am also the target—but he also knows better than to try to keep me from Emily." A dangerous shadow crossed Oliver's face, so dark and menacing and unexpected that Gideon actually retreated a step. "Ramsay does nothing without a reason." He stooped to pick up the letter that had fallen from Gideon's numb fingers and held both it and the waxed envelope with the women's hair. "He's saved us time and the possibility of injury while we attempted to garner the necessary information. Now, we have a starting point."

Gideon was nothing short of dumbfounded. His mind struggled to comprehend the entire situation. Suspending his disbelief, however, he clutched onto his desperate need to have Caro back in his arms.

"What do you require of me?"

"It is too dangerous for someone without training."

"Do you think I give a damn about that?" Gideon thumped his chest and advanced on his brother. "You know I can fight. And you would do anything to have Emily returned safely; I will do the same for Caro. I know you cannot tell me with any honesty that, were the roles reversed, you would sit by and allow me to handle things while you waited for word. Now, tell me what you need me to do." The last words were bit out in a tone that brooked no further argument.

Oliver turned down his eyes and examined the letter, his thumb tracing the bumpy borders of the black wax seal. Finally, he raised his eyes. The glitter he saw there told Gideon that he had an idea.

"WHY IS THIS happening?" Caroline whispered to herself over and over again as she hung her head and stifled useless sobs. She did her best to remain calm, but every deep, aching cramp of her abdomen released a fresh wave of panic inside of her. It was too soon. Too soon. The babe would not survive if he came this early.

She and Emily had been blindfolded and transported through London's streets after being bundled up and spirited away from Lady Night's. They'd been shoved to the floorboards of the carriage, cool metal blades pressed to their exposed throats. Hissed threats to remain silent filled their ears when all they'd wanted to do was scream for help. Caroline had had to bite her tongue so hard to keep herself from crying out that she tasted blood. Were she alone, were she not in mortal terror over the health and wellbeing of her unborn child, she might have screamed, regardless—better to fight for her life than allow this to play out. However, she knew she would never forgive herself if Emily was injured for her actions, and the babe in her belly had already taken a blow.

Please, she continued to pray silently; *please be all right*. A tiny flutter answered her, no stronger than the wings of a passing bird, but it was there. It gave Caroline hope.

Upon arrival at their destination, she and Emily were shoved down a hallway reeking of lacquer and wood dust, the tang of salt coated the back of her throat, and Caroline knew they were near the water—perhaps the docks. Soon, they were deposited into a room, their captors sliding a deadbolt home as they left.

As soon as the sound rang out, Caroline ripped the blindfold from her face and blinked into the contrasting darkness of the musty space and the shaft of late afternoon light piercing through the narrow slit of a window some six feet above their heads. They were in a storeroom of some sort, no larger than the formal dining room at Swanleigh House, but devoid of all furniture and comforts. The floor was streaked with grime and dust; a single bucket in the corner was the only item in the room. The exterior walls were made of stacked stone at the base and well-fitted wooden slats the rest of the way to the ceiling.

Emily stood a few feet away, turning in a circle as she, too, examined their surroundings. Caroline thought they were both a sight with their ripped and stained gowns, hair a matted mess, and tear-streaked faces. Simultaneously, they ran into one another's arms, holding tightly and trembling as each held the other up. They were one another's support, and neither could waver in this situation, or the other would fall.

They allowed themselves to indulge in their fear and anger for several minutes before—as if through unspoken agreement—they broke apart, dried their eyes, and began searching the room for any weaknesses. They spent what felt like hours scouring the corners for weapons, eyeing the height of the window, and examining the heavy, windowless door for any flaws, but they came up short. Their only method of gauging time was the fading light spearing through the narrow window.

Every so often, a pain would band itself around Caroline's waist, gripping her from back to front, locking her legs and causing her breath to hiss through her teeth. Emily paused each time and asked her if she was unwell. Each time, Caroline reassured her and vowed to bite back her reaction whenever the next pain came...because she knew it would come. She'd given up her hope that the cramping she'd experienced following the altercation on the stairs would subside; now, it was a matter of bracing herself for the time when the next one came. As near as she could tell, they struck with no regularity or rhythm, which was both a blessing and a curse. She had learned how a babe was near to birth if the mother's contractions were consistent and close together, but the irregularity of these also meant they were difficult to predict. She was worried enough; the last thing she wanted was for Emily to become concerned as well. They needed as much composure as possible to weather this situation.

Caroline finally gave in and huddled on the floor. She pulled her legs to her chest as best as she could, crossed her arms around her knees, and rested her head there in the cradle they created.

"Why is this happening?" she repeated, her voice breaking in the cavernous room.

"We will be all right," Emily said as she sat down beside her and adopted a similar position. The tremor in her voice made her words slightly less convincing than they might have been.

Caroline turned her head to face Emily. "Do you have any suspicions about who might be behind this? Why would they have infiltrated Lady Night's and taken us?"

Emily shook her head. "I'd never seen the man before—the one who came to the apartment under the guise of bringing our tea—and I know everyone who works beneath that roof."

"So what might his motive be?" Caroline lifted her head, her eyes going unfocused as she was lost in thought. "Money?" she said suddenly. "Ransom? Perhaps someone knew me to be the Marchioness of Swanleigh and thinks to demand Gideon pay a sum for my safe return?"

Emily bit her lip. "Perhaps..."

"Do you have other suspicions?" She didn't care for the hesitation before Emily shook her head. Neither of them openly addressed how, if Caroline was the target of the kidnapping, they would have known she would be at Lady Night's. She had never been there before and had made no advanced plans to do so. It was both baffling and terrifying.

Emily only shook her head in silent helplessness.

Caroline closed her eyes and breathed through another squeezing pain, exhaling in relief once it was finished. "How are you feeling?" she croaked out.

"Well enough," Emily said tremulously.

Caroline reached over and took her hand. "We must remain calm; hysterics will achieve nothing." The words were as much for Emily as they were for herself.

Emily nodded in agreement and squeezed her fingers back. "I am trying…only…" Her voice trailed off. She had to brace herself before she could begin again. "I haven't yet had an opportunity to tell Oliver about the baby. I kept postponing it. The time just never seemed right—I wanted it to be special."

Sensing Emily beginning to crumble, Caroline immediately wrapped her in her arms and held her. Hot tears dampened the front of her bodice, but she held herself together. "I know, darling. I know," Caroline murmured. "But you will." She closed her eyes, choked back her own tears, and comforted Emily, her mind racing with the desperate need to find a way to escape.

She'd had a nightmare once where she'd been on a small boat adrift in a black ocean of stars with no oar, no sail, no rudder. She'd screamed for help, but there was no one except the constellations to hear her. Just as she'd begun to lose all hope, Gideon had appeared beside her. She'd asked him where he'd come from and he'd replied that he'd always been there, even if she could not see him. He'd then handed her two oars made of clouds and pointed to the distance. "Land is that way," he'd said. "You are strong enough to find your way."

Caroline clung to that image as her mind grasped at any possibility of hope.

GIDEON ADJUSTED THE collar of his black woolen greatcoat. It was a tad too long in the sleeves, but its hem was the perfect length, dusting the toes of his borrowed boots. It was lucky that he and Oliver were of such a similar build; it made Gideon's disguise much easier to pull off.

While explaining his plan, Oliver had rummaged through trunks stored in an unused bedchamber and pulled out several items of clothing. "These should work," he'd said, eyeing Gideon up and down. The garments were worn and stained, but smelled clean enough after they'd been stored away.

Eager to begin, Gideon had immediately begun untying and unwinding his cravat, stripping all the way down to his small-clothes and donning Oliver's old clothing. The fabric was rougher than what he was accustomed to, but it fit well enough. Standing side-by-side in the mirror, Gideon had to give credit to his half brother. "We do appear quite similar," Gideon remarked. Oliver had also changed his clothing so they were near-perfect copies. Following his lead, Gideon proceeded to muss his own hair, so it was more similar to Oliver's. The length was slightly different, but it would not be noticeable in the gloaming light. Besides, he doubted anyone would be examining them that closely.

"Take this necktie," Oliver said without looking up. "As well as these boots."

"I cannot wear my own boots?"

"Too fine and too polished," Oliver grunted, still searching in the bottom of the trunk.

The boots felt heavy as Gideon held them up. He fingered a notch in one of the heels, only to have it separate with a metallic snick to reveal a small, removable blade. "And yet, they are much fancier than my own footwear," Gideon remarked with dark amusement, to which Oliver grunted in agreement. He fiddled the blade back into place and began to work the boots onto his feet. They were slightly large, but they would do.

Oliver then handed him a series of small blades and instructed him where to place them on his person in various pockets and pouches sewn into the borrowed clothing.

"Won't these be discovered?"

"It would appear odd if you *did not* arrive at least slightly armed."

Gideon could not argue with that logic, largely because he

was so out of his depth with this underworld he hadn't realized operated right beneath their noses. It turned out that Oliver was quite the accomplished committer of espionage and had made many enemies because of his talents.

"I often operated under an alias with a complex backstory and some alteration to my appearance—whether it be my clothing, a beard, shorn hair—but that does not mean I was never going to be recognized...not when my wife's mother's business happens to reside next door to a location where I was nearly killed during an investigation."

Gideon had seen his scars as Oliver had changed; a particularly nasty one was revealed when Oliver lifted his arms to slip his shirt over his head. The wound was positioned between his ribs and Gideon thought it was a wonder that Oliver had survived it.

Gideon loosed huff of incredulity.

"What was that?" Oliver asked distractedly as he continued his preparations.

"I've only just now realized that I never stood a chance in our wrestling match at Bray Castle, did I?"

Oliver's lips curled despite the seriousness of the situation. "You are lucky fisticuffs were decided against."

They continued discussing their preparations, running through their plan over and over again until Oliver was positive Gideon was familiar with every aspect. His body thrumming with anticipation and anxiety, they exited the townhouse just as the last blush of sunset began to melt from the sky and headed toward the river and the meeting place indicated in the note demanding the surrender of "Marcus Holden."

Several blocks before they reached the spot, Oliver peeled away from his side and disappeared into the shadows with unnerving ease. If he'd needed any further evidence of his half brother's talents, then that would have been it. Oliver had reassured him that he'd be nearby even if Gideon could not hear or see him. He took comfort in the soft triple trill of a whistle as it echoed against the buildings—a reminder that Gideon was not alone.

As he waited, stock-still as a headstone, the slick cobbles beneath his boots cooled rapidly. The early hints of fall were already creeping into London, adding a light chill to the damp air that carried with it the stench of the Thames and the overflowing gutters in this part of town. He released a long, slow breath and reminded himself of his task. He had to keep his head about him if he was going to distract these men and get them to lead Oliver to Emily and Caroline. Gideon would stand in as decoy, keeping them occupied until the women could be rescued. He would do whatever it took—endure whatever he needed—to know Caroline was safe once more.

Soon, man-shaped shadows peeled away from the dark buildings and alleyways…so many that he quickly lost count. His muscles tensed instinctively, but he knew he was no match for this many men, even with Oliver hidden away nearby.

"Marcus Holden?" asked one of the shadows in lightly accented English. Their plan hinged upon the fact that the men had either never had a good look at Oliver or had seen him months prior. It would be difficult for even their wives to tell them apart in a night this dark.

"You took something from me and I want it back," came Gideon's powerful reply. His fists clenched, but he was otherwise motionless.

"The women will be released," said another shadow.

"Only if you surrender quietly," added a third.

"Lay down your weapons and kick them away," the first figure instructed.

Slowly, so as not to startle anyone into retaliation, Gideon peeled open his coat and began removing the knives Oliver had tucked away. He did as he was told, dropping them to the cobblestones and using the toe of his boot to shove them, and they skittered away.

"Search him," ordered one shadow to another.

Gideon was roughly patted down and his every pocket was invaded by a barrel-chested man with bovine features. He couldn't help but notice a relatively fresh bandage wrapped around the man's left hand, noteworthy because he was otherwise remarkably dirty.

"She did that to you?" he muttered, not needing to clarify who "she" was.

"The red-haired bitch," the man grunted and then pulled a small knife from the top of Gideon's boot. Oliver had placed it there so they wouldn't search the soles more thoroughly. Gideon shrugged in a poor apology as the man pocketed the blade for himself. "She got what she deserved."

I look forward to killing you, Gideon thought as his hands were bound behind his back, a musty sack was placed over his head, and he was led away with a harsh shove to the center of his back that almost sent him sprawling.

THE SACK WAS ripped from Gideon's face and, though only two candles illuminated the large black space, he had to blink several times to regain his sight. He'd done his best to keep track of the turns and, as near as he could tell, they were at the docks. He'd lost count, though, after one man had slammed his head into the carriage floor. He hadn't seen it coming, so he hadn't been able to brace himself in the slightest...and it was difficult to recall much when one's ears rang like his head had been stuck inside of a church bell.

He was roughly carried and dragged into a building smelling of wood and salt where he was shoved down into a chair and strapped to it with thick, chafing ropes. His ankles had been pulled back until his knees were bent at more than a ninety-degree angle; they were then tied to his wrists, which had been stretched behind him over the back of the chair. In all, it was terribly uncomfortable, but he hadn't expected much better.

Gideon blinked at the men in the room—there were only two that he could see, but he knew there were more around.

"You do not seem like the vicious killer or the elite spy we were told to expect," observed the man with the thin mustache.

He recognized the voice as the first shadow.

"Are we supposed to have a certain look to us? I hadn't realized." Gideon's tone was remarkably flippant despite his pounding heart.

"He thinks he is a jester," remarked the second man—the one with the bandaged hand. Gideon was more pleased than he should have been to see him; it meant he did not have to seek him out to kill him.

"He will not for long," said the first man before he advanced on Gideon. "You killed Charles, Gilbert, and Paul," he snarled. "Henri died in your jail. *Le Général*…he, too, will be avenged. And you, you English excrement, will beg for the sweet release of death before I am through with you."

"That sounds markedly unpleasant," Gideon said flippantly. "I apologize for whatever happened to your friends, but can we not simply allow bygones to be bygones? From what I hear, they may have deserved—"

Crack!

Gideon's words were cut short by a vicious fist to his jaw. He tested his molars with his tongue, but none seemed to be loose. He did, however, taste the copper tang of blood where the inside of his cheek had been split on the edge of a tooth. He held onto his rage, bottling it up to save for later.

"*Cocky English pig*," growled the bullish man in French before he spat a wad of phlegm on the toe of Gideon's boot.

"*Now* that *was terribly impolite*," Gideon commented in the man's native tongue. "*These are borrowed, and I am certain the owner will not appreciate them being returned in such a sorry state.*" His French was imperfect from disuse, but he could still speak and understand it with relative fluency.

Both Frenchmen scowled before the first charged Gideon and pressed a blade to his throat. "*You arrogant pox-ridden filth,*" he hissed.

"*I thought the Froggies were more pox-ridden—*"

"*I should slit your throat right now!*" The blade pressed more deeply into Gideon's neck, and a warm trickle of blood began to soak into his neckcloth.

"No!" shouted the other man. *"They want him alive!"*

"For now…" He removed the blade and pocketed it. *"But that doesn't mean we cannot have some fun first. Give him what he deserves."*

Immediately, fists began to rain upon Gideon's head and chest. Still tied to the chair, he was knocked to the floor, unable to stop his head from striking the stones. The momentary blinding, ringing pain was a blessing before he once again felt every blow. A kick landed in his ribs and he heard, as well as felt, the crack of bone. He groaned and grunted, refusing to give them the satisfaction of crying out. It was hell, but he knew he could— he would—weather anything as long as it distracted these men long enough for Oliver to get Caroline to safety.

Chapter Twenty-One

"WE WAIT UNTIL they come for us," Caroline whispered. "Someone must come sooner or later; they will not leave us here forever."

"I will stand off to the side of the door and then strike him over the head with the bucket," added Emily. It was a weak plan at best, but it was all they had, and the bucket was the only item in the room. They had little to work with and, judging by the ache in Caroline's abdomen, not a great deal of time to escape to safety.

At least it was a heavy bucket…

Not long after, there was a metallic scrape as the door was unlocked. The women flew to their positions with Emily on the side of the door and Caroline standing before it, but well on the other side of the room to draw the man in. The man who stepped inside was lean and tall—too tall for Emily to properly strike him over the head. Instead, she struck his ear and shoulder. He bellowed in surprise and dropped to one knee.

"Again!" Caroline squealed. "Hit him again!"

Emily flinched but did just that. The second blow landed true and knocked the man face-first to the floor in a heap.

Thunderous footsteps pounded up the hallway. Panicking, Caroline snatched up the bucket and prepared to strike the next man. She didn't know how long they could fend them off, but they had to try.

The shadow in the doorway grew larger, looming like a

nightmarish demon. She began to bring down the bucket to strike, but it stopped dead, jarring her teeth, before it was wrenched from her hands.

"Caroline?"

She opened her eyes to find Oliver, dressed all in black, holding the bucket in one hand and a polished stiletto in the other. And…was that *blood* smeared on the blade?

With a cry, Emily launched herself into her husband's arms. Dropping the bucket with a clatter, he crushed her to him and held on as if afraid she might disappear into a puff of mist. The tender sight constricted Caroline's throat; her nose burned with emotion. The moment was short-lived, however, because another painful band of hot iron clamped down around Caroline's middle. She whimpered and clutched her stomach, nearly dropping to her knees.

Emily flew to her side. "What happened?"

"The baby," Caroline moaned as all the pain and fear began to slip past the wall she'd built. "I fell."

Emily looked up at her husband. "We must take her out of here."

Oliver scooped Caroline into his arms and she slung her arm around his neck. She tried not to listen as two other men met their deaths at the tip of Oliver's knives, thrown with deadly accuracy.

Soon, they were out into the misty night and spirited away in a dark carriage that would carry them far from their captors. Emily held Caroline's hand during their escape, comforting her as each spasm of her womb caused an unholy amount of pressure in her pelvis. She paid no attention to how far they traveled but was relieved when they rolled to a stop and Oliver lifted her out of the carriage. Tears and sweat blurred her vision as Oliver climbed several flights of stairs before she was deposited on a comfortable bed.

"Caroline, this is Dr. McCullom. He is going to see to your care," Oliver said, staring into her eyes to ensure she understood.

Caroline could only nod and turn toward the chestnut-haired man, silently pleading with him to save her baby.

"I will return as quickly as I can," Oliver said as he stood near the door to the room.

"Please do not leave me again," Emily begged, clutching the sleeve of his coat with white fingers.

"I must. I have to go back for Gideon."

Emily reared back. "Gideon? He was there as well? Why would you leave him behind?"

"Because he made me promise to put you and Caroline before him; he made me swear that I would save you at all costs. I would have told him the same if the roles had been reversed."

Finally, Emily nodded. They shared a deep, passionate kiss before Oliver slipped from the door like a shadow and Emily, with quiet tears falling from her eyes, hurried to Caroline's bedside.

"What is happening?" Caroline asked her. Both their hands were trembling as they held one another.

"Oliver has gone to retrieve Gideon; they will return soon."

"But—"

"They will return soon," Emily repeated adamantly, as if trying to also convince herself of this fact.

"I—I think I am losing my baby," Caroline said tremulously, feeling herself shatter as she spoke her worst fear into the world.

"Lady Swanleigh." The physician appeared at Emily's side. "I am Dr. Ian McCullom," he said, reiterating what Oliver had said. There was a slight melodic brogue to his voice, something soothing, and it briefly sliced through her panic. His eyes were clear and determined; his every motion exuded confidence. He was drying his hands on a pristine white cloth when he said, "I must ask some questions and examine you."

Caroline nodded, tears blurring her vision. Another wave of pain gripped her abdomen, making her moan more from fear than pain. She did her best to answer the physician's questions and Emily helped her to fill in the words she was unable to force from her throat. He asked her how she'd fallen, how frequently the pains in her abdomen were coming, and approximately how long they'd been occurring. He took note of the time when she indicated another cramp was seizing her belly and then compared it to the time when another came.

"Lady Swanleigh," he said, feeling the hammering pulse in her wrist. "You must try to calm yourself. I realize that is a ridiculous thing for a man to say to a woman in your condition, but it is of the utmost importance that you at least try. Your heart is racing and your condition can place stress on your unborn child." He looked down into her eyes, trying to impress upon her the seriousness of his words. "You have no signs of bleeding or dilation, and that is a *good thing*."

Caroline nodded along with him.

"I need you to breathe in through your nose, hold it, and breathe out through your mouth, like this." He demonstrated a prolonged inhalation, counted to four, and then exhaled slowly and evenly. Caroline tried, but her lungs did not want to cooperate.

"We will do it together," Emily chimed in and began mimicking Dr. McCullom.

"Yes, like that," said the physician. Caroline focused on Emily and was gradually able to perform the exercise correctly. After several rounds, he murmured, "Very good," in a soothing tone and returned to check her pulse. "When you have calmed, we will fetch you something to drink. Contractions can sometimes be worsened when a woman's body is lacking sufficient fluids."

"We haven't had anything to drink since this morning," Emily said thoughtfully, her hand flying protectively to her own belly.

"And you are expecting as well?" McCullom asked, and Emily nodded in reply. He peppered her with similar questions to those he'd asked of Caroline, but she hadn't experienced any pains and he reassured her that there should be no cause for concern. It was actually soothing for Caroline to focus on their exchange while she continued the breathing exercise.

He went to the door and peered out into the hall. Caroline heard him request fresh water for both his guests before he returned to the bedside.

"How are you feeling now, Lady Swanleigh?"

Caroline nodded. "Better. Less panicked."

"Good." His smile was as handsome as it was reassuring. "Your pains are spaced fairly far apart and appear to have no regularity. You say you have felt movement?" Caroline nodded again. "As have I. The little one you have in there has quite the kick. And you are nearly seven months along now?"

Caroline could feel Emily's eyes on her and her cheeks began to burn. "Very nearly," she answered truthfully, feeling low for having lied to Emily by omission.

"I am not saying the risks have passed, but I am hopeful. We will observe you as you continue to rest, and we will monitor your condition closely."

There was a light knock on the door and McCullom opened it to admit a beautiful, dark-haired young woman bearing a tray with a crockery pitcher of water and cups. Her bright-blue eyes surveyed the scene as she set her burden on the table beside the bed. Her green-gray gown was simple, but of obvious quality—not what one would have suspected from an assistant to a medical professional.

"Is there anything else I might help with?" she asked in a cultured accent.

"Thank you, no," McCullom replied as he poured water for both Caroline and Emily, and then tidied up the materials he'd used to clean and bandage the women's minor scrapes and bumps.

After being helped to sit up, Caroline drank the cool, clean water. It soothed her raw throat and quenched the desperate thirst she hadn't realized she'd been suffering. And, now that she wasn't in such a state of panic, she was definitely beginning to feel every one of those cuts and bruises McCullom had tended. Her left knee screamed when she bent it; abrasions on the heels of her palms burned, and she'd had quite the knock to her forehead. She had been so focused on the contractions of her womb and the blow to her abdomen to notice anything else, but every one of her injuries added up to a fair amount of discomfort.

Emily took Caroline's glass and set it aside. Caroline could see that the cut on her forearm had been bandaged, and the scrape on her cheek had been cleaned. She had complained of a battered elbow and a sore wrist, but she'd been otherwise without serious injury. As angelic as Emily appeared, she was a fighter—that much had been blatantly apparent as soon as she'd thrown that knife at their abductors.

"Where did you learn to wield a knife?" Caroline asked.

Emily appeared somewhat abashed by the question and did not reply until they were alone in the bedchamber. "Oliver taught me."

"Where did he learn such a thing?" The last word ended on a groan as her belly tightened again. She felt the panic stir once more, but reminded herself that she needed to breathe…that McCullom had reassured her that there was no imminent threat to her pregnancy…that the swift little kick she just felt was promising.

Emily was at war with herself, that much was evident. "It was part of his training," she finally said.

"Training? For the military?"

"Something like that."

Caroline sighed, realizing she would get no more information out of her, and she hadn't the strength to argue.

"I hope they return soon…" Caroline felt the sting of tears behind her eyes and pressed her hands to her face.

Emily shushed her softly. "They will. Gideon loves you and he is coming. Oliver will bring him back safely."

Caroline chose to believe the words rather than interpret them as Emily trying to convince herself of the same thing.

GIDEON'S EYES FLEW open at the flurry of thunderous footsteps and shouts. They sounded overhead in a growing cacophony of alarm.

The women were safe.

There was no other explanation for why such a ruckus would be raised.

A slow smile spread across his mouth, reopening his split lip so he tasted blood again. His jaw ached and his left eye was swollen nearly shut. Every joint screamed in pain; he could not take a deep breath without feeling as if his ribs were ripping through his flesh, but, despite all of this, he was relieved.

Now, he could stop his complacency and finally have his revenge.

His chair had been righted once more and he'd been left strapped to it in the same awkward position. Fortunately, this gave him access to the blade hidden in the heel of his boot. A flick of his fingers and the weapon was freed into his palm. He was fairly certain he had at least one broken finger, but he refused to let that stop him from quietly sawing away at his bindings with as little movement as possible. He focused all his attention on not dropping the blade. Luckily, the two men who'd had the pleasure of beating him were preoccupied as they traded hissed whispers with another man in the hall.

They had a decision: search for the women and whoever had helped them escape, or let them go and spirit Marcus/Oliver/Gideon away as they had planned. He hoped that whichever men had encountered Oliver had suffered appropriately.

Gideon nearly groaned in pain when his wrists were freed and proper blood flow and sensation began to return. Yes, he most certainly had two broken fingers. His spine popped as it was allowed to return to a more normal position rather than being bent back over the chair. He began sawing at the rope on his ankles next and made quick work of the binding just before the men shut the door and turned back to him. He'd spent hours goading them, taunting them, drawing their focus…he had also been collecting his pain and rage until such a time he'd be able to unleash it.

That time had finally arrived.

He looked between the men with his compromised vision—Thin Moustache and Bovine eyed him back. Bovine was the one who'd laid his hands on Caroline; Gideon had not forgotten that, no matter how many blows he'd taken.

"A problem, gentlemen?" he asked lightly in French.

"Not a problem," drawled Thin Moustache. *"Merely one less problem to deal with."* He pointed from the other man to Gideon. *"Release him from the chair. We will take him to the ship now and take the next tide to France."*

Bovine Man crossed the room and Gideon's pulse began to pound in anticipation, throbbing in his ears with deafening strength.

"Do you remember what you said to me when we first met?" Gideon asked him in a low, dangerous tone. *"That you were the one who helped abduct the women?"* The man did not so much as grunt in response. Gideon leaned forward…much further than he would have been able to were he still bound. *"Well, that was a mistake of unforgivable enormity."*

The man's round eyes widened when he registered that Gideon was free—which also happened to be the precise moment Gideon launched himself forward.

The small blade from his boot fell from his broken fingers with a clatter, but he was better with his fists anyway. He threw his considerable weight into a vicious uppercut that snapped the man's head back. White-hot pain ignited in his hand and radiated from his other injuries, but he did not allow it to halt his assault.

Thin Moustache launched himself at Gideon's side with a bellow and they tumbled to the filthy ground. Grime was ground into the wounds upon his face as they tussled, fists and legs flying. Each landed a few good hits, but Gideon tasted bile and blood in the back of his throat when the other man targeted his broken ribs. Utilizing a practiced maneuver with his legs to gain the upper hand, he flipped the Frenchman to the ground and struck his throat. The man began to choke and gag as he struggled to breathe.

Bovine Man had recovered and charged. This time, Gideon used the oaf's weight against him by tucking his shoulder down at the last moment to flip the man up and over. His shout of surprise was cut short as the wind was ejected from his lungs on impact. The man's coat fell open and Gideon recalled how he'd stowed one of Oliver's knives in his pocket. He wrenched it free and plunged it into Bovine Man's gut; the room echoed with his scream. Gideon leaned in until his nose was nearly pressed to this oversized one.

"That was for touching her." He gave it a sharp twist. *"And that is for calling her an insulting name."* Dark-red blood pooled around the knife; the man's hands scrabbled to remove it.

Gideon turned back to Thin Moustache, but he was left at a disadvantage with only one working eye. He never saw the chair flying at his temple, couldn't brace himself for the impact of the heavy wooden leg as it collided with his skull.

What vision he did have left went entirely black as he collapsed to the floor.

Chapter Twenty-Two

OLIVER CREPT INTO the eerily silent building from which he'd watched Gideon be taken into a few hours earlier and later, from which he'd evacuated the women. Nearly a dozen men had been prowling the darkened halls, perched atop the roof, and guarding the doors. Now that he'd returned, however, there was no one.

Still, he was cautious as he crept on silent feet from one space to the next. The three men he'd dispatched earlier still lay where they'd dropped, abandoned like rubbish by their cowardly comrades. Room after room was either empty or filled with crates, none of which had been moved recently, given the layer of dust coating them.

Finally, he located something promising.

The room was a perfect square, no larger than a small study. A splintered chair lay near the doorway, and the watery moonlight from the single narrow window set high on the wall cast just enough light to reveal a bulky form lying on the far side of the room.

The body groaned.

Oliver crept over the detritus and approached the man who was most assuredly not his half brother. His thick hands were coated in glistening blood as he futilely attempted to staunch the blood seeping from a wound in his abdomen. Oliver recognized the blade at the man's side as one of his own. Gideon had been there. He'd been the one to do that damage. Oliver looked back at the man's injury and knew without a doubt that it would be fatal. A blade in the gut like that would not kill instantly; death would come, but it would be a slow and excruciatingly painful process. The man groaned again.

Oliver crouched low and retrieved the discarded blade, wiping it on the sleeve of the dying man's coat.

"Come back to finish me off, English pig?" the man spat in French, his lips and teeth stained pink from blood.

"Where have they gone?" Oliver demanded. The man remained tight-lipped, though he squirmed in discomfort. Oliver tilted the blade at him again, allowing the moonlight to gleam off the tip. *"You are dying, but you are still alive right now, and I have plenty of time to have some fun. Should I flay your genitals? Make you a eunuch? Send you to hell with—"*

"La Genevieve!" The man released a wet cough and growled like a wounded dog.

"A ship? The Genevieve?" Oliver twisted his fist in the front of the man's damp shirt when he did not answer. *"Where is it anchored?"* he demanded and gave him a shake. The man's eyes rolled back into his head as he lost consciousness. Oliver dropped him to the floor with a curse.

The London dockyards were filled with dozens upon dozens of ships and boats of all sizes and ports of origin. It could take hours to locate the proper one onto which Gideon had been loaded, and if they planned to ride the tide out, then time was running dangerously short.

Oliver pocketed his blade and bolted from the building. His usual calm was beginning to wear thin. It was a relief to know that Emily was safe and in the care of a man whom he trusted, but now Gideon, his half brother, could be lost to him forever. They'd just found one another and, though Oliver had been wary and still struggled with letting him into his life, he was not ready to give up on the opportunity to have more family than he'd ever known. He would not fail Gideon; he would not fail to bring Caroline her husband.

He took a sharp turn down an alley which would have appeared nondescript to most passersby, but Oliver was no regular man…and he had no regular connections. He located the door at the dead end and rapped thrice in quick succession, twice more slowly, then thrice quickly again. It creaked open to reveal a room in far better condition than the building's exterior suggested it would be. What was once the kitchen and main living area of the flat had been converted into a safe meeting place for agents belonging to Ramsay's Spy Society.

The man himself was seated at the head of a table and lifted his dark head from the papers he'd been reading. No less than six other pairs of eyes lifted at Oliver's entrance.

"The women?" Ramsay asked, seeming not the least bit surprised at Oliver's arrival.

"Safe. But Swanleigh has been taken. I need to locate a ship called *la Genevieve* before she sails."

Ramsay nodded once and turned to the man on his left. "To the docks."

The man, dressed in the salt-stained rough clothes of a sailor, donned his knit cap and gestured for others to follow him. Oliver and the group slipped out into the night, some peeling away to collect more men for their search, others locating contacts who might know of the ship's whereabouts. If anyone could find the ship and Gideon before he was lost, then it was Ramsay and the complex web he'd woven over all of England.

Chapter Twenty-Three

GIDEON WOKE SLOWLY and regretted every second of it. His head pounded so badly that his ears rang. His face felt sticky with congealing blood, and his nose and mouth burned from the dust and dirt coating the inside of the burlap sack that had been shoved over his head. He'd been propped against a curved wall and it took him several minutes to realize it was not just his head spinning…the floor was unsteady because he was on a ship. It couldn't have been a very large one because the slight rocking of the water was still noticeable, but it was large enough that he'd been stored below deck like chattel; there was no light filtering through the weave of the fabric covering his head, nor was there a breeze to speak of, but a salt-and-pitch odor permeating the air confirmed his dawning realization.

Attempting to shove himself into a more comfortable position, he realized his boots were missing and he'd been stripped of everything save his shirt and breeches. Judging from the untucked state of his shirt, he'd been more thoroughly searched for weapons this time around. They were taking no more chances.

Gradually, Gideon managed to work the sack from his head. Shapeless forms filled the space around him and he realized he'd been tucked into a cargo hold. His hands were bound behind his back and his ankles had been tied together. His body ached in ways he hadn't known were possible.

Boots thudded overhead as men crossed the deck. He caught snippets of French and English words, none of them good. The ship grew louder with shouts and bangs as it came to life with sailing preparations. If they intended to take him to France as they'd indicated, then he'd be delivered there in a matter of only a few hours if the weather was right.

Refusing to dwell on that, Gideon relaxed his aching neck and allowed his head to thud against the hull—an action he regretted immediately as the unforgiving surface connected with a knot on his scalp.

Gideon closed his good eye and reminded himself to take solace in the fact that Caroline and the baby were safe. Oliver had kept true to his promise and brought the women to safety—they had been the priority. Now, buried in the bowels of the ship as he was, he didn't dare hope that Oliver or anyone else would return and locate him in time. He'd known this was a possibility when he'd agreed to play decoy to allow Oliver the opportunity to spirit the women to freedom, but that did not lessen the pain in his chest. He also hadn't believed just how much Oliver was hated by his enemies—and now he had the wounds to prove it.

He'd woken that morning longing to see and hold Caroline; now, the need struck him so fiercely that it made his eyes sting. Even if he could not see her again, he would hold her image in his mind and allow it to bring him comfort during whatever lay ahead. He was too exhausted, too battered to fight back. All he could do was gather the shreds of his strength and cling to them as long as possible.

One sound, incongruous with the din above his head, caught his attention and he opened his good eye. A muffled grunt and a thud. He frowned into the darkness.

Another choked grunt.

Another thud.

What the Devil—

"Gideon," hissed a voice barely loud enough to be classified as such. He sat up straighter, ignoring his muscles' protestations. His heart leaped into his throat when he heard it again.

Oliver.

He attempted to whistle, but his lips were cracked and parched. Licking them, he tried again. It wasn't perfect, but it was at least similar to the tune Oliver had taught him before this hellish mission.

"Again," hissed the voice as Oliver grew nearer, attempting to locate him in the hold. Gideon did.

The relief when he finally saw Oliver's broad-shouldered frame was nearly his undoing. "It's about bloody time," Gideon rasped, attempting to mask his emotion with humor.

"You're the one who allowed himself to be shut away on a ship bound for Calais," Oliver quipped as he sliced through Gideon's bindings. "Any broken bones? Can you walk?"

"I think just a few ribs and fingers." He rubbed the raw welts on his wrists and rotated his ankles to restore the circulation. His knee still bothered him, but, as Oliver helped pull him to stand, he thought it was manageable.

"Christ, you look like hell," muttered Oliver as a sliver of light from the deck above sliced across Gideon's face.

"I appreciate the sentiment. I shall keep it in mind the next time *you* are kidnapped, tied to a chair, and beaten for sport."

Oliver at least had the good grace to wince in sympathy. "Here," he said, handing over a blade and a pistol, primed and ready. "Took it off our friends after I boarded."

"Are you certain you are a spy and not a pirate?" Gideon jested, unable to help himself as his body began to sing with anticipation. Freedom was within his sights. As long as they could make it to shore, Gideon was confident he'd see Caro again.

"Not a pirate," Oliver said drolly. "A man with a knack for blending into the shadows and a few friends with rowboats." He paused, then added, "Men are poised to take the ship as soon as we escape. We weren't confident that they wouldn't immediately kill you once they realized the ship was being detained, so I volunteered to retrieve you first."

"Well, for that, I am supremely grateful. Now…let's get off this sodding ship. I've a terrible urge to see my wife. The women are well, are they not? Unharmed?" He knew in his heart that they were, but he had to hear the words.

"They are in a safe place," Oliver replied. Was it a trick of the light, or was there something evasive in Oliver's eyes? There was no time to analyze it, though.

Limping slightly, Gideon followed as Oliver led him through the hold and over the bodies of the men he'd dispatched on his way below deck. Peering at the rapidly moving legs darting from port to starboard, it was clear to Oliver and Gideon that no one had yet realized they'd been boarded and their prisoner was in the process of escaping. Ropes were hauled and coiled, last-minute crates like the ones with which Oliver had snuck aboard were secured for the short trip across the Channel, and men shouted instructions to one another, not sounding the least bit alarmed. Gideon filled his lungs with as much air as his ribs would allow. The hold had been thick and stifling, and, while the stench was little improved, at least the air was fresher on deck.

The plan was to climb to the small captain's deck at the stern and drop down to the rowboat tied there for transporting men and goods to and from shore. Gideon did not know how they would do so unseen, but he chose to buy into Oliver's optimism that the misty predawn gloom would help disguise them. It was nearly four o'clock, and high tide was fast approaching.

Oliver waited with preternatural stillness for the proper moment. When he finally moved, Gideon followed suit. All was going well until Gideon, still barefoot and vision compromised, tripped over an unseen coil of rope. He caught himself, but the lurching motion was enough to catch one man's eye and unleash a flurry of alarm.

Both he and Oliver cursed as they cast aside their caution and bolted toward the captain's deck. Oliver ushered Gideon up first and turned to face the men rushing toward them, brandishing knives and pistols. The ladder to the deck was only four rungs, so Gideon mounted it quickly and shouted at Oliver to move his arse. He turned just in time to watch him deliver a swift kick to the chest of the first man who reached him and a flashing blade to the arm of the next.

Oliver spun to climb up to Gideon, but he was wrenched back down again with a furious shout and the thuds of bodies colliding. Gideon rushed to help, but he was immediately thrown back by a man who'd stepped over Oliver to reach the captain's deck. Fists flew as Gideon leaned into his muscle memory from his years of pugilism and wrestling. One man dropped back like an anchor after Gideon's fist connected with his chin. Another was doubled over by a flurry of fists to his gut. Maneuvering closer to the edge of the deck, he saw Oliver had dispatched several men of his own; a spray of crimson blood was painted across his face like warpaint. Gideon realized with sinking dread that, while Oliver handled himself with impressive speed, agility, and ferocity, there were simply too many men.

One man charged across the deck toward Oliver's back, his vicious blade raised high, and Gideon took his chance. He pulled the pistol from the waistband of his breeches, took aim, and fired. Oliver's head whipped around at the weapon's bang and flash, then turned to watch the attacker fall backward to the deck in a rapidly spreading puddle of blood. The glance Oliver shot Gideon could only be viewed as grateful. That quickly dissolved into one of panic as he shouted Gideon's name. "Turn!"

Gideon did so just in time to evade the slashing blade of Thin Mustache. *"You are like a cat—so many lives,"* he snarled as he lunged again and again. The blade caught in Gideon's billowing shirt and prevented him from retreating just enough that the next swipe sliced across his abdomen. His shirt instantly bloomed with splotches of red. *"Tonight, you have used your final one."*

Gideon misjudged his next step and his injured knee gave out. He dropped to the deck with a roar of pain and frustration as his stiletto skittered away. He stared defiantly up at the other man, glaring at him as the blade was raised higher.

"My superiors will be disappointed that they did not have an opportunity to make you suffer, but they will have to make do with your

corpse.”

The knife began to descend, but Gideon saw only the curve of Caroline's smile, the cinnamon freckles on her cheeks, the way her hair glistened in the candlelight when they lay together, the way her hands danced across her rounded belly as if she were communicating with their child in a secret language of touch. Those were the images he chose to hold onto as he was welcomed into death's embrace.

Then, there was a flash of silver followed by a wet thud. Thin Moustache froze. A knife handle protruded from the left side of his chest.

His body collapsed like a ragdoll, and he moved no more.

Gideon turned to find Oliver had ascended the ladder and was holding his hand out to him. "Thank you," Gideon breathed, his heart daring to beat once more.

"I owed you," he replied and hauled Gideon to his feet. "Now go!"

Together, they rushed to the back of the deck and peered over the stern. Just as Oliver had said, there was a rowboat tied and waiting. They descended and dropped into the precariously rocking boat. Gideon landed awkwardly and grunted in pain. Oliver never stopped moving, untying them and shoving off with a series of sharp, loud whistles that echoed off the nearby hulls and lapping water.

Immediately, the French boat was overrun by men dressed in black. They clambered up the hull like deadly spiders and boarded it with shouted commands in both English and French.

Oliver rowed them away toward shore with sure, powerful strokes. Gideon couldn't help it; he collapsed back into the rowboat and turned his head up to the sky. The midnight-blue expanse was dotted with diamond stars, oddly peaceful and grounding in contrast to what he'd just endured.

"Are you alive?" Oliver grunted.

"Barely," Gideon groaned dramatically.

"Good. I promised to return you home; I'm just glad I made

no promises regarding your condition."

Gideon's chuckle died with a sharp protest from his ribs. "You make me laugh again and I shall be forced to hurt you as well."

That time, Oliver actually chuckled.

Chapter Twenty-Four

"Y OU'VE HAD YOUR damned way with me, now allow me to see my wife!"

Gideon believed he'd demonstrated an extraordinary amount of patience with Oliver, and then with the physician he'd insisted he see.

"I assure you, Lady Swanleigh is well and resting," said McCullom, the Scottish physician. The man was built more like a warrior than a healer, so his strength, coupled with Oliver's was enough to prevent Gideon from moving anywhere in his injured state.

"And you cannot allow her to see you looking as you do," growled Oliver as Gideon caught him in the abdomen with his elbow. His strength had returned in direct proportion to his proximity to Caroline. As soon as he'd been told she was in one of the bedchambers above, he could think of nothing other than reaching her. "Imagine what a fright it will give her when you reappear looking like a bloodied corpse." Only that was enough to make Gideon pause in his efforts, and eventually, he allowed McCullom to clean the dried blood from his face and prod the worst of his injuries to assess their severity. Despite the swelling, it did not appear to be a fracture in his knee. His fingers and a few ribs were, indeed, broken, but they could only be bound and bandaged.

"Am I free to see Caroline now?" Gideon ground out, his frustration barely held in check.

"You'll do for now, but I am not finished," McCullom said rather grudgingly.

"I'll not expire in the next hour, so I consider that good enough." He prepared to slide from the table, but Oliver placed a staying hand on his arm.

"Caroline…she was injured during the abduction," Oliver said gently.

Gideon's entire body flashed hot and then cold. "You said she was fine."

"She is," McCullom chimed in as he finished drying his hands. "She was knocked down and suffered a blow to her abdomen." The room tilted around Gideon. "That, coupled with the stress of the ordeal, caused some early contractions of her womb."

All the blood drained from Gideon's face. "W—What does that mean?"

"I have been monitoring her closely," the physician explained. "Her pains have slowed some, but they are still present. The babe's movements are continuing, which is a good sign; there has been no bleeding or loss of her waters. We will continue to watch for signs that she might—"

"Lose the baby," Gideon finished for him. Oliver's hand tightened on his shoulder.

Not that. He'd give his right arm if it meant saving Caro from that sorrow. She was safe and well, but he knew deep down she'd never be whole again if she lost their child because of this nightmare.

"Bring me to her," he rasped.

IT TOOK SOME doing, but Oliver and McCullom were able to assist Gideon in climbing the flights of stairs to the bedchamber where Caroline had been deposited. Each step sent a new throb of agony through his skull, the cut on his cheek pulled and seeped with every grimace, undoing all the cleaning that had been done, his left knee screamed in pain, but he continued on through sheer determination. He had to lay eyes on her. He had to see for himself that she was well.

He was nearly shaking with anticipation, pain, and anxiety when they finally reached the proper floor. The physician pushed the door open to reveal Emily, looking far less angelic with her mussed appearance, stained dress, and tear-streaked cheeks. She'd been seated beside the bed containing a quiet shape curled into a protective posture, red-gold hair spilling in messy waves across the pillow. Emily shot to her feet once she registered who had arrived. Gideon released Oliver and leaned more heavily on the sturdy Scottish physician. Out of the corner of his good eye, he saw Emily stumble into her husband's open arms and they held each other close, savoring one another's presence. Gideon's attention was riveted upon the woman tucked beneath the gray coverlet.

"She is finally sleeping," Emily said, her words muffled against her husband's chest. Oliver showed no sign of releasing her and Gideon could not blame him.

"Both Lady Swanleigh and the babe need all the rest they can get," added McCullom, helping Gideon into the chair Emily had vacated. It still wasn't close enough for him. He longed to crawl into bed with her and tangle their limbs, tuck her close until every possible inch of their skin met and they melded into one being. "Let me finish seeing to your wounds now."

"I am fine."

"You are not," McCullom said firmly, but low enough that Caroline was not disturbed. "I humored you belowstairs, but you are in my care. I will not allow your health to suffer. The gash on your cheek will require stitches at the very least or it will heal into an ugly scar. I must clean your eye to ensure no lasting damage was done to the—"

"Do what you must," Gideon snapped, unable to tear his eyes from his sleeping wife. She slept on her side with her cheek pillowed on one curled hand. Her long lashes fanned out across her cheeks, casting webs of dark shadows across her constellations of freckles. She looked exhausted yet peaceful. He was loathe to disturb her, but he could not resist taking her other hand in his and feeling the warmth of her skin beneath his battered fingers.

It was like a fresh wound upon his heart to see her in such a state, but he was also unspeakably proud of her for having survived it—not to mention inflicting a wound upon one of her captors. He could not live without her, that much had been confirmed that day. He'd gladly throw himself in harm's way; he'd topple empires to see her safe and happy. She spoke to a part of him he hadn't known existed. She gave him hope. She gave him purpose. She made him want to be a better man.

He hardly winced as the physician began cleaning his cheek and eye.

"I cannot begin to say how sorry I am for this situation—for the danger my past has put our wives in," Oliver said in a low tone. He had yet to release his wife, as if he was afraid she might vanish if he did. Gideon couldn't blame him; he'd have done the same if Caro were conscious. "It is my fault for believing I could ever lead a normal life and not have my sins catch up to me."

Gideon's head whipped in Oliver's direction, tearing his face free from McCullom's ministrations. It was on the tip of his tongue to damn Oliver for all the trouble his presence had caused; indeed, it would have been so easy for him to say that, with Caro lying helpless and Oliver's appearance so conveniently like their sire's. To direct all of his blind fury, his pain, his rage at Oliver would have felt so bloody good…but Gideon deflated instead.

"I do not blame you," he croaked and turned back to McCullom and Caro. Gideon spoke not another word as his wounds were tended. He focused on the even rise and fall of his wife's chest while Oliver and McCullom exchanged a few words around him. Dully, he heard Oliver and Emily leave for their home with the promise to return soon.

It was a painfully slow process as McCullom cleaned and bandaged Gideon's various scrapes and cuts, closed the wound in his cheek with no less than five neat silk stitches placed with a fine needle, and then quit the room to give him privacy.

No sooner had the door shut than Gideon was shucking his filthy clothing, cursing beneath his breath at every stab of pain the motions caused, and crawled into bed with Caro, curling up against her until they were fitted like two halves of the same whole. It would have been perfect and comforting, were it under different circumstances.

His fingers twitched as his hand hovered for several heart-beats before resting upon the swell of her abdomen and the child it guarded. He lay like that for several minutes, just existing, breathing her in and listening to the cadence of her life. He longed to hear her voice, but he dared not wake her. McCullom had said she needed her rest, and Gideon would be damned before he disturbed that.

There was a small ripple beneath his palm—a reminder of unseen strength and resilience that he could not ignore—and his heart skipped a beat.

"Hello, little one," Gideon whispered. The words felt awk-ward on his tongue, but also necessary. "I need you to be strong...like your mother. *We* need you to be strong. I realize that is a lot to ask of someone so small, but I promise in return you will have a life filled with the love and security I never knew. You are so wanted. Your mother fought for you, and I need you to fight for her, too. It is not yet time for us to meet, so stay safely in there for just a little while longer." A rolling movement like a stroke of acknowledgment from inside Caro's body was so strong that it lifted his hand. A hot tear slipped down Gideon's cheek and dropped from his nose into his wife's rose-gold curls.

CAROLINE AWOKE WITH her face buried against a warm, hard wall of masculine chest; crisp, dark hairs tickled her nose. It took her several moments to remember where she was and why, but her next thought was that she was in no pain. Well, except for those from her scrapes and bruises. The cramping in her abdomen had subsided sometime in the night enough to allow her to rest. She was stiff and sore, but to realize that Gideon had returned to her overwhelmed all of it. He looked terribly uncomfortable, wedged between her body and the wall on the narrow bed, and he smelled even worse, but none of that mattered in the face of her gratitude that he was there.

He must have felt her stir because his eye flew open—yes, singular eye. His left one was so badly blackened, it was swollen shut. A neat row of stitches followed the curve of his cheekbone.

"You're awake," he said, his voice thick with sleep. "Caroline, my love, you are awake." He cupped her cheek with a battered hand, three of his fingers tied together in some sort of splint. The relief shining in his silver eyes nearly moved her to tears because it was precisely how she felt upon seeing him, feeling him, hearing him. He enfolded her into his arms; though he squeezed her a little too tightly, she did not care one bit. It was right where she belonged.

"How are you feeling? No pains?"

She shook her head against Gideon's throat. "Not for a while. But I do not know if that is good or…or if there is something else wrong—"

"Do not work yourself up over this," he said before she could become overwrought and stroked her hair. "You rested, just like you needed to. The babe continued to move—so much, in fact, that I am baffled by how you were able to sleep through it."

There was no stifling her soft laugh at his affected indignation. Even as exhausted and injured as he was, he continued to put her first.

She stiffened as he pushed himself into a seated position with a groan. "Well, this is miserable," he mumbled as he tested his joints.

"Please do not leave." Caroline grabbed for his uninjured hand. She'd been so worried she would never see him again that she was afraid of letting him go just yet.

"I am only going to ring for McCullom, darling," he said and brought her hand to his split lip. "He requested that I let him know when you awoke."

Caroline tilted her head and cupped his cheek. "Your poor face. You fared better after your pugilism exhibitions."

"Yes, well, I was not bound to a chair during those matches."

"Bound to a chair?" she squeaked and sat up as slowly and carefully as she could. Gideon rose from the bed and, not only was she granted an unencumbered view of his sculpted back and taut backside, but also all the mottled bruises covering his body. "Gideon!" She clapped her hands over her mouth. "What happened to you?"

He pulled the rope with a sigh. "Quite a lot. And I'm tired and in a fair amount of pain, so I'd rather not recount every detail at the moment."

"And Oliver? Is he similarly…battered?"

Gideon scoffed as he pulled on his torn and soiled breeches with a mild sneer of exaggerated disgust. "Barely a scratch on him. The man's unnatural."

"I don't understand…" She pressed a hand to her forehead. "What do you mean? What was all this for?"

"As it happens, Mr. Black was quite the important man in his past profession and he made a great many enemies."

Caroline could only sit back in shock. So many questions spun 'round in her mind, but she did not have time to answer them before there was a knock on the door and Dr. McCullom entered. He was dressed the same as the night before in a fresh outfit consisting of a crisp white shirt, cravat, and black breeches. He was followed closely by the beautiful dark-haired woman who'd brought them their water. Again, Caroline's memory was tickled, and the woman's identity came to her in a flash.

"You are Lady Juliette? Sister to the Earl of Hopesend?"

The woman smiled warmly. "You are correct, Lady Swanleigh. Dr. McCullom is my husband."

"We do not spend as much time as we used to at this office; most of it has been taken over by my apprentice, Dr. Bianchi. He has been away on business these last two days, so I stayed here in case there were any urgent patients," McCullom explained.

"And I enjoy helping when I can, as well as a regular change of scenery, so I came along. Neither of us expected quite so exciting an evening. I do hope both of you are feeling well; you certainly look much better than last night." Gideon had made himself more presentable, though he looked rather more like a down-on-his-luck highwayman than a marquess with his injuries and deplorable clothing. Caroline was worried she did not look much better.

Lady Juliette held up the tray she carried. "I've brought some food for the both of you if you are feeling up to it."

"Thank you," Caroline almost sighed when she caught the scent of warm bacon. "You are a saint."

"Hardly," the other woman said with a laugh as she placed the tray by the bed. "I am merely a conveyance for sustenance—that takes little talent and even less sainthood. Mrs. Green, the housekeeper, should receive all credit for preparation. Cooking and baking are not skills I've mastered."

"Your pies have become a touch more palatable over the past few months," remarked Dr. McCullom in an unexpectedly light tone. Caroline was so caught off guard by his comment that she clapped her hand over her mouth to stifle a bubble of laughter. The physician's mien was so different from the previous evening—still mostly professional, still placing his patients' care first, but he was lighter with his wife around. To be honest, Caroline felt the same way. There was something soothing about Lady Juliette's broad smile, bright-blue eyes, and amiable personality. That the daughter and sister of an earl had fallen in love and married a Scottish physician—an utter scandal a few years prior—and that she was even enthusiastic about assisting at her husband's medical practice spoke of a woman who was unique…someone Caroline would love to know.

The lady swatted lightly at McCullom's broad shoulder. "You concentrate on doing your duties and I shall do mine, thank you."

His deep chuckle resonated through the room and he turned

his attention to Caroline. "How was your rest?"

"I hardly stirred."

"And your contractions? Have they abated?"

"They are a great deal more improved." She watched him check the water in the pitcher to determine how much she'd had to drink. It was nearly empty. Caroline had been parched from the ordeal and all the crying she'd done. Her body had felt like a wrung-out sponge and the draw to that cool, clear water was something she hadn't been able to ignore.

This seemed to please the physician and he nodded. "This is all quite promising. Do I have your permission to perform a physical examination?" he asked, pointedly looking at Caroline and not her husband. Most physicians consulted only the husband when making medical decisions, often not looking at or addressing the wife as if she were nothing more than a pet who had no bodily autonomy. Not that she for a second believed Gideon would deny her care, but she quite liked how McCullom treated her.

"Yes, of course."

"Is there anything you require, my lord?" Lady Juliette addressed Gideon. The man stood watch at the foot of Caroline's bed, arms crossed over his chest, his battered face turning all sorts of shades of yellow, green, blue, and purple. She had to give Lady Juliette credit for not shying away from his appearance.

"I need nothing other than to know my wife is well," he replied gruffly, but not unkindly. Caroline's heart fluttered in her breast.

"Take some time to care for yourself," said McCullom as he rinsed the mineral-scented soap from his hands with a fresh crock of hot water he'd carried up from the kitchens. "I will perform the examination and retrieve you when I am done so I can look over your injuries."

"If you care to wash, Mrs. Green has been boiling water, and there is a tub for your use," offered Lady Juliette when Gideon showed no sign of moving.

"I will be fine," Caroline reassured him.

Gideon looked about to protest until he caught a hint of his own odor. "Perhaps that would be for the best." He strode over and planted a lingering kiss on her lips.

"I agree," Caroline murmured when he finally pulled away.

He narrowed his eyes at Caroline for her quip in a silent, playful promise of retribution. "I will return in short order."

Chapter Twenty-Five

THOUGH IT CAUSED him no little amount of discomfort to leave Caro's side so soon after their reunion, she had been right. He needed a bath. Badly. While his wounds had been cleaned the night before, there was nothing quite like a good long soak in a tub until one's skin turned pink.

McCullom had offered him assistance down to the basement kitchen, but Gideon's pride insisted that he manage it alone. His knee bothered him with every step, but he was certain he could handle this much.

Mrs. Green, the plump, pleasant-faced woman he encountered after following the scents of frying bacon and oatcakes, took one look at him and began clucking like a mother hen. "The lady said ye'd need a bath, and sure enough you do," she tsked. Gideon was astonished by the speed with which she added boiling water to the wooden tub in the corner of the room. In preparation, it had already been mostly filled; the addition of the boiling water would balance with the cold to make it a pleasant temperature. "There's some of the doctor's special soap for ye. You'll want to use it on all your cuts and scrapes to keep 'em clean." She gestured to a yellow cake of the stuff set beside a crock pitcher for rinsing and a stack of clean toweling. "I'll be leaving for errands now so you'll have all the privacy ye need. Here," she added, as she placed a tin plate of food on the small table. "I had a feeling ye'd leave all the food for your wife upstairs—a lady in the family way must fill her belly—so I made a little extra for ye. Fill that stomach when you're clean."

"Thank you, Mrs. Green," Gideon said, his head fairly spinning with how she bustled to and fro.

"You're very welcome, my lord." Deep dimples were carved into her cheeks when she smiled back at him. With that, she ducked from the room and he heard the thud of the back door as she exited into the alleyway.

Shoving a thick cut of crisped bacon into his mouth, Gideon stripped bare and stepped into the tub. The water and strong soap provided stung his injuries, but the heat of the tub made him groan in pleasure. It soothed his sore muscles and the aching in his battered joints. Scrubbing the sweat and dried blood from his scalp went a long way toward making him feel more human. He'd bathe, eat more of Mrs. Green's cooking, and return to Caro's bedside. He needed to hear for himself that she and the baby were out of the woods.

"It would seem that the group has gotten quite sloppy since *le General*'s downfall," said Ramsay.

The spymaster had paid a call at McCullom's medical practice later that same afternoon, conveniently arriving less than an hour after Emily and Oliver had stopped by to personally check on Caroline and Gideon, and bring fresh clothing for them from Swanleigh House.

Gideon did not believe he'd ever forget the terror of discovering Caroline had been abducted, how close he'd come to losing her forever, but he had to acknowledge that Oliver was not to blame. As easy as it would have been to write a relationship with Oliver off as dangerous or not worth the risk, the man's wife had also been in danger. He knew Oliver well enough by that point to say that, had he known of a serious threat to the women's wellbeing, then he never would have allowed that day to play out as it had. Oliver was nothing if not exceptionally protective of and devoted to his wife—a trait they had in common.

Presently, Oliver, Ramsay, and Gideon were seated in the

small front parlor of the townhouse. The lower floor was dedicated to the physician's study and his medical practice, as well as Mrs. Green's kitchen. The main floor looked very much the same as any townhouse with a parlor and small dining room, while a couple of bedchambers were located on the topmost floor, where Caroline was resting with Emily and Lady Juliette to keep her company. McCullom was occupied tending patients down below.

Gideon felt markedly better after bathing. That, along with some willow bark tea, had gone a long way toward easing his aches. He could at least open his left eye now and confirm that the vision was intact. He'd recover, and he could not wait to bring Caroline home.

McCullom had reassured him that Caro's condition was promising. There were still no further signs of early labor and both she and the babe appeared strong. Neither he nor Caroline cared for it, but they'd agreed to the physician's recommendation that she remain abed there above his medical practice for at least a week or two to ensure there would be no relapse. He cautioned them that moving her too quickly might place undue stress upon her body. So, arrangements were made wherein Gideon would stay with her as much as possible until she was released.

"*Le Général*—one of the men mentioned that name." *Right before beating me*, Gideon thought sourly, but did not say aloud.

"He was a Frenchman posing as a purveyor of debauchery and vice," explained Oliver.

"The rest of his cell did not take kindly to his capture and eventual forced departure from this world." The iciness to Ramsay's tone was discomfiting. "Black was responsible for ferreting him out; they wished for revenge."

"Quite fervently, I might add," Gideon added sardonically. Now he better understood the viciousness of the attack. Revenge was a powerful motivator.

"They must not have realized the extent of Emily's involvement, or else she might have been a target as well."

Gideon's head whipped toward his half brother. "Emily was involved as well?"

Oliver made a sheepish shrug of one shoulder. "Not my most brilliant idea, but I was desperate." And that was all the explanation he offered.

"We have the ship. We have the identity of its owner. And now we know who to target in France," Ramsay said, ignoring Gideon and Oliver's discussion. His posture was impeccably straight—could his spine have been replaced with granite?

"Can you do that?" Gideon asked with a frown. "Travel to France and simply 'deal' with them?"

Ramsay leveled an unnervingly cool look at him. "My lord, I can do whatever I please. And when someone targets one of my agents, I take it very, very personally."

Gideon barely stifled a chill.

He did not doubt that in the slightest.

GIDEON RETURNED TO the room in which Caroline would reside for the next couple of weeks. It was plain and bare, but it was also clean and comfortable. And, judging from the tinkle of feminine laughter, she would have entertaining company to help pass the time. Oliver promised he and his wife would visit often; McCullom had said he and Lady Juliette would remain in residence for two more days before Dr. Bianchi returned and they left for their private residence.

"Our home is not far, so I would not be surprised if my wife is a frequent visitor during Lady Swanleigh's stay," McCullom had said. "She seems quite taken with her."

Gideon appreciated the support he and Caroline were receiving on all fronts, but what he truly wanted was to be alone with her in the comfort of their own home. Were her condition not so precarious, he'd have spirited her back to Bray Castle, where they could exist in peace and return to the last place the world had felt safe.

Emily and Lady Juliette were already standing when Gideon

entered the bedchamber.

"I will return tomorrow with that book for you," said McCullom's dark-haired wife. "For now, I will allow you to rest and see what Mrs. Green is planning for supper."

"I am sure we will come for another visit very soon," Emily chimed in reassuringly. "Let me know if there is anything you are missing from Swanleigh House. If you make a list, then I shall endeavor to obtain the items for you."

"Thank you...both of you," Caro said warmly just as the other women prepared to take their leave.

Caroline reclined against several pillows. She'd bathed, dressed in a fresh nightrail of pristine white, and her hair had been brushed to a crackling sheen, making it look like burnished bronze in the waning evening light. The days were growing shorter, stealing with them the warmth of summer. A fire had been set in the hearth in an effort to ward off the early chill, making the room feel comfortably close.

Her pale hands were crossed protectively over the mound of her belly. The smile she gave him was one of fatigued relief. Even bedridden as she was, she'd weathered an ordeal less than twenty-four hours before, and it had taken a toll on her body. He couldn't tear his eyes away from her long enough to bid the other ladies a proper farewell.

As soon as the door shut, he crossed the room to his wife and dropped into the chair beside the bed. She held her hand out to him and he took it, tracing her fingers and the fragile bones within before placing a kiss upon her palm and then pressing it to his beard-roughened cheek.

"I missed you," Caro whispered. His heart fluttered uncontrollably.

"I missed you as well," Gideon said honestly.

This was the first time they'd been truly alone since Caroline's escape and Gideon's rescue. There were no fewer than a thousand things to say, but they settled into a companionable silence, their eyes greedily drinking one another in. Caroline lay her head back as if her neck was suddenly too weary to hold it aloft. She sighed with a soft smile.

"Thank you for everything you did."

"You hardly need to thank me," he scoffed.

"But I do."

"You do not," he said more adamantly, leaning forward and squeezing the hand he still had not released. "I would do it all again for you. I would walk through fire. I would face down an army. I would—"

"Alright!" She emitted a single breathy laugh. "I understand." She sighed as if her heart overflowed with emotion and she was tired of holding back the flood. "Do you know how much I love you, Gideon?"

His world stopped.

He'd hoped. He'd dreamt of it. He'd wondered what it would be like to hear those words from her.

But he had told himself he could survive knowing Caroline cared for him, adored his friendship, desired him physically, and she would be the most amazing mother and wife. All of those things together were more than so many men could ask for.

But this? To have her declare her love for him?

It was as intoxicating as if he'd drunk an entire bottle of brandy in a single go. His veins now buzzed with it, his head swam with it, and he never wanted it to end.

He did not doubt that his cascade of emotions was playing out across his face because she took pity upon him.

"This is not a new occurrence either," she admitted. "Years ago, my heart refused to listen to reason any longer. No matter how many times I warned it that it needed to avoid you, lest it ruin one of the few wonderful things remaining in my life, it disregarded me. I blame you, of course." Gideon could not stifle a small chuff, but he remained otherwise silent for her to continue. "Do you remember when my horse threw a shoe as we were riding in the park?"

"What was that—three years ago now?" he asked.

Caro nodded. "You immediately dismounted to examine her and determined that she could no longer be ridden. You told me in no uncertain terms that I should take your horse and you would walk mine back to the mews at Swanleigh House. I tried to insist that I would walk with you, but you, stubborn man that you are, refused to hear me. We bickered until you finally pulled me down from the saddle, carried me to Posy, and deposited me upon his back. Thank goodness I wore my riding habit with the split skirts that day. You then attempted to shoo me on my way, but I refused..." Caro paused, her glittering eyes dancing over his face. "If you were going to walk, then we would walk beside you. The distance was greater than a mile and we spent the entire time in wonderful conversation.

"'How could a woman know this man and not fall in love with him?' I thought to myself. My heart fought the good fight in the face of your charm, good looks, and overwhelming thoughtfulness, but I suspected at that moment that those days of resistance were at an end. There was simply no help for it."

Gideon was in awe of her admission. Both his chest and his throat tightened with unfamiliar emotion, and even his eyes burned from it. To know she had loved him for so long and disguised it so well... God's wounds, it was humbling.

"I can see that I have been sorely remiss in my declarations of love, and, for that, I apologize. I shall do my best to remedy that from now until forever. I love you, Gideon Bray. I have loved you for years. I shall never stop loving you. You are selfless, kind, amusing, tenacious, and brave. You are everything I'd ever wanted in a knight in shining armor, and everything I thought I'd never deserve. And you saved me." She brought his palm to her abdomen. "You saved us."

Mouth agape, Gideon could only shake his head. "But you are wrong," he murmured. She shook her head. "You are wrong, Caroline. *You* saved *me*. Our friendship came at a time when I did not know who I was, other than a wretched man's heir. You called to a part of me and I could not deny the insistent pull. The hold began the very first day we met. I knew you were someone I could never walk away from. And I mean it when I say I would do it all again. All of it. I would spend evenings running rough-shod through London with you; I would celebrate birthdays and pass endless hours playing cards; I would knock Callbeck's teeth in over and over again; and I would, without question, place my life before yours whenever it was needed. Your friendship gave me joy, but your love has given me hope. I did not know what that was, and I needed you to teach me. Keep teaching me, darling, because I will forever be your pupil."

Caroline's tears were freely flowing by the time he finished speaking. Emotion was thick in his throat, but he managed to maintain control. He reached up and swiped at the offending streaks on Caro's cheeks with his thumb. "Do not become overwrought," he gently chided. "The last thing I desired was to overtax you."

"How can you expect me to not become emotional with a statement such as that?" Both of them choked on laughter, feeling lighter than they had in what felt like forever.

"And I will spend my days wondering how I was so lucky to be the one you chose," Gideon said, pressing his forehead to Caroline's before brushing his lips against hers in a reverent kiss.

She kissed him back, her tongue sweeping against the seam of his mouth. He nearly groaned. How he wanted her. How hard she made him with just that small a gesture. But he had to show restraint. He held her wrists, a pained groan rumbling through his chest, as he leaned back. "If you are in no condition to be moved to Swanleigh House, then you are certainly in no state to accept all the things I desire to do to you…"

Her pupils dilated when her eyes met his. "Then we shall bide our time. Isn't anticipation supposed to make the reward that much sweeter?"

"Nothing is sweeter than you are, that I can guarantee."

Chapter Twenty-Six

THE NEXT FEW weeks crept by with the painful slowness one only experienced during enforced monotony. Unused to the severe degree of inactivity, Caroline felt as if she were slowly losing her mind. She could only read so many books before her eyes crossed. She completed enough embroidery to provide Lady Juliette with a full collection of napkins—enough for her to host a dinner party. She did the same for Emily with pillow coverings in shades and designs that complemented her decor. She continued to tell herself that it was a wonderful break from the bustle of London life, but that exercise was wearing thin.

To his credit, Gideon spent as much time with her as he could. While his days were sometimes spent out of the town-house meeting with his men of business and seeing to other estate matters, he returned to her bedchamber each evening. They would share a meal, recount stories from their days, play cards or read side by side, and fall asleep in one another's arms. Though they grumbled about it, she suspected they'd both wind up missing the small bed when they were eventually allowed to move back to Swanleigh House—there was something so intimate about the forced proximity. Though they often both woke up aching and needy with arousal, it was far preferable to sleeping alone.

Though Lady Juliette and McCullom had returned to their own residence, she visited often and brought Caroline delightfully entertaining literature, as well as interesting stories from her ladies' reading society—which, she assured Caroline, she could attend just as soon as she was physically able. She'd read about the bold, outspoken Duchess of Morton, but she'd never been introduced to her. From the stories her friend told, Caroline suspected she and the duchess would get on quite well. Besides, the scandalous reading society seemed just the thing Caroline needed in her life.

The pains in her abdomen had subsided and the babe's movements increased, all signs which McCullom and his assistant, Dr. Bianchi, considered promising. Bianchi, with his classically Italian looks, dark hair, fathomless eyes, and musical accent was eminently professional and attentive during his monitoring of Caroline's condition. His visits were a brief respite in her day, and each time she saw him, she hoped he would tell her she would be released from her confinement. His smiles were kind and regretful each time he urged her to err on the side of caution and allow a few more days. This was not what she preferred to hear, but she told herself she'd rather suffer from boredom than cause her child any strain.

Emily and Oliver were also regular visitors. She knew Emily had shared the news of her pregnancy with her husband, but Caroline had yet to mention it to Gideon. It was not her place to reveal it, well remembering how it had felt to her when she thought the news of her own pregnancy had spread without her consent. Instead, she settled for watching Emily and Oliver together while they were blindingly thrilled with the future that lay ahead of them. It was a sight to behold. Several times, she caught an expression of tenderness on Oliver's face that was so similar to the one she often saw on Gideon that it made her breath catch. Two men from very different backgrounds—who knew so little about tenderness and acceptance—were remarkably similar in the way they'd overcome their respective adversity to forge their own paths…and learn what love truly meant.

The brothers had become closer in the weeks since Caroline and Emily's abduction, and it warmed Caroline's heart. Often when Emily came to sit with her, Oliver would leave them to their refreshments and amiable chatter, seeking out Gideon in the parlor belowstairs. Caroline did not know for certain, but she guessed they spoke of things most men did—hobbies, horseflesh, politics, how, when, and why Oliver had become involved in an elite society of spies (yes, Gideon had finally revealed to her the secrets of his half brother's history). Or perhaps they discussed their pasts, took turns learning from one another, and figured out what it meant to have a family who did not wish you ill or possess any ulterior motives. She liked to think it was a bit of everything.

One day, during Caroline's third week in McCullom and Bianchi's care, Gideon was sitting at Caroline's bedside, reclining with negligent grace as he read his book, when Emily and Oliver arrived for their visit.

They greeted them warmly and shared the expected pleasantries about their days. Emily had spent some time working through the books at Lady Night's, Oliver had accompanied her, and Gideon had spent much of his afternoon coordinating the sale of a small property near the Welsh border.

"And I have run out of crimson thread. Again." Caroline's voice was deceptively cheery as she provided her pathetic update.

"Oh, darling." Gideon kissed the top of her head and his words were covered in a healthy coat of sympathy. "It won't be too much longer now."

She certainly hoped not.

"Would you care to step out for a bit?" Oliver asked Gideon after a few more minutes of conversation.

Gideon's eyes darted to Caroline, and she knew it was on the tip of his tongue to refuse—not because he did not wish to spend time with Oliver, but because he knew how the time spent in that room was wearing on her. He felt guilty about being able to live his life while she was effectively frozen in time. "Go on," she shooed him. "Emily and I can share supper and chat. You have done nothing but spend every spare moment you have with me. I am certain the lads are about to storm the townhouse with torches and pitchforks and drag you from here. Unless I have lost track of time, it is Wednesday; they should be at Duke's. Take Oliver there on a visitor's voucher. I will be fine while you are absent for a few hours. Bianchi has no appointments this evening to take him away in case I have need of him."

Gideon eventually acquiesced and promised to return in a few hours' time.

"Thank goodness," Emily sighed and slumped back in the chair Gideon had vacated. "Oliver is thrilled about the baby, but my, he will drive me mad with his watchfulness!" Caroline laughed in sympathy. "He treats me with kid gloves when all I want is for him to…you know—" Emily's words died, and her cheeks turned a rather distinct shade of crimson.

"Oh, I understand. Believe me, I do." And did Caroline ever.

GIDEON AND OLIVER strolled through the doors of the exclusive Covent Garden gaming hell. After producing his membership token and alerting the manager that he would use his single annual guest voucher for Oliver, their coats were swiftly spirited away by the efficient staff and they were shown into one of the designated dining areas. A buffet of elegantly prepared dishes was laid out on the table spanning the width of the room. Oysters were nestled in a bed of ice—an astounding luxury that made an appearance at least once each week on Duke's table. A whole roasted pig, potatoes of all preparations, sole, squab, an array of vegetables and fruits, and an entire corner dedicated to a tower of pastries and chocolates rounded out that evening's offerings. It was opulence at its finest.

Gideon watched as his half brother absorbed their surroundings. From the fine papering on the walls to the polished wood bannisters, the expensive rugs, tapestries, and gilded sconces and polished crystal chandeliers, everything was impeccable.

"Have you been here before?" he asked Oliver. There was not the barest hint of condescension in his tone. In Oliver's line of work, who knew the places he'd been and the things he'd seen?

Gideon could only guess, and he suspected even his wildest imaginings were still nowhere near the truth.

"Only the exterior," he replied, eyeing the glistening surface of a halved oyster with either intense interest or disgust. "Lady Night's sometimes loans out employees for events. I have escorted them here before."

Gideon nodded just as they were approached by a few of Duke's other members. A steady stream of gentlemen made inquiries as to Caroline's health and his prolonged absence from Society and other social clubs. No one commented on his mostly healed injuries, though a few pairs of eyes flicked to the cut on his cheek. Other gazes were more drawn toward the man at Gideon's side. News of the Marquess of Swanleigh acknowledging his bastard half brother had made the rounds of the gossip columns. As expected, there were a fair bit of salacious whispers spread about the situation, but Gideon found it easy to set them aside when he knew the truth of it all. He was proud to have a brother—especially an unrecognized hero such as Oliver. Whether London knew it or not, Oliver was one of the many men to whom it owed its peace and way of life.

Blackwell and the others stumbled upon Oliver and Gideon as they sat down to eat. Soon, all of them shared a table, chatting and laughing amiably over their plates and the flowing drinks. Gideon noticed that Oliver never took more than a sip of any spirits placed before him—he was coming to learn Oliver was not a man prone to vices. It warmed Gideon's heart in to see his closest friends together with his brother, all of them sharing a meal and a table, accepting one another's presence as if they'd always been a part of each other's lives...and they did that for *him*.

Eventually, Gideon's friends returned to their planned evening of heavy gaming. Gideon and Oliver opted to remain at the table. Oliver lifted his glass.

"A toast," he said, and Gideon raised his own without question. "To family and friends, both of which I found quite by accident only a few short months ago." There was an openness to Oliver's face, a rawness to his tone that Gideon had not experienced before. The man was usually so cool and composed. "I was alone for so much of my life and I believed that was how it would be forever. Then, I found Emily. A year later, you chanced into my path…and you're bloody lucky I didn't pummel you like you deserved." Gideon laughed heartily at that—having seen Oliver in action, he could well appreciate that statement. "Now, I have the chance to right the wrongs of the people in my life because I fully intend to be a much better parent than those I've known. And I look forward to raising our children together."

The words sank in, and Gideon's smile burst into an enormous grin. "Emily is with child!" Oliver nodded and his grin was blinding. Gideon tossed back his drink and clasped hands with his brother. "Congratulations! When did you find out?"

"Just the other day," Oliver answered after he took a sip of his drink and set it aside. "I wanted you to be among the first to know."

This made Gideon pause. "Don't you have other friends? People whom you have known for many years? Wouldn't you wish to tell them first?"

Oliver shrugged. "The very nature of my life and my disposition prevented me from becoming close to almost everyone; as such, I have only one or two men I would consider *friends*." Gideon was humbled beyond measure to realize he was now officially among that select group, but he was truly taken aback by his next comment. "You are, after all, my little brother." Oliver's eyes glinted with a mischievousness Gideon hadn't known the man possessed.

Chapter Twenty-Seven

WHEN THE DAY finally came that Caroline was allowed to return to Swanleigh House—under strict orders to continue her rest, of course—she truly understood what Emily had told her of Oliver's "cloying carefulness" because Gideon proceeded to do precisely that.

He hardly left her side unless it was business he could put off no longer. She never had to ask for anything because he was always right there, predicting her every need and summoning the staff before she could so much as raise her finger toward the bellpull. She loved the man, but good grief! He was taking no chances when it came to her and their baby, who, by the way, was as displeased by the inactivity as she was, restless and moving almost constantly. Gideon's eternal presence might have annoyed her more, however, had she not known that it came from the purest love. He never missed an opportunity to tell her as much, to hold her close, to press tender kisses to her face, her neck, and even the burgeoning swell of her ripe abdomen.

This, of course, did not mean that Caroline did not suffer from bouts of frustration and melancholy.

One week after their return to Swanleigh House, Gideon joined Caroline on the bed and propped his head on his fist. "How are you faring, darling?"

"Well enough," Caro grumbled. It wasn't fair for her to be put out with him, but there were few outlets for her emotions at that point. With Parliament in session, he'd spent much of the day meeting with other members of his party to discuss a proposal for reforming the system in place to care for foundlings—a cause to which Caroline knew in her heart was worthy of lending her husband.

"Well enough to leave the bed so I might show you something?" His dark brows were raised in excitement.

That caught Caroline's interest.

"Of course," she agreed, though she was baffled. She was dressed in only her nightshift and, while she'd been allowed to return home, her activity was still restricted. Where could he possibly wish to take her?

He helped her rise and slip on her dressing gown before guiding her across the hall to a closed bedchamber door.

"Now, close your eyes," he said.

"Gideon—"

"Close them," he laughed, sounding every bit like a child who could not wait to present an accomplishment. She complied and heard the snick of the doorknob before his hands closed around her upper arms. He gently guided her into the space and positioned her just so before he said, "Open."

Caroline blinked into the warm afternoon light to discover that the bedchamber—once Gideon's childhood space—had been converted into a nursery, and a beautifully-appointed one at that. A bassinet swathed in ivory linens and a beautifully carved dark wood rocking chair took place of prominence in the space. She could smell the new papering in alternating stripes of fresh white and warm, dandelion yellow. Lace curtains were draped from the tall windows aimed toward the gardens below. A plush rug in blues and gold was laid in the center of the room, so soft she felt as if her bare toes sank into it like sun-warmed sand. She clasped her hands to her breast as she turned in the circle, afraid to blink lest she miss any detail. Everything she saw spoke of love and care. The gleaming baseboards, the oil painting of a bucolic field dotted with fluffy lambs, the little wooden figurines of cows, sheep, horses, and other livestock arranged so precisely on the windowsill; it was all so beautifully and carefully put together that it brought tears to her eyes and her throat clogged with emotion.

"Oh, Gideon…" she breathed.

He was at her side in an instant. "Do you not care for it? We can change anything you do not—" His words died when she gave a vehement shake of her head. It was so reminiscent of their first night of marriage—her walking into a new space he'd set up for her as best he could, nervous that she would like it, and she…utterly gobsmacked by the fact that someone had felt her worthy of the effort.

One of her hands drifted to her belly, rubbing in slow circles as she turned in awe, tears unheeded and trickling down her cheeks.

"I love it," she finally said tremulously and turned to meet his gaze. "I love *you*." Was it her imagination, or were his eyes suspiciously bright? "I love you so much, Gideon. I love you *so* very much, and I don't expect I will ever stop."

She stepped close to him and he immediately wrapped her in his arms, holding her tightly.

"I love you, too, Caro, to such a degree that it terrifies me."

"Love is not meant to be so scary," she replied with a watery laugh.

"It is for someone who has never known it."

Caroline tilted her head back to look up into his face, sympathizing with the sentiment. "Then we shall learn it together as we go." She stretched on her toes and pressed her lips to his until he groaned with need. His fingers tightened in the back of her dressing gown and every inch of their fronts were pressed together as close as possible with her stomach caught between them, but Gideon did not attempt to demand more. She could feel his tension in every one of his breaths, the tremble of his muscles against and around her.

Reaching around, she untangled his fingers from her clothing and brought his palm to her waist, positioning it just right and covering it with her own hand. The babe immediately unleashed a wallop of a kick.

"And this one, too. He knows his father, and we will learn to love together. The three of us."

"I like the sound of that," Gideon said as he swiftly bent and lifted Caroline into his arms to carry her back to their bed. He lay her down with infinite care, peppering her face with feather-light kisses while simultaneously lowering himself beside her.

They lost track of time as the world narrowed to the small space inhabited by the two of them. They touched and kissed, aching for one another, just savoring the nearness and openness between them. Gone was all the awkwardness of lying in bed with one's closest friend, replaced by the comforting companionship and unconditional love of family.

CAROLINE'S RECOVERY WAS slower than she would have liked, reinforced by Gideon's overprotectiveness. Other than Gideon's efforts, her saving graces lay in Emily and Lady Juliette. They made sure she was never lacking reading material or interesting stories while she was confined to her rooms. She found the stories from Lady Night's and Dr. McCullom's medical practice to be particularly interesting. Hardly a day went by that she didn't enjoy an amusing anecdote revolving around the colorful characters. All the distractions helped to pass her days; the nights when she was restless and uncomfortable in her own body, she would lie beside her husband and have silent conversations with the growing life inside of her. The movements, small and large, reminded her that she was never alone and that her future crept inexorably closer.

Finally, the long-awaited day came when Caroline was released from the restrictions that had so plagued her for nearly two full months. "The babe's movements are regular; your appetite and strength are hearty. I see no reason why you cannot return to some of your normal activities, within reason," Dr. Bianchi had said, much to Caroline's relief.

"What are her restrictions?" Gideon asked, looking less than pleased at the thought of his wife being unleashed upon the world once more. "Surely she should still take care?"

Caroline could have kissed the physician for what he said next: "None. By my estimate, nine and thirty weeks have passed. A healthy babe can be born any day. In fact, I encourage healthy expectant mothers to take walks and enjoy fresh air, to keep up on their physical activity at this point in their pregnancies; it often makes labor and childbirth easier."

She shot her husband a self-satisfied glance. "See, Swanleigh? I may resume my *activities*." The man knew bloody well what she meant and what she wanted—what she had longed for for weeks at that point and felt like she might burn alive from the inside out if she didn't receive soon.

The muscles of his finely-crafted jaw flexed and he looked back at Bianchi. "When you say she may resume her activities, that means…?"

The physician offered a knowing smile, likely having been volleyed this question many times over. "It means, you may resume relations, if you would like—"

"Yes!" Caro lurched forward with as much grace as a cow attempting to leap, and narrowed a determined glare at Gideon. "Yes."

Bianchi averted his head to pack away his kit and, she suspected, to mask his amusement. "You would be surprised how often I am asked this question, and how many husbands and wives are shocked when I advise them to indulge. In fact, it may even be beneficial—move things along."

"Meaning?" Gideon asked skeptically.

"There are cases where 'indulging' has helped lead to labor, especially in cases where a birth is overdue. You are not yet at that point, but your pregnancy has been rather fraught with difficulties. I suspect you would not be opposed to reaching the end."

That sealed it for Caroline. She was fully ready to have Gideon back in her bed and this baby out of her body.

If only Gideon weren't so bloody conscientious.

HER MADDENINGLY THOUGHTFUL husband did everything in his power to resist her attempts to draw him into her web of desire, often leaving her emotions stewing and her body humming and throbbing. He was far too careful for his own good. What she wouldn't have given to climb across his lap and ride him… But the man knew it, and he always found a way to escape. She knew it was not from lack of desire—she'd seen the thick outline of his arousal enough times to know that was not the case—but out of his fervent need to keep both her and the baby safe. Well, Caroline decided one week after Bianchi's visit that she'd had more than enough of that.

She chose her moment carefully, retiring early and then feigning sleep when Gideon finished the last of his correspondence in his study and finally came to bed. She listened to him enter the dressing room, the rustle of clothing and the gentle murmur of male voices as his valet helped him undress. She held perfectly still when she felt the dip in the mattress as he finally joined her in bed. Only when he pulled her into his body, as was his habit, did she move.

Caroline rolled to face her husband, slung her arm over his neck, and wrapped her leg over his hip so he could feel the heat of her sex hovering just above the part of him she craved with feral hunger. She wanted to leave no excuses to chance and had retired that evening completely nude.

"Caro! I thought you were asleep."

She loved how his arms instinctively enfolded her, but he stopped just shy of pulling her flush to him. The crisp whorls of hair on his chest tickled the erect, sensitive buds of her nipples and it was all she could do not to rub against him like a cat. Still, she closed the gap between them and thoroughly enjoyed the way his pupils blew wide within the molten silver of his eyes. His fingers flexed against her lower back, just above the curve of her bottom.

"I was waiting for you," she purred as she pressed slow, open-mouthed kisses against his jaw and throat.

"Hm?" His tone was distracted—especially when she ran her nails along the back of his scalp, stroking furrows in the thick, dark locks. She was pulling him in.

"Indeed. As a matter of fact, I have been waiting for you for far too long."

"I am right here," he breathed.

"And yet...I desire more..." She dipped her head and closed her lips over his flat male nipple. A rush of liquid heat flooded her core when he hissed a breath through his teeth. She suckled and nibbled while slowly trailing her fingers down past his clenching abdomen, finally locating the thick staff lengthening and throbbing between them.

"God, Caro!" he gasped as she wrapped her hand around him. She'd missed feeling him pulse against her palm, the velvet heat of his desire. He thickened further when she pumped her hand in three agonizingly slow strokes.

"Haven't you missed this as well?"

"You know I have," he growled even before she'd finished speaking. *Finally*, his hand drifted lower to her bottom, his fingers spreading wide and clutching her in a pleasantly possessive hold that made her molten core clench in anticipation.

"And you have made me wait far too long," she chided.

His hazy eyes met hers, so dark they were nearly completely black in the unsteady firelight. "You know why."

"And I appreciate your thoughtfulness, but right now, Gideon...I want you inside of me." His eyes rolled back with a groan at her words. "I need to feel you, and I am weary of waiting. There is nothing else I crave more in this world than your body—"

Gideon's mouth crashed down over hers. His tongue delved deep, mimicking the confident way she stroked his cock. She tightened her leg around his hip, pulling his pelvis closer to hers and allowing the broad head of his member to rub through her dripping folds with every stroke.

It seemed that Gideon's restraint had finally given up the fight because he nipped her lip, and nuzzled her nose, and commanded her to roll over. Too aroused to do anything but comply, Caroline rocked her body and did as she was told. Immediately, her husband moved flush to her back, grasped her hips, and brought her bottom in contact with his pelvis. He hiked up her top leg and hooked his arm beneath it to keep it aloft.

A deep rumble of pleased laughter tickled her spine when he discovered how wet she was for him. "You *have* missed this…" She could hear the pride in his voice. Each rock of his hips pushed him deeper into her folds, coating him in her nectar and rubbing against the pearl of her sex. Each movement urged her higher toward a rapid ascent the likes of which she'd never before experienced.

She arched back into Gideon as much as her ripe body would allow her to and he slid into her tight sheath in one long, glorious thrust. Caroline barely had time to catch her breath from the delicious stretch of it before he retreated and filled her again and again.

"Yes!" she cried, her nails clutching at his arm holding her leg aloft. "More like that."

He groaned into the back of her neck, burying his nose in her hair. "I won't last long. You feel too damned good…"

The pain in his voice, the bucking of his hips, the angle of his body inside of hers was overwhelmingly delicious. When he demanded she cup her perfect breasts and caress her nipples, her body zinged with awareness. When he described in great detail how she should touch herself, she began to pant for air.

"Pinch them," he commanded through clenched teeth. She moaned as she did as she was told. "Yes. You have the most delectable breasts. Merely the thought of them makes me hard. When I think of how those ripe nipples taste…" His breath caught, sending a bolt of lust straight from said nipples right to her center. "They are one of the sweetest things I've ever had on my tongue…aside from your cunny."

Caroline shattered. She fractured into a thousand stars sent spiraling outward in all directions. Her body bore down on his, grasping him with every thrust. She was still rippling from her climax when he buried himself to the hilt and flooded her with his seed, his hips jerking uncontrollably as he finally reached the release he'd denied himself for so long. His hand released her leg, but he wrapped his arm beneath her breasts to hold her close, his member still firm and throbbing deep inside of her.

They nestled into one another, eyes closed, bodies still wracked with the final ripples of pleasure as they drifted off into sated sleep.

GIDEON WAS QUITE content to indulge in Caroline's sexual appetites from then on. For all the restraint he'd shown over the previous months, he dove in with gusto. He recognized moments when Caroline was overly conscious of the changes heavy pregnancy had wrought upon her body, but he took every opportunity to tell her the truth—he found everything about her body to be enticing.

She drove him wild.

He took her with possessive passion, marking her as his own each time she screamed his name, came on his tongue or his fingers or his cock, or welcomed his spend into her body. It was *his* seed quickening inside of her.

His wife.

His child.

He felt a swell of pride whenever he brought her glowing, sensitive body to a shuddering, trembling release.

The night everything changed, Caroline rode out the tide of her orgasm as she rocked her body slowly atop his. She'd taken him deep and dictated the pace, chasing her own pleasure as he was content to be at her mercy. He couldn't help but follow closely behind his wife, each pull of her inner muscles dragging blinding bliss from his body.

Well pleased and exhausted, Caroline collapsed beside him as the final tremors of her climax drifted through her limbs like ripples in a pool. He pressed a kiss to her glistening brow and held her as close to his side as her firm, round stomach would allow. They panted together in the afterglow.

"That was…" she breathed. "I feel… My goodness…"

Gideon chuckled. "My sentiments exactly."

"I am—" Caro's words died abruptly, and her hand flew to her stomach. She looked up into his face when the pain passed.

"Was that…?"

"A contraction. I believe so." Their wide eyes met. Excitement and nerves roared through Gideon's blood in equal measure.

When another contraction came some fifteen minutes later, then again at increasingly shorter and regular intervals throughout the night, they both knew Caroline's time had come.

Bianchi had agreed to continue on as Caroline's physician—likely thanks in part to a sizable donation Gideon had made to McCullom's charity as a show of gratitude for all their help—and he was summoned.

It was not until the following evening, however, that Gideon was able to hold his mewling son in his arms. One look at the child's distinctive coloring gave evidence to his father's identity and, for the second time that year, Gideon knew what it felt like to have his family grow.

Caroline lay resting in the bed as he sat nearby in a wingback chair by the hearth. He hadn't wanted their son to become chilled by the dampness outside, so he'd ordered the fire stoked and the room kept at a comfortably warm temperature.

Staring down into the child's impossibly small face, examining the tiny shell of his ears, the perfection of his precious hands, the cupid's bow of his parted lips, the dainty nose so like his mother's, he felt supremely content and proud.

He was proud of his son's strong wail and sturdy build.

He was proud of Caroline's strength.

Perhaps it was strange, but he also felt pride in himself—pride that, as he stared into his son's face, he knew he would break the cycle of neglect his parents had begun. The absolutely overwhelming love he felt for this little soul in his arms told Gideon he could never treat the child as his parents had treated him. A cloud of sadness attempted to edge in, but he refused to blight such a beautiful moment wondering if his own parents had loved him at all. Instead, Gideon looked forward to spending the rest of his days proving he was a better man than his father had been. No matter how hard the old marquess had tried, he would never have the satisfaction of knowing that he'd warped Gideon into an image of himself. With Gideon's acceptance of Oliver and both brothers' determination to improve upon their pasts, his legacy would forever rest with him.

Gideon ran a finger along his son's alabaster cheek, marveling at the perfection he held in his arms, and forever grateful to the woman who'd given it to him.

CAROLINE WOKE TO find Gideon dressed only in his breeches as he paced slowly back and forth across the room. He held in his arms an impossibly tiny bundle of grunting, cooing newborn boy. She held very still so as not to alert him that she was awake; she enjoyed watching the scene far too much to disrupt it. She was exhausted, she was sore and in pain, but the sight was like a balm to all of it.

Neither she nor Gideon had had the benefit of a loving, supportive family. She'd been considered an inconvenient embarrassment while he'd been a pawn to cold, volatile parents. Still, she did not worry about their son in the least, and this belief was only solidified by the sight before her.

"Now you'll want to look into both the dam and the sire's lineage," Gideon explained softly. "Some will tell you to look at only the sire, but those shortsighted imbeciles should be disregarded—especially when placing a sizable bet." He continued on like that for several minutes, detailing all the best physical attributes to look for when selecting horseflesh. Caroline smiled;

some things never changed.

Finally, Gideon's eyes looked up from their son and he caught her watching. He had the good grace to appear slightly bashful.

"The topic is fine for now because he is too young to appreciate anything but the sound of your voice, but we will have to come up with more suitable subjects when he is older."

Gideon chuckled and crossed the room to the bed. He pressed a kiss to her brow and she caressed his cheek in return before holding out her arms for the baby.

"He is so beautiful," she whispered in awe, petting the black down on his head and running her finger along the sweet curve of his cheek. His eyes were a deep blue, but McCullom had said they'd likely change drastically in the coming weeks. "He looks just like his father."

Gideon chuckled. "Poor lad."

"We must settle on a name."

"Percy?"

Caroline wrinkled her nose.

"Bartholomew, Hadrian, Zeus—"

"Now you are being absurd," she said with a laugh and looked down into her son's face. "What about Theodore?"

Gideon paused as if weighing the name. "Theodore Bray, Earl of Easton and future Marquess of Swanleigh. It does sound nice, doesn't it?"

Caroline grinned. "Hello, Theodore," she whispered and kissed the top of his head.

Gideon climbed onto the mattress beside her and they lay there contentedly, the three of them, quietly looking forward to what the future had in store for their family.

Epilogue

September of 1824

Dearest Emily,

While it is my sincerest hope that you are enjoying your time at your cottage, we miss all of you quite fiercely! Does little Dalton enjoy the country as much as his father? I am sure he has already changed so much and I wonder if his looks have continued to favor Theodore's. I cannot wait to hold him and cuddle him—it feels like it has been a year rather than only a couple of weeks. I know you will be returning within the fortnight, but this letter simply could not wait.

Theo attempted his first steps today! To say Gideon was the proudest father in the world would have been an understatement. He scooped Theo up and spun him around; the room filled with laughter and squeals. To gaze upon my boys brings me boundless joy, and I am certain you feel the same with your family. As you know, these past eleven months as a family of three have consisted of a great deal of trial and error. Gideon and I have both been learning from the shortcomings of our parents, as well as finding our own way as husband and wife. Nowhere is this more evident in our quiet moments together— when I hold little Theo in my arms until he falls asleep and Gideon cannot help but kiss us both, when Gideon and I suffer a disagreement only to inevitably come back together because we miss one another far too much to stay that mad for long. We have learned to forgive. We have learned grace and patience. We have learned to bring joy and laughter into our home. Most of all, we have learned what it is like to love and be loved un-

conditionally. Theo is the epitome of that.

Our lives look very different from how they used to, but that has not prevented our adventures...or sneaking away to cause a bit of a scandal. Speaking of which...it is about time I inform Gideon that our family will be expanding in a little more than seven months. (Thank you for being such a loyal keeper of secrets!) I shall report back with his reaction, but I do not anticipate anything less than the most heartwarming elation from my marquess.

There may even be some tears of joy, though I will not disclose who sheds them. I will leave that up to your imagination.

Ever yours,
Caroline

Looking for more spicy romance and dreamy heroes?

The Rake Needs a Bride is the first in a new swoon-worthy "Reformed Rakes" series coming from Kelsey Swanson and Dragonblade Publishing in early 2026!

An impoverished viscount. An American heiress. A marriage for money.

But there is more to this rake than meets the eye...

Find out what happens when Viscount Blackwood must take a bride.

Acknowledgments

Caroline and Gideon's story changed so much from the first outline to this final draft. I usually stick to my original ideas pretty closely, but, as I wrote this one, some things did not feel right and true to their characters (especially Gideon's). I made the change and wound up writing my first-ever book *without* a third-act breakup! It can be done! Though I do *so* enjoy the drama of a good separation, Caroline and Gideon loved one another for so long and they had such a foundation of friendship and trust that they deserved something different. What resulted was a truly deep relationship and a hero who was more sugar than spice (at least, outside of the bedchamber).

I must extend my gratitude to everyone at Dragonblade Publishing who helped make this book happen. This "Spy Society" series was a new adventure for me and I could not have done it without them. I need to send a special thank you to my patient, talented editor, Brenda. You helped make these stories into what they are, and I am supremely grateful for your understanding when my deadline arrived and disaster struck. I don't think I've ever been so stressed about a due date in my life! Brenda talked me off a ledge and, with her expert help, I feel like this story is something special.

I am so appreciative to have the friends and family I do. They are unconditionally supportive of my work and my dreams. They cheer me on, give me grace when I am overwhelmed or preoccupied with work, and make sure I am watered and fed sunshine like the little potted plant I am.

As always, thank you to my husband and our son. I would not be where I am today without your love and encouragement. You make the future so much brighter.

About the Author

Kelsey is an Illinois native, author, wife, mother, animal lover, and owner of an obscenely large To-Be-Read book stash. She fostered her love of reading and writing after a heart condition sidelined her childhood. Early one, she learned the joy of living a thousand lives, experiencing hundreds of new worlds, and, eventually, the true pleasure of providing that same escape to others with her writing. Her passions continued to develop long after surgery restored her health and, to this day, it's difficult to find her without a book in her hands. She dove headfirst into the romance genre (perhaps) a bit earlier than the recommended minimum age and became rather adept at disguising her reading material. Once exposed to the glittering world of historical romance, she was forever changed. Her love of writing and all things British translated into her future collegiate studies in both English (with an emphasis on British Literature) and History (mainly British and European). She would go on to earn Bachelor's Degrees in both English and History, as well as a Master's Degree in English. She finished penning her first story fresh out of high school and has never looked back. Her debut novel, *The Baron's Folly*, was published in 2023.

When she's not reading or writing, she's usually watching reruns of her favorite shows, streaming just about any true crime show or podcast; obsessively collecting architectural designs, crafts, and recipes on Pinterest; or sketching, crocheting, cooking, and spending time with her family making the amazing memories she's always dreamt of. She is a diehard supporter of the Oxford Comma and is glued to the TV whenever le Tour de France is on. She is on a never-ending mission to convince her husband that they need pygmy goats, highland coos, and silkie chickens to make their lives complete.

authorkelseyswanson.my.canva.site